GEORGIA CATES

D1566242

Published by Georgia Cates Books, LLC

Sign-up for Georgia's newsletter. Get the latest news, first look at teasers, and giveaways just for subscribers.

Editing Services provided by Marion Archer of Making Manuscripts (www.makingmanuscripts.com) and Karen Lawson, The Proof is in the Reading.

Interior Design by Indie Formatting Services (www.indieformattingservices.com)

ISBN-13: 978-1514859988

ISBN-10: 151485998X

To those who don't crave comfortable;
you want mad passionate love even if it's harder and hurts more.

PROLOGUE

ANNA JAMES BENNETT

I SIGH AS I TOSS THE THICK LEGAL ENVELOPE ACROSS THE ISLAND IN MEREDITH'S gourmet kitchen. The proof of my marriage's dissolution barely comes to a stop before plummeting over the edge. "It's final, as of today."

My best friend, Meredith, squeals. "Yes. This calls for a celebratory drink."

The word celebratory implies happiness or joy. That isn't the case for me. My husband of twelve months left me for a nineteen-year-old. A kid. His former student.

Fucker.

He swears nothing happened while she was his pupil.

Liar.

He claims it's true love.

Dumbass.

Drake's relationship with Caitlyn is fleeting. She's an immature teen who wants to play house. The paint won't dry on the walls of their new apartment before she's ready to bail.

"I've been saving this one for a special occasion." Ahh. A bottle of Wittmann Westhofener Morstein Riesling. Always rich in body and texture. My favorite.

Gulp. Gulp. The bottle gurgles as Meredith pours far more than three ounces. My glass is three-quarters full when she presses two fingers against the base and glides it across the sleek Carrara marble toward me. I instantly salivate when the essence of honey, peach, mango, and flowers invades my nostrils.

Meredith lifts her glass, cueing me to the toast she's about to make. "Here's to the end of an error—your misconception that Drake Langston was a knight in shining armor rather than what he really is —a turd in tinfoil."

"I know that's the truth." I tap my glass against hers before taking the first sip of dry, fruity goodness. Damn, that's good stuff.

"Capone made sure you got everything you wanted?"

Alec Capone is the most successful divorce attorney in Georgia. He should be with a name like that. "I got more than I wanted, including custody of Little Bastard, since Drake relinquished ownership of him. Caitlyn's allergic." I'm epically pissed off about him dumping his cat on me.

"Are you keeping the lil' guy?"

"I haven't decided." Kermit, aka Little Bastard, has no love for me. Doesn't matter that I've been the one who has fed him his every bite, changed his litter box every time, taken him to the vet for every visit, even the time he was deathly ill from eating part of my foam flip-flop.

"You won't have a problem if you decide to rehome him. He's beautiful. Plenty of cat lovers would take him just because he's a Bengal."

Kermit was Drake's trophy cat. Pretty to look at and that's about it. Much like Caitlyn.

I have no emotional connection to Little Bastard. I've tried to bond, but he's resistant. That's why I'm so surprised by the way I feel when I think of giving him away. *He's resistant to loving me. Just like Drake.*

"I got my name back." That's what I wanted most. Bennett. My daddy's name.

The wrinkle in Meredith's brow serves as a warning. It's always a prelude to something serious. "I understand those papers feel like a painful ending, but that's because they're disguising what today is. A new beginning. Grayson and I think it's important for you to treat this as a fresh start."

Meredith disappears into the dining room and returns with a gift bag covered in curly ribbon and filled with tissue paper.

"Your divorce gift. Read the card first."

I open the envelope and read the message aloud. "Congratulations on your divorce. We hated him."

"No secret there." I already knew Meredith and Grayson despised Drake.

I rip into the bag, tossing aqua and lime tissue paper in every direction. I'm worse than a child when it comes to tearing into gifts.

I take out each item and place it on the countertop. Sunscreen. Ray-Bans. The ridiculously expensive bikini I lusted for at that expensive boutique in Buckhead. And condoms.

"Sur . . . prise. Grayson and I are taking you to Jamaica with us next month."

Umm . . . not just no. "Forget it. Not happening."

"Oh, it's happening. We've already booked two suites and your airline ticket. First class."

She's out of her mind. I'm not going to *that place*. "Cancel one. Unless you and Grayson plan to use separate suites."

"Can't cancel. It's Wicked Week at the resort so both rooms had to be paid for in full. Nonrefundable."

This is her way of guilting me into doing what she wants. She thinks I'll say yes if her money won't be returned. "You're so wrong for doing this to me."

"You need a getaway, and we knew you'd never agree otherwise. Don't be mad."

I'm not mad. I'm pissed. I've already made plans for the next three months. "I'm taking a second job while school's out for summer. There's no way an employer will give me vacation time four weeks after hiring me."

"Maybe not, unless your bosses are Meredith and Grayson Faulkner. Come to work for us, and we'll guarantee you the time off. There won't be a reason in the world you can't go."

Right. No reason in the world unless you consider the fact this all-expenses-paid vacation is for a getaway at a hedonism resort. A freaking no-holds-barred sex retreat.

I'm neither a hedonist nor a swinger.

Meredith Faulkner has been my best friend since ninth grade. We've been through thick and thin. There's nothing she and I haven't shared, apart from one huge exception.

Meredith and Grayson practice hedonism. They chase pleasure in any form it presents. They're also part of a local community known to many as *the lifestyle*. They're swingers. Wife Swappers.

Whatever floats their boat is fine by me. I don't judge. But hedonism and swinging ain't my thang. I'm not into casual sex. I prefer intimacy with a man I love, and always within the boundaries of a committed relationship.

Call me old-fashioned but I need more than a physical connection. A quick fuck with a person I've just met isn't my cup of tea. Neither is having sex with someone else while my husband watches. Or the other way around.

"Don't be worried about the money. Indulge is all-inclusive. You won't be out a dime."

I am cash-strapped, but Meredith knows my resistance is unrelated to my financial status. "I don't practice hedonism, and I'm not a swinger. I have no business going to Indulge."

"It's Jamaica, mon! There are plenty of activities that have nothing to do with hedonism or swinging." She picks up the top of the bikini she just gifted me and holds it up over my shirt. "Think of how great you'll look on the beach in this."

I'm not denying I need an escape from this hell I call reality, but I don't want it to be at Indulge, even if all expenses are paid. "Seeing you and Grayson with other people will be a problem for me."

"Then we'll ensure you don't."

"What kind of things would there be for me to do?"

"Let me grab my laptop, and I'll show you."

The website for Indulge makes it appear to be a classy establishment. But looks can be deceiving. "This isn't what I was expecting."

"Hedonism resorts are like anything else. There are different levels. Go to a hundred dollar a night establishment and you'll get what you pay for. Indulge is five stars all the way so it's only the best accommodations and amenities for its guests."

Meredith navigates to the page of offered activities. The list is huge. "You've always wanted to try snorkeling and scuba diving."

"True." I wanted an island honeymoon where Drake and I could do those things together. He took me to the mountains instead, the last place I wanted to go, because it was cheaper.

"I know you don't think so, but this is your kind of vacation, Anna James. The pools are luxurious. The beaches are white with the bluest water you've ever seen. You're provided with all the alcohol and food you can hold. Calories don't count there."

"Well, that changes everything."

"The service is magnificent. You can lie on the beach, in this new bikini, and have drinks brought to you by a handsome cabana boy. Who wouldn't enjoy that?"

I imagine the serenity of being on a Jamaican beach. I envision the sun warming my skin. It lightly glistens with sweat, but I'm not hot because the breeze cools me when it blows against my sun-kissed skin. The rush of the waves rolling in and out is steady. It's my favorite sound in the world. A perfect recipe for relaxation.

My lovely imagery is interrupted by a notion—some old naked coot standing beside me where I'm sunbathing on a lounger. I look over to see who's blocking the sun, and his spunk spitter is staring me down. "I don't want some dude's frank 'n beans in my face."

Meredith bursts into laughter. "Despite what you think, the men don't go around shaking their balls like maracas."

"I won't be hounded?" That would piss me off. And completely ruin my good time.

"You're a beautiful woman. I don't think it's possible for you to not be propositioned."

I've spent my life being compared to a life-size version of Barbie. Long blonde hair, blue eyes, but petite. At five four, I don't have those mile-long, lean legs like the doll.

I've never had a problem with men finding me attractive. Except my own husband. *I must have aged out for him since he likes 'em young.*

"There's a policy in place and everyone adheres to it. All you have to say is 'I appreciate your interest, but no thank you.' They won't bother you after that. Harassment isn't allowed. Anyone who doesn't abide by the rules is asked to leave."

"But what about the one refusing to take no for an answer?" It never fails. There will be one in the bunch.

"There's always someone at Indulge who will say yes. They don't waste their time on uninterested people." Well, that makes sense.

I hear the garage door lifting. "Sounds like G's home."

Meredith beams. Three years of marriage and she still lights up like a candle for him. Yet she'll have sex with another man. Their marriage is an enigma I don't think I'll ever understand.

"Grayson's comfortable with me going to the resort with y'all?"

"It was his idea. He wants to do something nice for you. Let him."

G's a good friend. Loyal. Protective. So much so I thought he was going to kill Drake when he found out what he'd done to me. I adore him for that; it was nice to know I had someone in my corner.

Grayson enters from the garage and is nearly tackled by their golden retriever, desperate for his daily dose of petting from his master. "Hey, Howie. Were you a good boy today?"

"No, he damn sure wasn't," Meredith calls outs. "He snuck into the laundry room and stole my favorite panties from the laundry basket. He chewed a big-ass hole in the crotch."

Grayson chuckles loudly before giving Howie one last scratch behind his ears.

"It's not funny. It's the third pair this week."

My best friend's husband comes to her and kisses the side of her face. It's so loving. Normal. Someone looking in from the outside couldn't possibly imagine the things they do behind closed doors. "Howie knows I like you in crotchless panties."

Meredith gasps and slaps his arm. "Stop. Don't say things like that in front of Anna James."

Grayson grins in my direction. He's so handsome. Dark hair graying at the temples. Bright blue eyes. I wouldn't dare share him with another woman if I were Meredith. "My dear wife would totally say something like that in front of you."

He's almost right. "No. She would say much worse."

Meredith winks at me. "I absolutely would but only because I can. I'm her best friend."

Grayson gestures to the gift bag on the counter. "Is AJ still calling you a friend after opening our gift?"

I pick up the card. "I loved this. And the bikini."

Grayson smirks. "What about our offer?"

I don't know what to say. To decline feels like a shitty, ungrateful thing. To accept feels wrong. Wicked.

"Don't think about what kind of resort it is or what goes on there. It's the change of scenery and escape from life that you need. Think of it as a palate cleansing."

All valid points.

A palate cleansing. I like that idea. A lot. "Okay. I'm in."

Meredith squeals and darts to where I'm sitting. She throws her arms around me and squeezes tightly. "You're going to have the time of your life. This is going to be a getaway you'll never forget. I guarantee it."

I'm certain it will be an experience I'll never forget. Even when I try.

Now, to find someone to keep Little Bastard.

CHAPTER 1

ANNA JAMES BENNETT

IT'S NIGHT ONE AT INDULGE, AND I'M HANGING OUT IN MY ROOM. MEREDITH and Grayson have gone out on the prowl. Not a problem. This suite is lavish. Spacious living room. Separate bedroom. Bathroom with an enormous double shower and soaker tub. It looks the part of a luxurious boutique hotel until you notice the mirrors. There are many and they're mounted at all angles. I guess this resort wants you to be certain what's getting slipped in where and by whom. The thought makes me shudder.

I'm starving. I had an early lunch but that was seven hours ago. That means my backbone is in danger of being eaten by my stomach. I need to get something in my belly soon so that doesn't happen. I'll need a strong spine for when I return to school in August.

Yesterday's news included Drake's refusal to leave his position as head football coach. That means I'll have to work side by side with him every day since he didn't have the decency to move on to another school.

Selfish twittlefuck.

I thumb through the resort binder to check out my dinner options. I was fairly set on staying in and ordering room service until I see the menu at a restaurant called Consume. "Hmm. Witty name."

Meredith has given me the heads-up on resort policies, so I'm already aware that clothing is required in all restaurants. Thank God. I don't want to see anyone's junk while I eat.

Ethnic food is my weakness, and my craving for jerk chicken and a pineapple-coconut martini has convinced me I can't stay holed up tonight.

Attire is smart casual, so I change out of my traveling clothes into one of my favorite sundresses. If I were home, I'd put on an uncomfortable strapless bra beneath it. But here, I'm going braless, erect nipples and all. Makes me feel like a damn rebel. And I like it.

I'm hardly out of my hotel room when I run into a bare couple at the elevators. Both are attractive. Maybe mid thirties.

"Hello," they say in unison.

"Hi." I'm confused about where my eyes should be, therefore I look down at my phone. It's always a perfect diversion in an uncomfortable situation.

The elevator doors open, and the three of us step inside. Awkward doesn't begin to describe how it feels to be enclosed in a box with this pair wearing only their smiles. "Lobby?"

"Yes, thank you."

I still don't know where to look, so I stare at the elevator floor. Without thinking, I step back and lean against the handrail. I consider all the naked asses that have probably been pressed in this same spot and jolt away. Gross. The germaphobe living inside me isn't going to fair well these nine days.

I'm thrilled for more than one reason when I walk inside the restaurant. Number one: there's food. Two: everyone is wearing clothes. "Good evening. Do you have a reservation?"

Wow. I didn't consider the possibility I'd need one. "I don't. Is that going to be a problem?"

"Let me have a look." The hostess studies her computer screen. I notice her nametag. Michaela. Same as my mom. *Reminds me. I need to call her and Willa to let them know I arrived safely.*

I cross my fingers hoping it'll help Michaela find a table for me. "You're looking at a minimum of two hours before I could seat you."

Shiz. That means I won't eat for almost three hours. "Good grief. Are the other restaurants packed like this?"

"Likely. It's the dinner rush but also guest census is at its highest since Wicked Week is beginning soon. Things will be even more crowded next week. I highly recommend making reservations as soon as possible."

"I don't really know what I want to do." Maybe there's a snack bar or something. I'm not choosy at this point.

"Would you like me to check to see if there's an opening with a single diner?"

In a normal world, I would assume she's referring to a seat but I'm not so sure about this place. "I'm sorry. This is my first time at Indulge. Can you expand on what you mean?"

"Some single diners may choose to offer available seating at their table to other lone guests. I can see if there's an open seat that way." I'm certain splitting a table during dinner doesn't hold a candle to all the other things that get shared around here.

I don't think I can wait two or three hours for food. "What is your opinion on the speed of room service?"

"It's hard to say. I'm guessing at least ninety minutes." Then I'm not much better off. And I went to the trouble of getting ready.

"I'll give this single diner thing a try." I'm not the least bit excited about sitting with a complete stranger. It's weird.

"Let's see what we can find for you." Michaela studies the computer screen again. "You're in luck. I have one single diner agreeing to share. Right this way."

Quiet, sultry jazz tunes tantalize guests. The tables are dressed in white and crystal while little pops of red décor scatter the room. Elegant black and white damask wallpaper covers its walls. Enormous chandeliers provide soft light, and the glossy black marble tiles underfoot beautifully complete Consume's décor. Mesmerizing.

White. Black. Red. If sin had a color palette, this would be it.

I stare at the sensual black and white art on the walls as I'm led to my table. I'm so engrossed by the nudie photos that I bump into a server carrying a full tray of food. "Oh my God. I'm so sorry. I wasn't watching where I was going."

This server looks so young. I'm certain he must be at least twenty-one to work in an establishment like this, but I swear he doesn't look a day over sixteen.

"No. Pardon me, Miss." Ah. He has a lovely Jamaican accent.

"It was all my fault."

The hostess gestures toward the empty seat. "Kevin is your server. He'll be with you shortly. Enjoy your dinner."

"Thank you."

I settle into my seat and observe the man sitting across from me. One look and I'm able to form an opinion: He's too damn handsome for his own good. Thick, dark brown hair. Hazel eyes surrounded by lush black lashes. Rosy cheeks. Full, pink lips.

His rakish smile completes the package. "You sound just like a Georgia peach."

He's hit the nail on the head. *How unsettling.* "I'm sorry?"

"Your accent. Can't mistake it for anything else." His voice is deep. Smooth. Southern just like me.

"You sound a little peachy yourself."

His smile broadens, deepening the dimples in each of his cheeks. "Guilty as charged. Buckhead, born and bred."

Buckhead. Born. Bred. The three B's.

Buckhead is an affluent uptown district of Atlanta, which tells me two things: this guy is probably wealthy. And by default, he's likely a total jackass.

He tilts his head to the side and lifts his brows. "And you?"

"Buford." I say the word and immediately regret it. I should have lied. He has no business knowing where I'm from.

"Been to Buford many times."

Buckhead and Buford are close, only about forty minutes apart. I'm not sure how I feel about meeting someone who lives so close.

I need to chill. He's likely feeling a little uneasy about me as well.

"I occasionally shop in Buckhead. My best friend and I love their boutiques." It's rare that I'm able to afford anything so I mostly look when I go with Meredith.

He holds out his hand over the table. "I'm Beau Emerson."

I consider lying about who I am. This guy's well within stalker distance but I wasn't blessed with thinking fast on my feet. "Anna James Bennett."

My double name is confusing for people since James can be both a man's name and a last name. "My friends and family call me Anna James. Or AJ."

"Very nice to meet you. I'm pleased to share a table with such a lovely woman."

Is that a move? I'm not certain, but it's probably best to nip this in the bud now. Beau Emerson doesn't need to be under the impression this is anything but two people sharing a table because of a crowding issue. "I appreciate your interest, but no thank you."

He leans back in his chair, his arms crossed over what I'm guessing is a well-built chest beneath his white linen shirt. He studies my face for a moment before a lopsided grin appears. "Miss Bennett. That wasn't even close to being a proposition."

Heat pulses in my face. I would love to crawl beneath this table. "I'm sorry." I can barely breath the words through my embarrassment.

I feel obligated to explain. "I'm not familiar with the typical practices here; I've never been to a place like this."

"Clearly." Both of his dimples are back on display now; I'm amusing him. I'm not sure if I should be angry or embarrassed.

Humiliation wins.

I'm normally confident in all I do, but I'm out of my element. This is his world, and I'm an outsider. "You find my ignorance entertaining."

"You're wrong. I find your inexperience intriguing."

"What part of that could you possibly find intriguing?"

"You're new to hedonism."

Oh. I get it now. He sees me as a newcomer. Fresh meat. A shiny new toy. "You've got this all wrong. I'm not here to participate. This is a free Jamaican vacation for me. A treat from my best friends."

"Your friends brought you to a place where crazy stuff happens. And by that, I mean lewd sexual acts."

"Meredith and Grayson warned me."

"Are your friends trying to recruit you into a polyamory relationship with them?"

Polyamory is the hard-core stuff. Meredith says she and Grayson will never go there. Too much commitment for them. "Oh, God no! Meredith has been my best friend for nine years. She and her husband just wanted to do something nice for me."

"Right." He's wearing a different kind of smile now, the skeptical kind.

"I know what you're thinking but they're really not."

"If you say so."

I don't know why I feel the need to convince him. "I had a shitastrophe in my life. This trip is their divorce gift to me. They thought the sun and sand would do me some good."

"Has it?"

"I don't know. We only arrived a few hours ago."

"Then welcome to Indulge, where your fantasies meet reality."

"Thank you." I think.

Our conversation is briefly interrupted when our server appears. Good thing I already know what I want because I've not even looked at the menu.

After placing my order, I resume my study of the nude photography on the walls. They're actually tasteful and elegant.

"Like what you see?"

Oddly, I do. "I've never seen anything like them. They're lovely."

"Third one on the left. That's me."

I search the walls and find the one he's referring to. Holy shizzle. That erection is enormous.

I swallow. "It's very nice." Shit. That was a dumb thing to say. "The picture, I mean. It's artful."

He bursts into laughter. "I'm kidding. I just wanted to see your reaction."

The heat has returned to my cheeks. "Well, aren't you the comedian?"

"I'm a good-time guy who enjoys a laugh. And that was a fine one."

"At my expense." I think he enjoys laughing at me.

"Sorry. Not sorry."

"Right."

Kevin returns with our drinks, a pineapple-coconut martini for me and a draft beer for Beau.

I sample my cocktail. It doesn't disappoint. "Are you a frequenter?"

"I don't know what makes one a frequenter, but I typically come four times a year."

"That qualifies you as a patron in my book. Is this your quarterly visit or a special trip for Wicked Week?"

"I, too, had a shitastrophe in my life. I thought the sun and sand would do me some good."

He's using my words. "Divorce?"

"No." That's all he says. No explanation. I'm curious to know what he means but not rude enough to ask him to expand if he doesn't volunteer the information.

I decide to steer the conversation in a safer route. "What do you do for a living?"

"Real estate agent but I also flip houses with my brothers." I'm guessing Beau has a lucrative business. He'd have to if he comes here four times a year. This place isn't cheap.

"What about you?"

"High school teacher. English and creative writing."

"So you're out for summer."

"Yup. Can't lie. Summer break is a huge perk for being a teacher." It's one of the things that drove me to choose that profession. That and my love of words.

Words are powerful. They can evoke countless reactions. Joy. Pain. Arousal. Make a heart skip a beat. Or shatter it into a million pieces.

Dinner arrives quickly considering the crowd. Our conversation never slows despite the fact we're stuffing our faces. "You mentioned divorce. Is it safe to assume that a split from your husband is the shitastrophe you were referring to earlier?"

"Yeah."

"How long were you married?" He's asking more questions than I'm comfortable answering.

"Our divorce was final a week after our first anniversary."

"Irreconcilable differences?"

Yeah. All that and a bag of chips. "I guess you could call it that since I was unable to accept him screwing one of our former students. And he had a bad case of douchebaggery."

"That's fucking low. And illegal. I hope the prick is being prosecuted to the fullest extent of the law." I'm a little surprised by his annoyance. It can't possibly be out of concern for me, but I can't ignore the slight ping of joy to hear someone else's disgust.

"Technically, his relationship with Caitlyn isn't illegal since she's nineteen. They both claim their relationship started after she was of age and had graduated so there's nothing to pursue from a criminal aspect."

"And you believe that?"

"Absolutely not." I'm no fool.

"You seem like a great girl, so your ex must be a dumb bastard. I don't have to spend more than a few minutes with you to come to that conclusion." He's quick to defend my honor. Sort of reminds me of Grayson.

Everything about Beau seems normal. I could almost forget where we are and that his tastes are likely something I'm not accustomed to.

"Are you married?" He's dining alone, but that means nothing in a place like this.

"Almost. I was engaged until a month ago." I'd like to know what happened but I don't want to pry.

"I'm sorry."

"Don't be. Best thing that could have happened to me was not marrying her." I recognize bitterness when I hear it.

My curiosity is piqued. "The almost Mrs. Emerson must have done something really bad."

Beau goes completely still and closes his eyes. "Unforgivable."

There's only one thing worse than losing one person you love to cheating: it's losing two people you love. "She cheated with a friend? Or relative?" Oh, God. I hope it wasn't one of his brothers.

"Cheating would have been much less painful." I can't imagine what he means. There's very little that could hurt worse than being scorned by the one you consider your soul mate.

"My bad. I just assumed."

I give him a moment to expand on what he meant, but he says nothing. Guess he's not in the mood to talk about it so I take our chat in a new direction. I'm interested to hear someone's opinion besides Meredith's.

"My friend swears that swinging makes her marriage less complicated. She's a full-on advocate."

"I wouldn't know. I've never been married nor am I a swinger."

Well, he isn't a four-times-a-year attendee for nothing. He's some kind of sexual deviant. "My mistake. I assumed you were because you're at a hedonism resort."

"Not everyone here comes to do that."

I point to myself. "I can testify to that."

Our server comes by to clear our plates. "May I interest you in some coffee or dessert? Perhaps another cocktail or beer?"

I'm feeling my four martinis. A fifth probably isn't a good idea. "Heat and hangovers don't mix, so nothing for me, thank you."

Beau flicks his hand. "Nothing for me either."

This is the part where we go separate ways. "We should probably get up and give our table to two of those hungry people out there waiting to be seated."

"Right."

We exit the building and stop on the sidewalk to say goodbye. "It was a pleasure dining with you, Anna James."

Beau Emerson is handsome. Kind. Intellectually stimulating. The way he spoke to me made me feel the way a woman should. More like the old me. Not the one still licking her wounds because she was dumped for a toddler, but the woman I was before Drake. Confident.

"Thank you for offering your extra seat to a stranger. I'd still be waiting for a table if you hadn't." In some ways, even though I am thanking him for his seat, he has actually given me more.

"I hope your stay is a pleasant one."

"And yours as well."

"Goodnight," we say in unison.

I want him to say something more, such as "take a walk with me" or "can I see you tomorrow?" But he doesn't. I'm tempted to turn back for a glance as I walk away. But I don't; he's a hedonist. Spending time with a vanilla girl like me isn't deemed worthy of a blip on his radar. And spending time with a hedonist as handsome as he is not on mine either.

CHAPTER 2

ANNA JAMES BENNETT

IT'S GROWING DARK. THE OCEAN HAS ALREADY SWALLOWED THE SUN. BEAU AND I talked much longer than I thought.

I'm not ready to return to my room to sit alone so I decide to explore the resort despite the warning Meredith gave me about the risqué things happening at Indulge after the sun goes down.

This is a huge resort; it isn't a bad idea to scope it out. Identifying the places I can and shouldn't go is essential.

The first sign I stumble upon directs me straight ahead for the beach area. Perfect. I would love to feel the sand under my feet.

I reach the beach's edge and bend down to remove my shoes.

"Taking a walk on the beach?" It's that deep, smooth, southern voice again. Beau.

Tingles dance across my skin. I nibble my bottom lip to suppress the delight I feel. "Yeah. I'm too anxious to wait until tomorrow."

"Mind if I join you?"

"I'd like that."

Beau holds up a finger. "Give me a few minutes."

He disappears and returns a few minutes later holding a drink in each hand. He holds out a cocktail for me. "Pineapple-coconut martini."

"How did you pull this off?"

"Magic."

I look around and spot a freestanding bar. "The only magical thing about this will be if I don't have a huge hangover tomorrow." I sip the fruity concoction. Yummy. "I believe you, Mr. Beau Emerson, are a bad influence."

"Not the first time I've heard that."

"I bet not."

"In case you're unaware, there are two beaches. Planning to go nude or prude tomorrow?"

Those are my only options? "Choosing to cover my T&A doesn't make me a prude."

"Maybe not anywhere else in the world but it's different here. Covering your tits and ass means you're uptight."

I haven't been a goody-goody a day in my life, but it seems I could be labeled a saint by these standards. "I won't be getting naked so show me the way to the prude side."

"You got it." Beau leads me down a path lined with glowing torches and trees. The overhead foliage is so heavy I can no longer see the sky or stars. It's an odd sensation, like walking through a tropical labyrinth.

We come to the end of the maze where the path meets the beach. With shoes in one hand, and my martini in the other, I step into the sand. Beau stands with a hand in his pocket, unmoving. "Now who's the prude? Roll your pants up and come with me."

I advance toward the water, leaving him behind. I rake my toes through the sand. I close my eyes and listen to the rush of water. Its pattern is predictable. Anticipated. I like that.

Peace. Tranquility. Deliverance. This is what brought me to this place.

"I love the feel of sand at night. The sun has gone down, and it's had time to cool. The deeper you dig your toes in, the cooler it gets."

He plunges his toes in. "I've never given that any thought but you're right."

"Shh. Be still and listen for a moment."

Beau stands beside me, shoes off, pant legs rolled to mid calves. Silent.

"I love this sound. I have a noise maker set to ocean waves, but the real thing is so much better."

"Then we should listen for a while." He lowers himself to sit in the sand.

I plop down to join him. Nothing graceful about it. The martinis have made my joints loose and turned my bones to gelatin. "We lived on the Mississippi coast until I was fifteen. Our house was across the street from the beach. I could look out my bedroom window and see the ocean until it dropped out of sight. My dad was still living then. My happiest memories are from when we lived there. Maybe that's why I find the sound of the water so soothing. It feels like home."

"I thought your Georgia peach accent was a little on the thick side. That explains it. You're a transplant."

"I've lived in Georgia for nine years but my Mississippi twang still pokes its head out to make its presence known. I'll never shake it. Trust me. I've tried."

"I like it."

"Drake didn't. He said it made me sound like a hick."

"Your ex sounds like a real ass."

"He is, but all the shit he did provided me a vacation in Jamaica. I can't regret that part." At least not yet.

"This is the right place to help you forget your troubles."

I want to know what brought Beau here. "This conversation is one-sided. You never told me what it is you're trying to forget."

He doesn't take the lead to talk so I backpedal. "We can talk about it . . . or we can get up and run into the ocean."

"I vote for skinny-dipping."

"I said run into the ocean. There was no mention of getting naked." Just like a man to assume that.

"Go in your dress if you don't want to take it off."

I stand and use my contortion skills to lower my zipper down my back. "I love this dress. It would be a shame to ruin it."

He watches me struggle. "Want me to get that for you?"

Letting a stranger unzip me doesn't feel right. "Nah, I'm good. I got it up by myself. I can get it down."

My brain is screaming that skinny-dipping with a stranger is a terrible idea, but the liquor I've consumed convinces me it's brilliant plan.

Beau removes his button-down and pulls his undershirt over his head. He tosses both and reaches for the button of his gray trousers. He pushes them until they're crumbled with his boxer briefs at his feet.

What I'm about to do suddenly becomes a little more surreal. I'm questioning my actions. I hold the front of my dress, thinking it over. It's not too late to turn back.

"You're not changing your mind?"

"I've skinny-dipped plenty of times but never with a stranger."

"This was your idea. Not mine." He's standing completely bare, illuminated only by a sliver of the moon.

"I know."

"Listen, Peach. I don't have to get a girl like you liquored up and naked to score some ass." He waves his hand toward the resort. "There are plenty of women up there who'd be more than happy to give me whatever I want, so let's just forget this."

Beau reaches for his clothes, and I realize him leaving is the last thing I want. "No. Don't go."

I let go of my dress. The top catches on my hips so I push it down until it drops on top of my feet. Since I went braless, I'm standing before him wearing only my panties. "You didn't even have to buy me dinner to get me naked."

"You're not naked yet." He turns his back on me and goes toward the water. I'm grateful. I didn't want to wiggle out of my panties while he pretended to not ogle.

I bolt into the water. The temperature has dropped with the night, but I drudge through so I'll have its coverage. "This is a helluva lot colder than I expected."

"The sand isn't the only thing to cool after the sun goes down."

I go out far enough to submerge my breasts. The girls pull the buoyancy card and float so I go in a little deeper.

"You have great tits. It's a damn shame you don't plan to observe the clothing optional choice."

Is he kidding me? "I'd call this clothing optional. I'm pretty sure I can't get more naked."

Beau cackles. "You have the coverage of night and water. Not the same thing."

"You seem to have no problem checking them out by moonlight."

"That's because I have excellent night vision."

"So do predatory animals."

"You consider me a predator?"

"I don't know what I consider you right now."

He goes under the water, disappearing for longer than I'm comfortable with. "Come on, dude. Not funny."

I spin around to see if he's hiding behind me. "Beau."

No answer. This is so not funny.

"Beau," I call out louder.

I see nothing. Hear nothing. My heart takes off in a sprint. "Beau," I scream.

He bobs up directly in front of me, after what feels like an eternity, and grabs my waist. "Miss me?"

I push at his shoulders, making him stumble backward. "Asshole."

He gains his footing and reaches for my midsection. "I'm sorry, Peach. Don't go."

My back is to him, but he holds my hips firmly. I imagine what it would be like if he took one step closer, maybe two, and our bodies touched.

Damn. It would feel so good to be touched again. *It's been so long.*

This is crazy. Completely irresponsible. I'm showing no better judgment than the kids I teach.

"Why should I stay?"

"Because I like you. And I enjoy talking to you."

"I think you like listening more than you like talking."

Silence.

He doesn't get to inquire about my personal life and spill nothing in return. "I think I should turn in for the evening. It was really nice to meet you."

He releases his hold on me. I spin around to leave but stop when he calls out, "Her name is Erin."

He has my attention. "And?"

"We were together for three years. Engaged for one. We were part of two separate polyamorous relationships over the last year and a half. Both went sour but the last one was the final nail in the coffin."

Holy shit. He's into poly relationships. I'm not sure about the ins and outs of what they do, but I know it's the big time. It's even too much for Meredith and Grayson. "Two women at once. I hear that's every guy's fantasy."

"The sex part is a fantasy come true. Won't lie. Being with two women was a sex fantasy realized. The relationship aspect, a total nightmare

I'm curious about this lifestyle. "How so?"

"What should have been a sexual partner in our bed quickly

turned into a second woman in my life. She became a part of everything in and out of the bedroom."

A triad relationship. I can't begin to imagine how that works. Or maybe it doesn't. He said it went bad.

"When I love, it's wholeheartedly, and I demand the same in return. I have to be everything or nothing at all. I could never share. I'd be consumed with jealousy and tied in knots all the time." I know firsthand from my experience with Drake's infidelity.

"Erin was my primary and could be territorial when it suited her. Jealousy was an issue."

I'm calling bullshit. "She couldn't have been too territorial if she allowed you to bring another woman into your bed."

"It wasn't me. Erin's the one who introduced Jenna into our lives."

"Mind. Blown." What kind of woman would do that? Maybe a bisexual one.

"It was great at first but then Erin's job became more demanding. It consumed the majority of her time. Being alone with Jenna so often brought us closer."

"Meaning more sex between you and Jenna without Erin."

"Right. Erin despised us sharing something special that didn't include her." Sounds like she considered herself the hierarchy on the sex pyramid.

This is a no-brainer. "I can see where that would go over like a turd in a punchbowl."

"You say some of the damnedest things." Beau's words are nearly drowned by his chuckles, and I'm reminded of how it feels to make a man laugh. No sneer. No smirk or cruel smile. Just a simple expression of amusement.

I spend the majority of my time with teenagers. After a while, a bit of their adolescent behavior tends to rub off. "I'm sorry. I sidetracked you. You were telling me about Jenna."

"Right. Jenna was thinking long-term. She started talking about getting married and having children, so Erin forced her out of the relationship."

That doesn't explain the terrible thing Erin did. "But that wasn't the end of it?"

"I thought it was. I expected to get married and put our poly life on the back burner for a while."

I can see where this train wreck is going. "She brought another woman into your bed."

"You're half-right. It was a man the next time. Heath."

If he didn't already have my full attention, he'd damn sure has it now. "Dude-on-dude action. The plot thickens."

"I don't do dick. It's pussy only for me." Good grief. That mouth.

I don't know jack shit about this multiple partner stuff, but I understand a scorned woman's mind and how it works. "Heath was your punishment for growing close to Jenna."

"That's the understatement of the century. She sure gave me a taste of my own medicine."

"I'm not sure that's a fair statement since she's the one who did the soliciting. But one thing's for certain. Invite trouble inside and it will enter every time."

"It gets so much worse."

"You watched your fiancée have sex with another man. I can't imagine it getting more unpleasant than that."

"Erin was pregnant. It was mine. We know because the timing made it impossible for the baby to be Heath's."

I was wrong. It can get so much worse.

"I came home from work one day last month and Heath had taken her to the abortion clinic. The procedure was done before I knew about it. The kid was mine, and I didn't get a say if it lived or not."

He's hurting, and I don't know how to respond. Something inside me wants to comfort him, but to say "I'm sorry" feels so insignificant. So empty.

This man isn't wounded over a woman. He's grieving a loss sex won't cure. "Are you sure you should be here?"

"I came to fuck ninety-nine different ways. This is definitely the place I need to be."

He can't fuck away this kind of pain. "How many of those ninety-nine ways have you gotten under your belt so far?"

"None yet. I just got here."

That seems like an excessive amount of sex during a getaway. "How many days are you staying?"

"Nine." Same as us.

"I'm no mathematician but you're here nine days, counting today. That means you have to fuck eleven different ways per day if you're going to squeeze in ninety-nine. You better get crackin', sir."

"There's no hurry. There'll be plenty of opportunities after midnight. That's when things heat up." I'll definitely be safely tucked in my bed long before then.

I'm guessing I'll be sick of this place by the end of nine days. It all seems so extreme. "Do you typically stay so long?"

"No. I've always done long weekends because of work."

I recall the variety of people I've seen since my arrival. "Do you have standards for the people you have sex with or is a vagina the only requirement?"

He chuckles. "Of course I have standards. Don't you?"

"Absolutely. High ones."

"What does a girl like you look for?"

He's lumped me into some kind of category. "A girl like me? What does that mean?"

"A vanilla girl."

I am vanilla but I've not yet decided if I'm going to be pissed off about having that label placed on me. "Call me old-fashioned but I don't long to be double penetrated."

"You might like it if you tried it."

I hate being judged. "You assume I haven't."

"You assume I have." He totally has me there.

"You're the one who was in a sexual triad involving two guys and a girl. Two dicks. One vagina. Three assholes. I already know you aren't into dudes so my assumption was made by process of elimination."

He laughs. "You sort of have a dirty mouth."

"Not dirty. Innocent-challenged." He hasn't heard shit out of me yet. "I'm curious to know what you thought of it."

"It feels great."

I hear a silent *but* in there somewhere. "But you hated her being with another man?"

"Of course. She was going to be my wife. I loved her. Every time Heath came into our bed, it was a reminder I was never going to be enough to satisfy her."

Does the poly want out?

"Be happy you figured it out before you married her instead of after."

"My affection for her slipped a little further away every time I saw them together. The love I had for her eventually drifted beyond my grasp. I tried but couldn't get it back. She became nothing more than a body to me, an object I used for getting off." I can believe that.

"Will your next relationship be polyamorous?"

"I have no idea. I only know I came here to fuck the two of them off my mind. That's as far as I've gotten."

Sex isn't a fix for what's going on in his head. And heart. But he has to figure that out for himself.

"I don't want to talk about those fuckers anymore. I rather hear about your vanilla girl high standards."

"I want true and beautiful." I bet he thinks that's unrealistic.

"Total myth. Doesn't exist in today's world." Pessimist. He's probably a glass half-empty kind of guy.

"It does. I saw it between my mother and father. The fairy tale is real, and I won't settle for less."

"This is a different generation. But I wish you the best of luck with that."

"Tell me your standards since you have so little faith in love."

"I could tell you but it would be so much easier to show you."

My stomach flips; I don't know what that means. "A verbal description would suffice."

"Come on. It'll be fun. You can help me choose my first of ninety-nine fucks."

Oh. That's not what I thought he meant. It's a total wakeup call for what Beau likes. "I don't think so. It was lovely meeting you but I think it's time for me to go in for the evening."

"Don't go, Peach. It's still early." All the more reason for me to get back to my suite before things heat up around this place.

I leave the water and go to my dress and panties on the beach. I shake my dress before pulling it over my head.

He comes out of the water and is by my side stepping into his trousers. "Did I say something to upset you?"

"Nah. It's all good." I've enjoyed my non-hedonist time with Beau, but he's ready to go on the hunt. It's time for this to end.

Despite attempting to decline, Beau insists on walking me back to my room. Claims he wants to ensure I make it there safely. That may or may not be the truth but it doesn't matter.

He's a hedonist.
Hell, he's poly.
I'm not.
No way we're happening.

CHAPTER 3

ANNA JAMES BENNETT

It's eight in the morning. That's early for a resort like Indulge, so I'm surprised to see the restaurant packed with a breakfast rush. I understand this is Indulge's busiest time, but I thought more guests would be sleeping in this morning after partying long and hard last night.

There are familiar items on the breakfast menu. Bacon. Ham. Eggs. I can get all of those foods at home but I want to try new things.

"What do you recommend I sample first?" Meredith and Grayson are both chefs so they never steer me wrong.

"My favorite is the sweet potato pudding. But the cornmeal pudding is fantastic as well." Meredith has a ginormous sweet tooth so I'm not surprised by her suggestions.

"They are good but a little sugary for my taste. The fish dishes are delicious but the callaloo and cheddar quiche is probably my favorite," Grayson says.

"What in the world is callaloo?"

"It's the Jamaican version of spinach."

I'm all about exploring new foods, but I'm just not sure I can do fish for breakfast, especially after all the drinks I had with Beau last night. I'm not feeling my best. "I think I'd better go with the quiche today."

"How was dining a la room service last night?"

Mere's going to love this. "I wouldn't know. I ended up going out for dinner."

Meredith's mouth gapes. "Shut up! Which restaurant?"

"Consume."

Meredith narrows her eyes. "We walked by and saw a huge crowd waiting to be seated. Who'd you have to blow to get a table?"

Ugh. That's just gross.

"I was told I would have to wait two hours to be seated or I could share a table with another single diner. I was too hungry to wait." I say it nonchalantly, like dining with a stranger was no big deal, but my gal pal should have told me about that option.

"Shit. I forgot to tell you they offered that here during busy times. Just so you know, they do the same thing with rooms."

"You mean strangers share rooms?"

Meredith tests the coffee placed in front of her before replying. "Yup."

I go to work concocting the perfect cup of coffee with creamer and sugar. I have to add more than normal since it's nearly black as tar. "I can't believe people would do that. It's so bizarre."

"What did you think of the dinner companion you were paired with?" Grayson asks.

"He was very pleasant."

Meredith smirks. "He."

"Yes. A very handsome he." Meredith looks pleased as punch.

"Tell me more about this handsome man you dined with." She makes it sound like a date with potential.

"His name is Beau Emerson." I watch Meredith's face for some type of recognition. Nothing. Good. "He's from Buckhead. What are the odds of that?"

"I'm not really surprised. Atlanta and its surrounding areas have a big swingers population. Since this is the most luxurious resort, I'd expect to see the Buckhead hedonists population here rather than those mediocre places in The Bahamas."

"Beau's not a swinger; he's poly."

Mere's eyes widen. "Then he's here with his partners?"

"His trio broke up a month ago. It ended poorly, particularly for him."

"Those kinds of relationships rarely end well, and it's the reason we'll never go that way. Odd numbers never work," Grayson says.

"You know an awful lot about this guy to have only had dinner with him." Meredith is fishing for info.

She's half-right. And I can't stop smiling about the part she has wrong.

Meredith reaches over and punches my upper arm. "You're blushing. What did you do?"

I smile, remembering the fun night I had with Beau. "We talked. We drank. We may have skinny-dipped."

Meredith's mouth gapes. "You little harlot!"

I wish. Maybe. "It was all innocent. Nothing happened."

"And you look totally bummed about it."

Bummed isn't the right word. I think jilted is a better choice. "We were talking and having a great time when the conversation steered toward our standards for sex partners. He said he'd rather show than tell me. I thought he was flirting." I recall the way it made me feel—good for the first time in months. "But then he told me I could help him choose his first fuck. It felt like I'd been doused with a bucket of cold water. I was reminded of the kind of game he was here to play, and the type of man I was dealing with, so I left him to do his thing while I came back to my suite."

It was easy to think of Beau as a normal guy while we were having a regular conversation that didn't include sexual tastes, but I slipped. I allowed myself to enjoy his company a little too much. My mistake.

I have no right to be upset; Beau told me of his true colors. He never pretended to be anything he wasn't.

"He's a hot guy. I'm sure he found plenty of willing women to do whatever he wanted." I'm a little surprised to be bothered by that prospect.

Our conversation is briefly interrupted as breakfast is placed in front of us but Meredith is quick to return to our previous conversation. "I'm certain he didn't mean to offend you."

"My bet is he was probably trying to warm you up to the idea of a threesome by having you choose the other woman."

Grayson's idea might hold water if I'd not been crystal clear about being non-hedonistic, non-swinging, and non-poly. "I don't think so. He called me a vanilla girl after I told him I wasn't into any of the things that go on here."

"Maybe he likes a challenge." Meredith is looking at Grayson instead of me. I suspect there's an underlying conversation I'm not hearing.

I enjoyed talking to him, but I don't plan on being anyone's challenge to be conquered. "This is a big resort. I doubt I'll see him again."

"That would be a shame. You connected with this guy, despite your differences," Meredith says.

"I enjoyed talking to him. I could see us being friends." His lifestyle doesn't bother me, just as Meredith and Grayson's choices don't change my feelings toward them.

"The resort isn't that big. You could run into him again." Meredith is always the optimist, and I know she wants me to move beyond Drake, but I'm confused about why she'd push this. She knows I'll only consider a monogamous relationship.

I shrug my shoulders, trying to appear as though I don't care. "Meh. If I do, okay, and if I don't, okay."

"Right." As my best friend, she can see right through me. "Still planning to hang out at the beach today?"

"Yeah. The *prude* one. By the way, I hate that name."

"It's a great beach. You'll enjoy it." It looked nice from what I could tell last night.

"What's on today's agenda for the two of you?" I asked the question without considering the possible kinky answer I'll get.

"Couples scuba diving."

"That sounds like a ton of fun." I've always wanted to try it.

"We should probably get a move on, Mere. Our lesson begins in twenty minutes."

Meredith takes a last chug of orange juice. "Want to go to dinner with us tonight?"

I hate eating alone. Makes me feel like such a loser. "Sure, if you don't mind me being a third wheel."

"Shut up. You're never a third wheel."

~

I DECIDE to wear the new bikini Meredith gifted me—a black push-up halter top with a white tie between my breasts and the matching black bikini bottom with white ties on each hip. It sits super low so I'm rather proud I allowed Meredith to talk me into doing the full bikini electrolysis a few months ago.

I quickly discover I'm not the only goody-goody around here

when I arrive at the prude beach. It's early but there are so many people that only a few empty loungers remain. I choose a lone chair on the end since I'm hoping unwelcome company won't bug me.

I untie the strings of my top behind my neck and stretch out on the lounger to soak up some rays. I'm not there five minutes before a cute cabana boy stands over me asking what kind of drink I'd like. "Bay Breeze, please."

My drink is delicious, but I'm sipping since I plan to be careful. Heat and alcohol can be a dangerous combination if you don't have the good sense to drink responsibly. And it would suck to get drunk, pass out, and deep-fry my ass in the Jamaican sun.

I relax, close my eyes, and listen to the waves. The sound is soothing but the people around me are disrupting my serenity. *Shut up, people.*

I enjoyed this beach more last night. I'm not sure if that's because it was void of all the current distractions or if Beau's company simply made it more appealing.

I suspect both.

Damn. It's hotter than a whorehouse on nickel night. *Slurp!* I finish my drink quicker than intended. I need a bottle of water next time hottie cabana boy comes around taking drink requests.

Is a gentle breeze too much to ask for?

My back needs sun so I roll to my stomach and stretch my arms overhead. I'm hopeful eliminating the direct exposure on my face will cool me down. It doesn't.

Just when I think I can no longer take the heat, I'm abruptly shaded. "Peach. You could almost pass for the nude beach in that swimsuit. I can see your ass crack."

There it is again. That deep, southern voice. There's just something so warm and smooth about it, like a good whisky making its way down my throat.

I feel something in the pooling sweat at the dip of my lower back. It glides downward, moving into the waistband of my bikini bottom. I think it's his finger. And it's almost in the top of my butt cleft when I jolt straight up. "Hello? Boundaries! Do you have any?"

He's laughing. "I do but they're fairly limited."

I definitely believe that.

My top is untied so I have to hold it in place. "No worries, Peach.

I've already seen those."

I haven't forgotten. "Maybe but not in daylight."

He taps my ankle with the back of his hand. "Scoot over."

I wiggle across the lounger and secure my top behind my neck. He parks himself on the foot of my chair, turned so he's facing me.

Shouldn't he be sleeping in from his late night of whore hounding? "What are you doing out and about so early?"

"Been up since six. I'm an early riser."

I know what he did after we parted ways. "Even when you stay out all night partying and chasing booty?"

"No one has to chase booty here. It's pretty much available twenty-four-seven to anyone who wants it."

"Yeah. You keep telling me that." I'm certain plenty was thrown in his direction after he escorted me to my room last night.

"Only because it's true."

"I assume you were able to find your first fuck without my assistance." It isn't my intention but I come off sounding bitter.

"It was a bust. I couldn't find anyone to suit my fancy."

I'm surprised how much that pleases me. "Then your standards must be exceptionally high."

"They are."

I'm curious about his night. "What did you end up doing after walking me back?"

"Jerking off in the shower."

I conjure an image of what that must look like. If my face wasn't flaming before, it is now. "My God, Beau! You have no filter."

"You're blushing. You're thinking about it, aren't you? Me stroking my cock?"

He's so damn inappropriate. But right. "No! Of course not. My face is red because I'm sitting in the sun." Total lie.

"You're welcome to come to my room and watch if you like. I wouldn't mind."

Oh, my. I wouldn't mind either, in fact, I would love that visual. "No, thank you."

"Anna James. Are you always such a polite, vanilla girl?"

I love the sound of my name on his lips. "Yes. You might try it sometime."

"Try being polite and vanilla or try out a polite, vanilla girl?"

Am I wrong to hope for the latter? Definitely. "Doesn't matter which. I'm guessing you'd not be happy with either."

He leans back on his palms, looking as though he doesn't plan to leave any time soon. "No. Probably not."

He didn't have to agree so quickly. "You're a very rude boy."

"I haven't been a boy in quite some time."

I didn't think so. "How old are you?"

"Old enough to know better."

I don't understand what he means but I'd like to. "Know better than what?"

Those damn dimples make another appearance. They're such a distraction. "Nothing. I'm thirty-five."

I knew he was older than me but I wouldn't have guessed that. He has a much younger face. "I was thinking late twenties or early thirties."

"I'm guessing you're mid twenties."

"Twenty-four."

He nods, looking completely unsurprised. "I'm eleven years older. You might not want to hang out with an old geezer."

"There are old geezers here, but you're definitely not one of them."

"A lot of the women who come here are only interested in the twenty-somethings. They're under the impression they have bigger, harder dicks." He peers over the top of his sunglasses. "They're wrong."

"I can't compare the two, but I'm guessing a thirty-five-year-old with more experience knows just how to . . ." I feel heat rising in my cheeks again so decide not to continue that thought.

Beau chuckles. I see a single brow lift behind his sunglasses. "Yeah. I know just how to . . ."

I bet he does.

"My ex was twenty-five, and he was always far more concerned with how he was going to get off than how it felt for me." That was probably TMI.

"Guys are sexually selfish during their twenties. I don't think we figure things out until we reach thirty, give or take."

"Then that would explain all the mediocre sex I've had." I can't believe I just admitted to that.

"You should never settle for sex that doesn't curl your toes."

This conversation feels like it's rapidly leaving the friend zone. I need to change that. "What are your plans for today?"

"There are not a lot of activities going on right now. Mind if I hang out here with you?"

Beau's looking pretty cozy on the foot of my lounger. "Umm . . . I think you already are."

"Rephrase. Do you mind if I *continue* to hang with you?"

"That's fine but I'm burning up. I've gotta go into the water to cool off."

He peels his shirt from his body and tosses it on top of my bag. "I'll go in with you."

Damn, I was right. Beau's body is muscular. Very nicely chiseled.

His rounded pecs beg to be caressed. His nipples all but scream for me to lick them. But that isn't the kicker. It's that damn V peeking out above his waistband, taunting me. It needs the attention of my hands and mouth as well.

He's almost completely slick. Not a bit of hair on his chest but he has that cherished trail below his belly button leading down to whatever treasure he has inside those trunks. I love that.

Not a bit of ink on his body. Surprising. I thought surely the cover of darkness last night had disguised a black tribal tattoo on his arms or chest.

The water is cool, refreshing. "I should have done this sooner."

I bend at the knees and lower myself until my shoulders are submerged. My top soaks up the cool seawater, and my nipples become hard. Great. It's something embarrassing for him to comment on so I go deeper to conceal them.

I'm keen to know more about this man, something besides his sexual tastes, but he's already proven he can be closed off. I recall how I persuaded him to spill the beans about his fiancée and my confidence grows.

So far today, Beau has been charming and open. Flirty too, which has been nice for the self-esteem. I wonder if he would answer anything else about himself. "Tell me about your family."

His head cocks as his brow creases beneath his sunglasses. "I'm the oldest of five. Three brothers and a baby sister." I like the way he calls her a baby. Sounds like the protective older brother I always wanted but never had. "Judd's thirty-three. Next is Hutch who's thirty. Then there's Wilder who's twenty-eight. Caroline just turned nineteen."

"Thirty-five to nineteen. That's a big gap."

"Yeah. She was a surprise for my parents."

I bet she was. "A pleasant one, I'm sure. Any of your siblings married?"

"No, but Caroline has a baby. A ten-month-old girl named Ashlyn."

I'm guessing that was another surprise. "Wow. That seems like such a young age to be responsible for a child."

"It is, especially since Ashlyn has Down syndrome. Caroline's been forced to grow up faster than most girls her age."

"Does Ashlyn's father help her?"

"No. He's a total asshole."

"That's a typical teen father for ya."

"Anderson's twenty-two." Beau looks heated. "As you can imagine, I was exceptionally pissed off about him messing around with my teenage sister. I wanted to kill him, especially after I found out he had knocked her up. I still consider it when times are rough. But I wouldn't change anything in the world for Ashlyn. She's the apple of my eye."

Protective brother and uncle to a niece with special needs. He just stepped it up another notch on the hotness meter. "Sounds as though you help with her."

"We all do. It's what family does." It's odd to consider Beau a family man. "What about you? Any brothers or sisters?"

"One younger sister. Willa. She's twenty-two."

"Do you see her often?"

"Not as much as I'd like. She and my mom moved back to Mississippi a few years ago."

I miss my mom and sister so much. I wish they didn't live six hours away.

I've considered moving back to Mississippi to be near them but I have a good life in Georgia. No husband or family, granted, but many beloved friends. None as good as Meredith and Grayson by any means, but I can't forget my co-workers and students. I adore them.

"I'm close with my family. I fish, hunt, and play golf with my brothers and dad all the time but football is what brings the whole family together. We're diehard UGA fans."

I'm no diehard fan but I am an alumna "I'm a bulldog too. Graduated from there two years ago."

I have Beau's undivided attention now. "Hell yeah! Ever go back for football games?"

"I've been once since I graduated but only because a friend had an extra ticket."

"We have seats in one of the suites. Never miss a game."

"Champions Club?"

His eyes widen and he's all smiles. *Those damn dimples are killing me.* "Yeah. You know it?"

I have no doubt his family is well off. A donation for just one of those seats is crazy high, far more than my teacher's salary will afford. "I was invited into one of those with a friend once. It was a pretty spectacular experience. I had no idea you could watch the game like that. I think I was most impressed with the food." No hot dogs and chips being served in that place. Catered food only. And a dessert bar to die for.

"It's not bad." Beau is unpretentious. I like that.

"Not bad, my ass. It's awesome."

"I'll take you to a game this fall . . . if you're interested. If not, no big deal." And there it is. The invitation to extend this relationship, whatever it is, on the outside of this resort.

This feels like something different. Not a hedonist who practices polyamory inviting a vanilla girl to a Georgia Bulldogs football game.

I'm intrigued.

I don't think it's possible for me to decline his invitation. "Sure. Sounds fun."

I move to lie on my back to float on the surface of the water. I close my eyes behind my sunglasses and my ears fill with the ocean. I hear nothing. See nothing. Think nothing. I'm weightless, floating like a particle in the air you can only see illuminated by sunlight.

I float for a while before a huge splash of water lands on my face, rushing straight up my nose. The saltwater immediately burns my sinuses. "What the hell, Beau?"

"Go dancing with me tonight."

I don't know what's happening here. "Sure you want to waste

precious time with me instead of working on those ninety-nine fucks?"

He shrugs. "I did the five-knuckle shuffle last night. If I'm being completely honest, I did it this morning too, so I'm good."

Well, hell. That image is in my head again. I hope he doesn't tease me again about coming to his room to watch. I might consider taking him up on the offer.

"Come on. Go with me, Peach. It'll be fun."

His dimples are far too persuasive. There's no hope for me. I can't resist. "Yeah, okay."

CHAPTER 4

ANNA JAMES BENNETT

"WHAT IS THE DRESS CODE FOR THE DANCE CLUB?" SURELY THAT ISN'T CLOTHING optional as well. If it is, forget it. I don't want to be in a place where naked body parts are jiggling.

Meredith lifts a brow. "Depends on which one you're referring to."

"I have no idea."

"There are two. One is on the dressier side while the other tends to be more casual. Sensual elegant works for both. Why do you want to know?"

"I'm going with Beau."

"Then we need to be in my room. I saw what you packed and ain't none of it gonna work for dancing." Meredith moves toward the door.

"I can't go outside like this." I'm still in my tank and boxer shorts.

"Really, Anna James? You think what you're wearing is inappropriate for stepping outside to go into the room next door?"

I look down to inspect myself and point to the problem. "Yes. You can see my nipples through this."

"Again, you think that's a problem for here?" She's laughing at me.

"It's indecent for me." I grab a T-shirt and pull it over my tank before following Mere to her suite. "I happen to like the clothes I brought. I bought most of them specifically for this trip." My budget was basically next to nothing, but I found a lot of summer items on clearance.

"The clothes you brought work fine for home but not here. You'll stand out like a sore thumb. The vultures will circle if you look like a newbie and be quick to call dibs on you."

"Umm . . . not up for grabs here."

"They won't understand that. And I know you'll be annoyed if they bother you."

I don't want to be harassed. "Then show me what you have."

She spreads an ensemble of at least fifteen dresses across the bed. "Shit. This collection looks like you beat a hooker's ass and then stole her wardrobe."

"Shut up and pick something."

I choose a black one shoulder with slits in the sides. I hold it up for inspection. "Think I'd look okay in this?"

"You'd look killer in any of them." One of the great things about having Meredith for a best friend is that we're very close in size. My butt is chunkier so this dress will fit tighter. Sometimes that's good but I'm not sure with this one.

"I don't know, Mere. I'm afraid it's going to be tight and ride up my ass."

She takes it off the hanger. "The only way to know is to try it on. If it doesn't work, we'll move on to something else."

I strip down and slip into the spandex sheath. She's beaming so I know this one is a winner. "It's a hell yes from me. What do you think?"

I step in front of the full-length mirror for inspection. "I like it."

"Like, hell. You should love it. It looks fantastic. It's way better on you than me."

I remove my ponytail holder keeping the messy bun on top of my head in place. "Okay. I admit. I love it. Hair up, down, straight or curly?"

"Big loose curls. No doubt."

"I think so too." I don't do it often because it's so much work, but I have plenty of time to get ready.

Meredith's eyes meet mine in the mirror. "You want to look great for this guy. I can tell."

I spin around to meet her face to face. "I do not. I like talking to him. That's all."

She's reading far too much into this.

"You're such a liar. A bad one. You really like this guy."

"I do, but only as a friend. He knows I'm not up for anything kinky."

I'm oddly comfortable with Beau but I think I know why. He reminds me of Grayson.

"Be careful with him. He's a different kind of animal you don't understand."

I get it. Beau's a beast of prey . . . just like her husband. I remember telling Meredith the same thing about Grayson when she told me about his sexual preferences.

Look at how that turned out.

Meredith was barely twenty when she walked into Grayson's class at the culinary institute. Her spark for him was instantaneous, despite the thirteen-year age gap. Poor guy never had a chance. She saw him, wanted him, and was determined to make him hers.

Meredith always finds a way to get what she wants.

The swingers thing came as quite the shock to Mere, but she wanted G so badly she was willing to give it a shot. I still remember what she said about him when she told me he enjoyed swapping sexual partners. *"Grayson makes me feel a little dirty. I fucking love it. And I fucking love him."*

Her wry smile betrayed her and I knew she had agreed to try it. Turns out, swapping suited her.

That was almost four years ago and their relationship is stronger than ever.

Married. Successful. Happy. They have it all. It's difficult to not envy them.

They're happier than a tornado in a trailer park. But sharing would never suit me. Ever. So, that means Beau Emerson is off limits.

And that's . . . very disappointing.

~

I HARDLY ATE anything at dinner. The thought of going out dancing with Beau tonight has me in knots. Of course, Meredith noticed and gave me shit about it. I'm grateful Grayson stepped in and told her to cool her jets about the whole thing.

I appreciate her concern, but I'm a big girl. I can handle whatever comes my way.

Beau knocks and my heart instantly speeds. It's been more than four years since I've opened the door for a date, other than Drake, and it's still a dreaded moment for me. The guy is obligated to remark on how great you look. It's awkward.

Shit. I just referred to this as a date. It's not.

I open the door and begin chattering so we can avoid that uncomfortable moment where he's obligated to comment on how I look. "Hey, I'm ready. Just give me a sec to grab my clutch."

I go to the bathroom to fetch my bright pink lipstick and take one last look at myself. Loose curls. Smokey eyes. Slutty dress. Ridiculously high fuck-me pumps I'm going to regret after about a dozen steps. I'm primed and ready to dance my ass off.

"Just so you know, I haven't been dancing in years. I may be a little rusty." Drake hated clubbing. Every time we went, he'd sulk in the corner so I eventually stopped asking to go.

Wanker.

I chuckle, thinking how Sweetie Pie Caitlyn must be coping with Mr. Snooze Fest.

I come out of the bathroom to find Beau inside my suite instead of where I left him at the door. This is another thing I've not done in a while—been behind a closed door with a man who isn't my husband.

I hold up my clutch. "Got it. I'm ready."

He's unmoving. "Something wrong?"

He twirls his finger in a circle. "Spin."

I do a three-sixty, stopping to face him. "Up to snuff?"

He's unblinking. "So fucking beautiful it hurts."

Total. Panty. Dropper.

I'm taken aback by his words; I've never been told anything like that before. Drake seldom complimented me, but when he did, it always felt . . . forced.

Shouldn't a husband find his wife beautiful, because she's his precious treasure, and tell her often? My father did. I heard him tell my mother countless times how lovely she was.

So fucking beautiful it hurts. Geez. Those words make my skin warm and my heart skip a beat.

But I can't afford to be carried away by pretty words. Beau Emerson is fluent in charming woman. In fact, he has to be twice as good as any other man if he's to charm two women at once.

I look down and dig through my clutch. I'm not looking for

anything in particular. It's a diversion so he won't see how affected I am by his words. "Thank you."

He lifts my keycard from the table and twiddles it between two fingers. "Looking for this?"

"Yeah, thanks." I take the plastic card from him and drop it into my purse.

Beau gets the door for me, another thing Drake seldom did. "You're quite the gentleman."

His hand comes to rest on my lower back as we exit, and chills erupt all over my body. No man's touch has ever done that to me. I don't think there was ever a time when Drake's made my body react this way.

"Gentleman in public. Alpha in the bedroom." His words are accompanied by a seductive chortle.

Alpha in the bedroom?

That sounds hot, not like anything I experienced with my four years of mediocre, missionary-position sex.

Sheez. That gives me way too much to think about tonight.

The club is already packed when we enter. "Is this normal or is it extra crowded because of Wicked Week?"

"I've never seen it this full." He takes my hand to lead me through the mob. "Come on. Let's get a drink."

He pushes his way to the bar. "What do you want?"

I feel like a beer. "Stella."

"Nice choice. I think that's what I'll have too."

I move away from the bar to stand out of the path of drink seekers. I feel safer in the corner. I'm not a fan of how some, men *and* women, brush against me as they pass.

I wave my hand when I see Beau searching the crowd. He gives me a quick upward nod of acknowledgement when he finds me.

He holds out my Stella. "We're not going to get a table . . . unless you want to be a little friendlier."

"No, thank you." I'm good.

"You might change your mind after you stand in those heels for a while." I'm predicting he's right. I'm already experiencing some discomfort.

"I'll be okay."

We move to the quietest spot in the club, but we're still forced to yell over the music. We chitchat about this and that. Before I know it, we've each had four Stellas. "You drink beer like a man."

I shrug. "I've always been able to keep up."

Beau passes off our empty bottles to a waitress as she walks by. "Dance with me."

Four doses of personality enhancement. I'm so in. "Sure."

A fast-paced song with a lot of bass is thumping. It's a great tempo for moving my hips. I know the lyrics by heart so I sing along. Of course, it's too loud for Beau to hear me, which is good since I can't sing worth a damn, but he watches my mouth and facial expressions. He grins and I'm reminded of how animated I can be when I get carried away over a great song.

I move close to Beau. Very close. The dance floor is the one place in my book where it's deemed acceptable to dry hump in public so I take advantage.

I turn around and sway my hips, wiggling my bottom against him. He hooks his hand around my waist and pulls my body firmly against his. He grinds hard and there's no question about what I'm feeling pressed against my ass.

Being with someone like Beau is a game I don't understand; I've not been taught the rules. I only know I like him and what's happening between us.

Beau holds my shoulders and guides me to turn around. He then moves his hold to my waist and drags his mouth down my front as he lowers himself in front of me. He moves his hands to my ass and pulls me against him so his face is pressed to my groin. I can feel his warm breath between my legs through the thin fabric of my dress.

Oh, fuck. This is hot.

He rises slowly. On the way up, his mouth hovers over mine. So close, yet so far away.

The intimacy of the almost kiss is often times more powerful than the kiss itself.

I want his lips on mine so badly. And I think he does, too. There's a hunger in his eyes, but even if I couldn't see it, I can feel it pressed against my stomach.

My heart is pounding in my chest. He's looking at my mouth so I lick my lips in anticipation. I'm waiting, expecting it any second, but the moment is lost when I feel someone dancing behind me. Or rather on me.

I look over my shoulder and see some random guy thrusting his cock against my ass. Gross.

I look at Beau to gauge his reaction. Does he like watching another man do this to me?

This is a telltale moment. It will define this relationship and the immediate place it's going because I'm not at all into what this guy is doing behind me.

Beau leans forward and says something into his ear. The man gives me a nod and swiftly leaves.

"I don't know what you said to make him move along, but thank you."

"Some fail to recognize, or acknowledge, when their advances are unwelcome so they need a little push in the right direction." He takes my hand in his. "Come on. I want to take you somewhere special."

"Are we leaving?" I'm having a good time. I don't want to go yet.

"No, but I know places where we won't be bothered by people like that."

He leads me to a staircase where we run into a huge, muscled man with a head shaved slicker than an onion. He steps out of our way when he sees Beau. "Welcome back, Mr. Emerson."

"Thanks, Romario. This is Anna James Bennett. She's my guest tonight."

"Welcome, Miss Bennett."

"Thank you."

Beau holds my hand as we ascend the staircase. "Where are we going?"

"Can't tell you. You'll need to see it to understand."

We enter a dark room. The wall to my immediate left is made entirely of glass overlooking the dance club. "I didn't notice this when we were downstairs."

"Most people don't."

I'm confused by what I'm seeing.

The room is completely black and white and accented with pops of red. Sin's palette colors, again.

To my right are rows of booths, very much like restaurant seating but with one huge exception. Beds are in place of tables. "What in the world is this place?"

"A private couples lounge. Only guests who pay an access fee are allowed inside."

Each space is enclosed on three sides by walls with an opening facing the glass over the club. I notice several are closed off by thick velvet drapes.

He's still holding my hand when he leads me down the aisle in front of the first row. We pass several occupied booths. Some couples are having drinks as they observe the dancing below while others are involved in their own activities.

Shit. I can't wrap my mind around what's happening *publicly* inside the enclosure we just passed.

Beau stops at the booth on the end, right next to the couple having oral sex.

Great. I'll never unsee that.

"This one is mine." He tilts his head in the direction of the cunnilingus couple. "I lease it by the year so I don't have to share a space with people like that."

Can't say I blame him for that.

I'm not able to resist peering over my shoulder at the show. It's like a car wreck you can't look away from. "They get off on being watched. That's why their drape isn't closed."

I feel dirty for looking.

Beau gestures for me to go in first. "After you, Peach."

I ponder the best way to get inside. I'd get on my hands and knees and crawl in if I were wearing pants. That's not a possibility with this dress so I guess it's sit and scoot.

I slide back a few inches at a time, pulling my dress down as I go so I don't show him everything I have beneath.

"I'll get these for you." Beau grasps the backs of my heels and slips them off. "Better?"

"Yes! It was sort of dumb to wear them out dancing but I love the way they look with this dress."

"The dress. The shoes. You. All perfection."

Is that a line? If so, it's a great one. And I'm falling for it. "You're sweet."

He crawls in beside me on his hands and knees. "I'm being honest. You're one of the most stunning women I've ever seen."

Swoon.

Beau Emerson makes me feel like a woman. A *desired* woman. His words. The way he looks at me. His body language. Everything he does is a huge turn-on.

We're sitting close. All he'd have to do is lean over to kiss me. And I realize I want him to.

"Drinks?" I jolt when a cocktail waitress appears at the foot of the bed. She's dressed, if you can call it that, in what looks like an ensemble made from black electrical tape. There are a few strips here and there with very little left to the imagination.

Beau doesn't appear the least bit interested in her near bareness. He's overlooking her because his complete attention is on me. I like that. "Beer?"

"Sure."

We sit at the head of the bed, our backs resting against the stacks of pillows while having another Stella.

Marian Hill's "Got It" thumps below. Moaning from the neighboring couple carries into our booth. My every nerve ending is stimulated. Humming. Buzzing. Craving.

I need a distraction.

"Is Beau short for something?"

He shakes his head. "It is but we're not going there."

"Beaumont?" It's the obvious choice. Maybe.

He says nothing so perhaps not. "Beaudon? Beauchamp?" No response so I elbow him. "Tell me."

He chuckles while saying, "Big Beau." I barely know him but I'm not the least bit surprised by his big cock remark.

I giggle and choke on my drink. My mishap sends beer into my sinuses, causing me to accidentally snort. I cup my hand over my nose but do it again. "Sorry. I really didn't mean to do that."

"This is a tight space. If you fart next, you're outta here, Peach."

Omigod. I'm laughing so hard I lose my breath and tears pool in the corners of my eyes. "Dammit, you're going to make me mess up my makeup."

I love Beau's sense of humor but he's trying to distract me from guessing his full name. "I think Beau is short for something dapper. Regal. And you hate it." I rack my brain for a minute. "I forgot about Beauregard."

He chuckles, a low sound deep in his chest. "I'll never tell."

I think I've hit the nail on the head. "Beauregard. That's what I'm calling you unless you tell me otherwise."

He shrugs. "Whatever butters your bread, baby."

He holds out his drink. "A toast to Peach and Beauregard."

"To Peach and Beauregard. Now, that's a pair." *Clink!* We tap the necks of our glass beer bottles.

We suck those down in no time, and as though on cue, electrical tape woman appears with more. "Anything else, Mr. Emerson?"

"We're fine. I'll ring if that should change."

"Very good, sir."

I wait until she's gone to ask. "You'll ring her?"

He points to an intercom on the wall. "Call system." Of course. How silly of me.

We work on our fresh beers while watching the show below on the dance floor. The dry humping I was doing against Beau earlier has nothing on what's happening right now. Which reminds me of earlier. "What did you say to that man on the dance floor to make him go away?"

"I told him your pussy and ass were mine and I didn't share you with anyone."

Holy shit. My stomach just did something. Maybe a backflip?

"That ass monkey pushed himself on you without an invitation or permission. I showed him kindness by not punching him in his face, which is what I really wanted to do. But violence is grounds for being thrown out of the resort and that would mean I wouldn't get to see you this week. And I would really like that . . . if you're open to it."

He wants to see me this week?

I'm pretty sure a feather could knock me over right now.

"I don't know what spending time with a person like you means." Is Beau looking for a friend? A lover? Or a new partner for a triad? It's definitely a no to the latter.

"We don't have to put a label on what it is."

Beau has desires I'll never be able to satisfy. What most men consider a fantasy is his reality. I'd be wise to not forget that no matter how much fun we're having.

"I like you, Beauregard." We both smile when I use his new nickname. "I enjoy spending time together. But you, and the things you like, frighten me."

He grazes the back of his fingers down my cheek. "Does my simple touch scare you?"

I look down. "Yes."

He grasps my chin and forces me to look at him. He rubs my bottom lip with his thumb. "And this too?"

I nod.

He takes my beer from my hand, placing it on the shelf inside the booth. He leans in for a kiss, the one I've been dying for since he told me I was so fucking beautiful it hurt. But if I'm being honest, I wanted it long before that.

I'm trembling. My breath is rapid. I may even be a little lightheaded.

He stops before his lips touch mine. We're so close I can smell the Stella on his breath. I want to taste it. "How does this make you feel?"

"It scares the hell out of me."

His bottom lip grazes mine but he still doesn't kiss me. "I'll back off right now if it's what you want. We'll leave this lounge. I'll escort you back to your room and say goodnight. But if that happens, I'm going back to my suite for a cold shower so I can jerk off while fantasizing about what might have happened if you had told me to kiss you right now."

Gush! The crotch of my panties just became drenched.

This is it. The second moment of the night that will define where this relationship is going. "Kiss me."

He laces his fingers through my hair and holds me prisoner when he lowers his mouth to mine. I open to invite his tongue inside. It meets mine and together the two become erotic dance partners.

Ah. A first kiss. Always the last to be forgotten.

He stops, his lips hovering over mine. His breath is warm against my skin. "More or stop? Your call."

I'm standing at a crossroads. He's asking me to venture further with him but my heart tells me one more step will take me beyond the point of no return.

I'm twenty-four, divorced, in Jamaica, and kissing a seriously hot man. *Why the fuck would I say no?* "More."

His mouth leaves mine and travels down my neck. "Your lips make me wonder what the rest of you will taste like."

I close my eyes and debate what I'm doing. This goes against everything I believe and all the things I want for myself.

This man knows the power of seduction. He's giving me exactly what I want, so slowly, it's taking my breath away.

This isn't love. Nor is it true and beautiful. But I want it more than my next breath.

I have no idea what it is I think we're doing or what we can ever become. I only know I like it a whole fucking lot.

Beau tugs at the strapless side of my dress until my breast pops out of the top. His hand encompasses the mound and squeezes rhythmically as he moves lower. He pushes it up and sucks my nipple into his mouth, circling the hard pebble with his tongue. When he finishes, he drags his teeth over it.

Every touch, lick, and suck has a direct link sending a message to the center of my groin. *Get ready for what's coming next.*

He rolls my body so I'm lying on my side.

What's he doing?

Oh, hell. He can keep doing that.

His tongue, which has been darting in and out of the open slits down the side of my dress, touches my hipbone. I tremble from its contact against the sensitive skin there.

I open my eyes and see the silhouette of a woman standing at the opening of the booth we're in. I jolt up, covering my exposed chest with my hand, and she moves away.

"What's wrong?"

"There was a woman standing there watching us." Creepy.

"Probably Shayna from the next booth. She likes to watch in addition to being watched."

"Well, I don't like to be ogled." The curtain is open but it's still a complete violation of privacy.

He moves to the end of the bed, pulls the plush velvet drapes together, and fastens them with a hook. "Easy fix."

He turns around but doesn't come back to me. Instead, he sits back on his feet, placing his palms on the top of his thighs. "I know you're not sure about this. Or me. That's why I'm not going to fuck you tonight."

I admire his confidence. "You assume I'd let you."

He crawls in my direction on all fours before hovering over my body. "Trust me when I say you're going to wish I would."

He puts his hands on my knees and pushes my legs apart. Like cracking open a book he can't wait to read. And I let him. I'm trembling, impatient to experience what he has in store for me.

He hoists my dress to my waist. My entire groin throbs as he lightly strokes his fingertips over the wet crotch of my panties. "See? You're already drenched, and I've barely touched you."

I can't get enough air in and out of my nose so I open my mouth to breathe. I work to gain control, but it still results in an embarrassing pant.

He cups his hand over my groin and pets me through my wet panties. Every nerve ending between my legs is alive. "I don't think I've stopped thinking about you for a single minute since we met."

He pushes the wet fabric aside and groans beneath his breath. "You're so smooth. I love that."

He glides his fingers up and down my center. His fingertip grazes my clit with every upward stroke, enough to stimulate but not nearly enough to satisfy. It's torture, the sweetest kind.

I tilt my hips and rock against his hand. I lift my arms over my head and grasp the pillow under my head, turning my face into it. "Omigod."

Beau thrusts two fingers in and out of me while working my clit. At least that's what I think he's doing. I can't really be sure since it's something I've never had done to me before.

I've not been blessed with generous sexual partners. Only takers.

He lowers his mouth to my neck and kisses me just below my lobe. His words are a seductive, breathy whisper traveling from his lips to my ear. "My cock is going to feel better than this when I get it inside you."

His cock. Inside me.

Oh, yes.

I'm losing, no finding, myself in what Beau's doing. I'm discovering a part of me I've never known. "Oh. My. God. Please don't stop."

I tense all over, including my curled toes, when the rhythmic contractions in my groin begin. Once. Twice. I lose count of how many times my internal body squeezes around Beau's fingers. "Don't stop coming yet, Anna James. Ride it all the way."

I couldn't stop this fast-moving train if I tried. I've never experienced toe-curling ecstasy that is this orgasm.

How the hell have I missed out on this?

I bite my lip and grasp him tightly around his neck to pull him close. He wasn't kidding. I do want him to fuck me.

I relax when it ends. My entire body goes lax. That includes allowing my legs to fall completely apart. I don't have it in me to care if he sees my goodies.

I would let Beau do that to me again anytime. No question.

He moves up my body until he's lying on top of me, his erection pressing against my crotch. "The way you respond to my touch is sexy as fuck."

I want to touch him, see if he has a similar response.

I push my hand between our bodies so I can reach his dick. I stretch my neck so my mouth reaches his earlobe. "I'm going to make you come so hard."

He growls and flips us over so I'm on top. I'm straddling him so my dress is jacked up to my hips. Perfect opportunity to grind my crotch against his cock. "You are killing me, Peach."

I sit back and push my hand down the front of his trousers. He's full and warm inside my palm. I grasp firmly and move my hand up and down in a steady motion.

"Being inside me is going to feel so much better than this." I'm the one using his words now. Dirty ones. And I like it; it feels right.

"My cock was so jealous of my fingers when they were in you."

I stop stroking it and rub his tip over the crotch of my underwear. All it would take would be to push the fabric of my panties aside and he could be inside me. "You were right when you predicted I'd want you to fuck me."

"Yeah. He has a way of doing that."

What the fuck?

I'm startled to hear a voice inside our booth so I jerk around to see what's going on. Someone is standing at our booth entrance holding the drapes wide open. "Honey, I'm home."

CHAPTER 5

ANNA JAMES BENNETT

"SHIT." I'M SHINING MY ENTIRE ASS TO WHOEVER THIS IS SO I QUICKLY ROLL OFF Beau and yank my dress down.

"Get the fuck out, Linc." I jolt when Beau raises his growly, authoritative voice.

Our intruder doesn't budge so Beau kicks one of his feet in the guy's direction, narrowly missing his crotch. "Christ on a cracker. You could have kicked me in the balls."

"That was my intention." Beau groans beneath his breath.

"Simmer down, Bobo."

"I *had* a beautiful woman sitting on top of me with her hand around my cock. Simmering down is the complete opposite of what I want, hence the reason I'm telling you to leave. Now."

"No, motherfucker. I have a beef with you."

Beau shakes his head. "And I have a grievance with you."

"You walked right past my booth with this lovely lady and didn't stop to say hello, kiss my ass, or anything."

"That would be because I didn't want you scaring the hell out of Anna James, which I imagine you're sort of doing right now."

"I'm Linc. It's a pleasure to make your acquaintance." The man offers his right hand for a shake, and all I can do is look at it. Really? I just had my palm wrapped around Beau's cock and he wants to shake hands? That's just nasty.

I shake my head. "Probably not the best time for a handshake."

Linc comes into the booth and stretches out next to me.

Freak!

He interrupts our intimate moment and then climbs into the booth with us? Unbelievable.

I bug my eyes at Beau so he'll know I disapprove. He better not think this is going to turn into a threesome.

He pats my leg and leans over to whisper in my ear. "Don't worry. I'm going to get him out of here."

"You didn't come to the pool party last night." Well, at least Linc is validating what Beau told me. Looks like he did turn in after he escorted me to my room. It's a little silly but that makes me smile inside.

"I had a late evening out with Anna James."

"I heard you put Erin and Heath out on their asses." Oh. Linc must know Beau well.

"Sure the fuck did."

"What happened?" This guy's a nosy bastard.

"Not going there with you, Linc."

"Are the two of you starting up a new poly trio? If so, I want in." Wow. I think he's totally serious. And I suspect it's the reason behind his rude interruption. He came to call dibs before anyone else had a chance. *Apparently, these kinds of people like laying claims on others.*

Beau swats away the hand Linc rests on my thigh and replaces it with his own. "Forget it. I'm not sharing her with anyone."

Chills erupt down my body; I can't help but like the hint of possessive, alpha-tone in his voice.

Linc nibbles his bottom lip while looking me over, head to toe. It's unsettling to be undressed by his eyes. "Mmm . . . can't say I blame you. I'd keep this one all to myself too."

He stretches and groans before scooting to the edge to leave. Thank God. "Do let me know if you change your mind. I'd love a taste. You know how much I visually enjoy blondes."

He isn't gone a second too soon. "What a whack job."

"Linc's not so bad . . . when he isn't interrupting one hell of a hand job."

I wanted to make him come. Hard. And I would have if we'd not been interrupted. "We didn't get to the best part."

"No, we didn't." Beau leans over and kisses the side of my neck. Makes me want to climb on top of him again to finish what I started. But, not here.

"Can we go somewhere else? Maybe a place with a little more

freedom from disturbance?"

"Our rooms are the only places we'll find privacy."

I don't respond because I'm torn.

"Don't worry, Peach. We can go to my room, and you can leave whenever you want."

Choosing to go to a suite with a man I just met, especially one like Beau, is a big decision. Scary stuff. I've never done anything like that; I've always exercised extreme caution in everything I do. And look where that got me. Dumped within a year of marriage.

Beau's already given me one toe-curling orgasm, and he's offering more. *Is there really a choice, Anna James?*

"I want to."

"Thank fuck." The words barely reach my ears before Beau grasps the back of my neck and pulls me in so his lips can reach mine.

Aah! Every woman dreams of being kissed like this, just once in her lifetime, so hard and deep she can feel it down to her toes.

Time to throw caution to the wind and live for the moment without worry for potentially ruinous consequences.

Beau's suite is on the opposite side of the resort from mine, but it's close to the club, so the walk isn't far. I'm thankful since my feet are already protesting.

He holds my hand on the way. It's sweet and romantic, but I'm not plagued with the misconception that this budding relationship is either of those things.

We enter and I'm confounded by the differences in our suites. His is much roomier with a kitchen and dining area. There are a lot of doors so I'm guessing he has more than one bedroom. "Hot damn! Is this the presidential suite?"

"Maybe."

I go to the sheer drapes in front of his windows to see what kind of view he has. I find French doors leading out onto a balcony facing a beach. No surprise there. "Nude or prude view?"

"Prude."

"Awe. That's too bad."

"Not really. It enabled me to watch you today."

I should be a little disturbed to learn that. But I'm not. "You didn't spy for long; you showed up about thirty minutes after I arrived."

"Because I didn't want to see you from a distance."

He says things like that, and I'm further confused about what is happening between us. "You could be with any woman of your choosing at this resort, yet you're with the one and only non-hedonist at a hedonism resort. Why?"

"I was intrigued by you from the moment you sat at my table." I'm reminded of the conversation I had with Meredith and Grayson this morning at breakfast.

I won't be anyone's challenge to conquer.

"Is that code for seeing me as a conquest? Someone you want to seduce into your world of hedonism?"

"No. It means I like you and enjoy our conversations."

A roguish grin spreads beneath his stubble as he approaches. When he reaches me, his hands go to my hips and pull me close. His mouth hovers over mine, his warm breath teasing my lips. "Perhaps you're the one trying to seduce me into your vanilla world."

Hands cup beneath my ass and I'm lifted so my legs are wrapped around him. I hold on tightly around his shoulders as he carries me to the sofa. He falls back onto the couch, and I'm straddling him again. Good. It means I'm the one in control.

He places a hand on each side of my face and gazes into my eyes. "You are so fucking beautiful."

The expression I see there tells me everything I need to know. This man, despite his usual preferences, wants the vanilla me just as I am.

I squeeze him tightly, pressing my body hard against his. I rotate my hips in a circular motion against his hard cock pressing into my crotch. I reach between us to slip my hand into his trousers, but he flips us over so I'm on my back. I should have known he wasn't going to let me be in charge for long.

His hand disappears beneath my dress and navigates its way down the front of my black lace panties. Looks like I was wrong in believing we came here to finish what I started. Seems we're starting over from the beginning. No complaints here. He can use those magic fingers to touch me any time he wants.

I spread my legs wide, giving him full access to my body. My breathing has turned to panting as I anticipate what he's going to do next.

He slides a finger down through my slick center and back up once in a slow, torturous stroke. My clit is barely grazed. I strongly suspect that is purposefully done. But I like it. I'm desperate for more so I move my hips against his fingers.

"I want you to be mine this week. No one else's."

He's stroking me faster. It feels so good I can hardly register the words I hear. So I say nothing.

"Answer me, Peach."

"Hmm?" It comes out as a delicate whimper between breaths.

His finger finds my erogenous switch. I jolt from the surprise of its sensitivity as he rubs it in a circular motion. My back bows as my legs part even farther.

"Tell me what I want to hear. Say you'll be mine."

No way I can agree to anything while he's doing this. "I can't think straight right now."

He stops the circular pleasure and his fingers retreat. "This stops until I get an answer."

He's just being irrational. "This is coercion."

"Use any term you like. I call it utilizing whatever means necessary to get what I want. And that, my beautiful peach, is you."

I grasp his wrist and push his hand back down in my panties. "Don't stop."

He strokes my clit a few times before coming to a standstill again. "Give me the answer I want, and I'll keep going."

I can say yes now and back out later if I change my mind. But seriously, who would want to renege on this for the next week?

"Yes."

"Yes to what?"

I'm squeezing his wrist. Hard. "I'll be yours this week."

And just like that, I bend to his will. Fuck.

"You've pleased me, Peach. Now, I'm going to please you."

Beau moves to his knees and pushes my dress above my hips before grasping the sides of my panties and dragging them down my legs. He presses his lips to my inner thigh and places a kiss against my scalding skin. "I treat everything belonging to me with great care."

I shouldn't like hearing him refer to me as his possession. But I do.

He trails kisses up my inner thighs. "We'll have eight nights of this. Do you think you can handle all the orgasms I'm going to give you?"

I don't know. I could very well lose my mind after this one, but I damn sure want to give it a try. "Abso-fucking-lutely."

"Love that attitude, Peach."

He places his tongue flat against my center and swipes upward in slow motion until he finds my clit.

"Tastes." *Lick.*

"So." *Suck.*

"Fucking." *Bite – oh, hell.*

"Good."

He then uses the tip to lick me in a circular movement. A moment later he spices things up by going side to side as his fingers simultaneously thrust in and out.

He has a magic tongue to accompany those magic fingers. I wonder if he has a magic cock too. I plan on finding out.

The initial, tingly sensations of an orgasm make their presence known. I simultaneously want to suppress them so this can last longer while I pine for the earth-shattering flutters I'm certain will curl my toes. *Again.*

The decision isn't mine. Beau is the one in control. And he's holding nothing back.

I push my fingers into his hair and fist the top while I squirm beneath his grip. Some form of garbled sound escapes my mouth when the rhythmic flutters in my pelvis begin. Beau sucks my clit hard and slows the movement of his fingers. His movements are methodical. Deliberate. And all about bringing me pleasure.

I'm utterly spent and boneless when the rhythmic contractions cease.

Beau crawls up my body until we're face to face. I'm so dazed I have to blink several times to focus on his face. And those eyes. My God, those big, beautiful hazel eyes have the ability to hypnotize me.

He rubs my lip with his thumb before leaning down for a kiss. I smell me on his breath. It's weird. Not something I'm used to. "You won't regret saying yes. I'm going to give you the best week of your life, Peach."

I reach up and run my fingertips along his stubbly chin. My confidence is at an all-time high. I feel brave. "Maybe it's me who will give you the best week of your life."

I kiss him quickly before cueing him to flip with me so I'm back on top. I kiss the spot below his earlobe and whisper, "My turn to please you."

"Fuck, yeah. I'm up for that." Yes, he is.

I move to straddle him. He tugs the shoulder of my dress down and covers my nipple with his mouth. He sucks air in through his teeth when I grind against him. "You have no idea how badly I want to fuck you."

"Then do." I don't reach into his trousers this time. I yank the button open and lower the zipper. I push the front of his underwear down so he's freed.

He growls beneath his breath. "I told you I wouldn't fuck you tonight."

He's torn about keeping his word. That says a lot about his character but I'm not looking for integrity right now. "You did, but you also said you'd make me want you to. And I do. Desperately. That has to count for something."

He grasps both sides of my face and pulls me close so we're eye to eye. "But you're still not sure about me."

"I agreed to give myself to you while we're at this resort. I don't think I'd have done that if I wasn't positive about what I want." Beauregard Emerson. He's what I want, and I plan to have him, starting now.

I fist his cock and stroke up and down. "My hand might feel pretty good but being inside me will be so much better. Tighter. Wetter. Deeper."

"Fuck, I can't wait until tomorrow," he growls.

He loops one arm around my waist, and I hang on to him as he thrusts upward to retrieve his wallet from his back pocket. When he lowers us to the sofa again, he releases my waist and leans back. He takes the square package out and tears it open with his teeth. One fluid motion and he's sheathed in latex. Dude is fast.

He thrusts upward again to rid himself completely of his pants and underwear. He's still wearing a linen button-down but not for long. I start at the top and work my way down. "Every button you undo brings me closer to coming undone."

"I can't wait to watch you come undone."

I push his shirt from his shoulders when I'm finished and toss it to his growing pile of clothes on the floor.

Beau Emerson is all man. And all naked beneath me. I can't resist my urge to reach out and touch his muscular chest. Flat stomach.

God, he's beautiful.

He grasps the bottom of my dress and pushes upward. "This is coming off. I'm dying to see you naked again."

Beau has already stripped me of my panties, and I came braless, so I'm completely bare when the dress comes off with the exception of the fuck-me pumps. Those stay on.

Beau pushes my breasts together and presses his face into the center of them, moving his head back and forth. His facial scruff is scratchy but feels good. "These tits . . . they're magnificent."

He sucks them briefly before moving his mouth upward to kiss my neck. Always an enormous turn-on for me.

I love foreplay, but I'm ready to have Beau Emerson inside me. I rise on my knees and grasp the tip of his rock-hard cock so I can guide it to my entrance. I slide the tip through my slick center before slowly sinking down. He groans loudly after he's deep inside.

I wrap my arms around his shoulders and move up and down, sliding him almost completely out before lowering myself down again. I ride him slowly. Deliberately. I want to make this last for as long as possible.

"This feels so fucking good, but I really need to be in control."

His hands grasp my hips and we roll so I'm on my back. Again. He uses his legs to push mine apart and positions his erection against the very wet center between my legs. He bites his bottom lip and shakes his head as he groans, "Peach, I'm about to fuck you so hard. You have no idea."

He drives into me with one smooth motion—hard, just like he promised. He warned me but I was not expecting this kind of power behind his thrust. The noise forced from me sounds something like a cross between a gasp and moan.

He pulls back with deliberate leisure. It feels like he's going to slide out completely, but then he thrusts into me again with even more domination.

I'm surprised when he reaches for my feet and brings them over his shoulders so he can get deeper inside me. His pace is slow, but every stroke is deliberate. And, oh so powerful. This man wasn't kidding when he said he was going to fuck me hard. And I'm loving it.

His fingertips find my most sensitive area. He's going to try to make me come a third time instead of concentrating solely on his own orgasm. Incredible. I've *never* been with a man who cared if I came the first time.

"Is that good for you?"

"Very." It's crazy good. I have no idea how he's managing this maneuver, but the combination of him rubbing my clit while he's thrusting in and out of me is amazing.

"I'm about to come again." The words are barely out before the muscular contractions deep within my pelvis begin squeezing around Beau's cock.

He pulls my legs down from his shoulders and thrusts as deep as his body will allow.

"I feel it, Peach. Ride it out. Come all around me." Beau shudders and groans as he drives into me the last few times.

I'm fully satiated and relaxed. A euphoria I've never experienced is spreading from the center of my body toward my limbs. Bliss.

Beau sinks over me, his body relaxing between my legs. Wait for it. Wait for it. He'll pull out and get up to redress at any minute. Probably dismiss me back to my room.

Doesn't happen.

He remains inside me while softly tracing his fingertips up and down my arms. It feels . . . intimate. And unexpected.

I wish I knew what he is thinking right now.

He nuzzles the side of my neck with his facial scruff. "I like the way that feels."

His hand finds its way between my legs to cup my groin. "Mmm . . . I like the way that feels."

Beau has a crude edge about him. And I like it.

Plump lips kiss the side of my face. "Turn with me."

He pulls out and we roll so his front is to my back. *Spooning.*

His arm drapes over me and finds my hand, lacing our fingers. "Will you tell your friends about our arrangement for the week?"

"Of course. I'd never keep something like that from Meredith and Grayson."

"You don't anticipate them giving you shit about it, do you?"

Hmm . . . I'm not really sure after the conversation we had this morning. "I guess we'll see."

Beau brings my hand to his mouth for a kiss. "Spend the night with me."

Whoa. Wasn't expecting that. "I don't have any of my stuff."

"You don't need a thing tonight."

"Staying means I'll have to do the walk of shame in the morning." I hate that. It's so embarrassing.

"Shame doesn't exist at Indulge." He kisses my shoulder. "Please stay."

I don't guess there's any harm in staying over; we've already had sex. "All right, if it's what you want."

He kisses my back this time. "You won't regret it."

His cock rubs my ass cheek. "I need to get rid of this."

Beau climbs over me and walks naked across the living room into the bathroom. He's right. Shame doesn't exist here; I feel none as I ogle his naked body. *Damn, he's hot.*

I'm stretched on my side when he returns. I scoot back as far as I can, giving him as much room as possible to lie beside me.

He grasps my hands and pulls. "Come. Let's go to the bed. It'll be much more comfortable."

I'm staying. Might as well get comfortable. "Sure."

I climb into Beau's bed and tuck the sheet under my arms only to have him yank it away. "I didn't bring you in here so you could cover yourself. I want full access to these."

I reach over and yank the sheet down to his knees. "Fine. But what's good for the goose is good for the gander so I want full access to that."

"Gladly. I grant you all the access you want."

I settle into the mountain of pillows behind my head and look up at the mirror above the bed. That should be interesting later on.

"I'm thinking of renting a Jeep for the week so we can leave the resort to explore beyond the walls of Indulge."

This man. He's amazing. "I would love that."

Anna James, this is the start of something good, but let's get this straight right now. It's just sex. Don't forget that. No hearts involved.

"The things we could do this week are endless. Swim with dolphins. Go cliff jumping. Rafting. Visit the mineral springs or luminous lagoon. Some of those would require a little driving, but there's also the local stuff like reggae clubs and bars, some with karaoke if that's your thing."

I'm dependent on him to fund these things. He should pick. "What do you want to do?"

"I already have what I want for the week so you get to choose our activities."

Beau came to Indulge for its hedonistic atmosphere, yet he's willing to leave it behind to spend time with me outside its parameters. "You're kind and considerate. Thank you."

"You make me want to do nice things for you, Peach."

Peach. I adore his nickname for me.

I inch closer and kiss his chest. "And that makes me want to do nice things for you."

He rises and covers my body with his. "Want to work on the second of ninety-nine ways?"

I giggle when his reference sinks in. "Yeah. You have some catching up to do."

CHAPTER 6

ANNA JAMES BENNETT

PING! I WAKE TO THE ALERT OF A NEW TEXT MESSAGE FROM MEREDITH.

Everything go ok last night? Want to talk about it over breakfast?
8:00 at Devour?

Beau and I never made final plans for today, and I don't know if meeting Mere and G for breakfast will work. He may have made other arrangements.

I lie on my back and look at the mirror mounted above the bed. Damn. Watching the things Beau did between my legs last night was sexy but the view this morning isn't so great. I'm a hot mess.

I finger comb the rat's nest on the top of my head and smile when I recall how it got there.

Beau was right. I don't regret saying yes. This is going to be the best week of my life.

Last night's beer is making my breath taste like ass. I badly need a toothbrush. And a shower; I smell like sex, lots of it.

Beau is sleeping peacefully. I hate to wake him, but I need to know our agenda for the day so I can respond to Meredith.

"Beau-re-gard." He doesn't stir so I slowly repeat my new nickname for him. It takes a third time to rouse him.

He smiles the moment he sees me. "Mornin', Peach."

He stretches and his hand goes straight for my ass, grabbing a handful. He drags me close and kisses my neck when I turn my face away. "Aren't you a beautiful sight to wake to?"

"I doubt that, judging by the reflection I see above."

"Wrong. You look lovely." He runs his hand over the top of my hair. "And very well fucked."

Indeed, I have been. And it's a first.

"Meredith asked me to breakfast. I need to know our plan for today so I can respond."

"We can do breakfast with your friends before leaving the resort. I'd love to meet them if you're open to that."

"I had planned on telling them about our arrangement over breakfast. Sure you want to be there? I'm certain they'll drill you about your intentions toward me." It might be awkward so I'm giving him an out.

"I can handle whatever they dish."

"Okay. I'll let them know you're coming so they aren't completely shocked."

I respond to Mere's text.

8 at Devour is fine. Table for 4. Beau is coming.

Ping!
U spent the nite w/ him!!??
I thumb a reply.

Yes & it was magnificent!!!

Ping!

DIRTY WHORE!!!

Swoosh!

Exceedingly so. :)

I type out *He gives me butterflies* but delete it before hitting send.

"They'll be okay with me crashing breakfast?"

I have no idea. "Absolutely."

Meredith and Grayson are protective of me. They have been since my mom and Willa moved away. In a way, they are my family.

They promised my mom and sister they would watch over me,

and they've been true to their word. A little too true. Their concern borders on annoying since Drake fucked me over.

I move to sit on the edge of the bed and realize how sore my inner thighs are. Damn, Beau had me in positions I've not been in for a while. Or maybe never.

"Want me to come back here when I'm finished getting ready so we can walk over together?"

His hand snakes around my waist. He kisses the dip in my lower back and my body instantly erupts with goosebumps. "Yes, but I think you can stay for a few more minutes."

He wants to have morning sex. I'd be all for that if we had time but it's already seven. I have to walk to my room, get ready, and walk back. "We'll never make it on time if I don't leave now. It takes a while to tame this mop on my head."

He twirls one of my locks around his finger. "You have beautiful hair."

"Sometimes I wonder if it's worth the time I spend on maintenance. Everything about it takes forever. Washing. Drying. Curling."

"It's worth it 'cause it's sexy as hell." I'm happy he thinks so.

"We should probably decide now what we're doing today so I'll know what to wear and what to do with this." I point to the top of my head. No way I'm spending an hour curling this stuff if we're riding around in the Jeep with the top off.

"I told you, Peach. Your choice."

I don't even have to think about it. "Swim with dolphins."

"Done."

Swimming with dolphins makes the top ten on my bucket list. But it's something I've always imagined doing with my husband, not a man I met days ago.

I go in search of my dress still lying on the living room floor.

"You have a great ass. Reminds me of a juicy peach I want to bite into."

"I believe I recall an incident very similar to that last night."

He chuckles loudly. "Sweetest Georgia peach I've ever tasted."

I slip into my panties and dress while he watches from the other room. "I'll be back at a quarter 'til. Wear something bulletproof."

"That bad, huh?"

"No." I don't know. Maybe. Guess we'll see.

~

MEREDITH AND GRAYSON seem genuinely pleased to meet Beau. I think they may even like him. That's certainly a one-eighty from their feelings about Drake.

Even if it's only for a week, it will be nice to have a companion who isn't constantly preaching to me how I have no business hanging out with sexual deviants like Meredith and Grayson. Such a fucking mistake to tell Drake about their relationship.

"What have you two have been up to?" Meredith can hardly contain her excitement.

I can't recall the name of the dance club we went to so I look to Beau for help. "Which club did we go to?"

"Debauchery."

Meredith snaps her fingers and slowly rolls her wrist. "Bow chicka bow wow."

Sounds like the anthem for a bad porn movie but there's a reason for that kind of response. Meredith has to know what's upstairs.

"Beau took me to his booth in the private couples lounge." I think I may be blushing.

"I've heard about it but never been. Too rich for our blood." Mere shoves my arm. "Damn, girl. I'm jealous."

"It was . . . fun." That's not the right word. Erotic is a better fit.

Meredith lifts one brow. "I bet it was."

I'm certain Meredith wants all the deets but we can have that conversation when the boys aren't around.

I'm not really sure how to broach the subject of my agreement with Beau so I'm just going to throw it out there. "We've enjoyed each another's company thus far, and we've made the decision to spend the week together instead of us both being alone."

Meredith is all for this. I see it in her smile. "I think that's a wonderful idea. No one should be alone at Indulge."

She winks at me and I have an epiphany. *Beotch* knew this would happen. That's why she brought me.

I'll need to thank her later.

I'm so giddy about today I can hardly stand it. "Beau's taking me to swim with dolphins." I squee like a little girl.

Meredith beams at Beau. "You have no idea how badly she's always wanted to do that."

With the worry of our announcement out of the way, the rest of our dining experience is pleasant. Turns out that Beau, Meredith, and Grayson know a lot of the same people. Some from Indulge, others from back home. Makes for some interesting conversation.

Meredith hugs me when we part ways. "Glad you came now?"

"I am. Thank you for bringing me."

"Happy to."

Meredith glances over at Beau and Grayson. They're in deep conversation about something. "I can see why you like him."

"I know. He's a nice guy, and we talk like we've known one another forever."

"I have a good feeling about him."

A good feeling about what? That he won't turn out to be a serial killer? "What do you mean?"

"He lives forty minutes from you. If things go well, maybe you can continue your relationship at home."

"He may not want that." And I won't either if he goes home and starts another threesome.

"You don't know that he doesn't. Maybe he's open to a one-on-one."

How many times has Meredith told me monogamy is the death of a relationship? Countless. "I'm not sure a man who has practiced polyamory for as long as Beau could be satisfied with one woman."

"He was looking pretty satisfied just now."

He certainly seemed satisfied last night.

"We've fucked a few times. I still qualify as a new toy." Those words sting a little as they leave my mouth.

"I guess we'll see." We sure will.

Beau and Grayson come over, interrupting our girly chitchat. "I know it seems early to hit the road but we have to catch a taxi to the car rental place and then drive about an hour and a half."

Perfect. I'll get to sightsee on the way there and back.

Grayson shakes Beau's hand. "Take care of our girl."

He sounds like a father passing his firstborn off to a boy for the first time.

"Absolutely, man."

Mere hugs me. "Have a great time and drive carefully."

We luck out at the car rental center and get their last Jeep. Very little would suck more than getting stuck with a mommy mobile in Jamaica, so I'm ecstatic since I really wanted something without a top.

We drive along the coast to reach our destination in Ocho Rios. White sand. Blue water as far as the eye can see. The drive is breathtaking, but it's hot without the top on the Jeep. I take off my shoes and put my feet on the dash so the wind can blow up my dress. And it does, exposing me all the way up to my bikini bottoms.

Beau puts his hand on my thigh. "You better watch it, Peach, or I'll be running this thing off the road trying to catch another peek at what's under that dress."

"I might let you have more than a peek tonight. If you're a good boy today, maybe you'll get to touch it."

"Ahh, Peach. You can't say things like that when it's going to be at least seven hours before I get you back to the resort."

"Then I guess you'll spend all day thinking about it." I love teasing him.

"Which means I'll be hard all day without a bit of relief in sight."

"Then you should think about something else. Maybe a granny in rollers wearing knee-highs under her zippered housecoat."

"Nope. I have a fetish for old ladies."

I'm sure he's kidding, I hope, but I'm curious about any real fetishes or tastes he may have. "I know last night probably wasn't what you're used to." I consider not finishing my thought but decide to go for it. Curiosity and desire for validation exceed my fear. "But it was really good for me."

I hate second-guessing my sex appeal and ability to please Beau. It's because of what Drake did to me. But I can't help myself. *How does a woman not question everything about herself after she's betrayed by the person she thought she couldn't live without?*

He squeezes my leg. "It was great for me, too."

I want to believe him. "Was it really?"

He briefly takes his eyes from the road to look at me. "Why are you asking me that?"

"Because you're accustomed to kinkier sex than what we had last night."

"I like the kind of sex we had. I mostly like that I, alone, was enough to please you. Just me."

Did Erin make Beau feel like he wasn't enough? If so, that couldn't be further from the truth, and I'm going to spend this week proving that to him.

I'm still curious to know his tastes. "Is there anything special you like?"

"During sex?"

"Yeah. Is there any kind of kink you want to try on me?" He's grinning so I know there's something on his mind. "Don't be afraid to ask. I'm vanilla but not a total prude. The worst thing I could do is say no."

"I don't know. I wouldn't want to scare you."

I lean over and run my hand up the leg of his shorts. "I think I can persuade you to tell me."

"What I think is you can keep doing that and I'll be convinced to pull this Jeep over to a secluded area to fuck you."

"Temp-ting," I tease. Very tempting indeed.

"Might take you up on that when we drive back."

A girl can hope. "I dare you."

He puts his hand over mine. "Do you like anal?"

I had a sneakin' suspicion that's what was on his mind. "Don't know. Never tried it."

"It's really good."

Yeah. I suppose it is for the man. But what about the poor woman getting something shoved in her ass? It's hard for me to think that could feel great.

"If you're willing to try it, I'd love to be your first." I bet.

I've heard good and bad about that so I don't know. I'd prefer to talk it over with Meredith before agreeing or declining. Although I'm not sure she's the best person to ask. I already know she's a huge fan. "Not sure. Let me think about it."

"Sure. But keep this in mind when making your decision. I promise I'll never do anything to hurt you, angel."

Angel? Maybe an angel with a hint of bitch.

Beau Emerson is complex, generous, and sexy-as-hell. He showed me what Drake and I had been missing: fervid passion. My body has been craving what Beau provided.

But what about next week when I'm back at home? He only promised me this week. Will I be able to walk away and go back to my role of dumped ex-wife? Will my heart allow that? He says he'll never do anything to hurt me, but does that count for my body *and my heart?*

~

WE COMPLETE our thirty-minute demonstration, and we're ready to go into the water with Esmerelda and Seraphina, the two resident dolphins for our swim experience.

Our instructor, Karen, enters the water first. I lower myself in behind her, using the dock ladder, and Beau follows next. We bob up and down in our life jackets, waiting for our second instructor, Jonathan, to cue the dolphins. I'm shaking from the excitement.

"Are you guys here on your honeymoon?"

"Sure are," Beau answers before I can reply. He grabs my hand and brings it to his mouth for a kiss. "Been married to this beautiful woman for three days." What is this feeling running through me? I have no idea. And I'm scared to try to identify it.

"How much longer will you be in Jamaica?"

"We have seven more glorious days here together." Beau's so convincing he's almost fooling me. But I guess lying is a better alternative to the real story.

"Have you had a good time so far?" Karen asks.

I want in on this little deception. "Yes. It's been a lovely honeymoon. I'm so glad we chose to come here. Aren't you, honey?"

"Best decision ever." He strokes the back of his fingers down my cheek. "Just like marrying you, my beloved."

"Where are you staying?"

Uh oh. I should have kept my mouth shut. I'm blank because I'm a horrible liar. "Umm . . . shoot. I keep forgetting the name of our hotel." I look at Beau for help.

"It's the Grand Rose, darling." He doesn't miss a beat.

"What a beautiful hotel. Perfect for honeymooners."

"It is indeed. So romantic."

Jonathan blows a whistle, and our two dolphin friends swim toward us. "Meet Esmeralda and Seraphina, our two reigning princesses of Dolphin Bay."

The pair come right up to us and I'm amazed by what beautiful creatures they are. "I've never seen a dolphin so close."

Karen reaches out to rub the top of one's head. "You can touch them."

I touch the side of Esmerelda's neck. It's rubbery and slick. "Her skin feels just like I imagined it would."

Beau touches Esmerelda's nose. Or snout. Whatever it's called. "That's just how I imagined it as well."

Beau and I take turns being pulled across the water by the pair while holding their top fins. It's like a different kind of water skiing.

The only camera I have is on my phone, and it's under lock and key inside the locker room so I'm pleased that Dolphin Bay offers photo ops by a photographer. "Give Seraphina a kiss," she says.

We take several photos, but my favorite pose is the one of Beau and me in the center with a dolphin on each side of us, kissing our faces. "I'm buying that one for sure."

"You're getting all of them. That was too much fun to not take home a reminder of this day." Totally agree. We had thirty minutes with Esmerelda and Seraphina but it was over way too quickly. I wish I could roll back time and do it all over again.

Dolphin Bay isn't just about the dolphins. We can interact with sharks and stingrays, or do some kind of boating. "Whatcha want to do next?"

"The glass bottom kayak sounds fun. We can do some fish watching. And then maybe some fish eating. I'm getting a little hungry."

We go through the activities one by one, including lunch, until the beach is the only thing left to do. "Want to swim or are you ready to head back to home base?"

It's only five o'clock. I'm in no hurry to return to Indulge. That place doesn't excite me.

"The beach works for me."

We find a couple of loungers next to each other. I suspect the only reason we're able to secure them is because it's late in the day. I bet you couldn't find one vacant chair three hours ago. "This is more my speed. Adults and children in swimsuits. That's what you expect to see when you go to the beach."

"You like children?"

"I must. I chose to spend nine months out of the year with them."

"Yeah, but you teach high school. Completely different than being around kindergarteners all day."

That's debatable. "There are days when I could argue with you about that."

I take the bottle of sunscreen from my bag and rub it over the front of my body. It would suck to burn when I have seven more days in paradise.

Beau is very tanned but anyone can blister in this sun. "Want some?"

"Yeah. Probably a good idea."

"Will you get my back first?"

"Sure."

Beau takes great care in covering every inch of my shoulders and back. Starting at my neck and shoulders, his hands soothingly rub sunscreen into my body. His hands caress lower, gently kneading my spine, my back, to the point I am nearly moaning it feels so good. I can add masseuse to his many talents. "Mmm. You can stop doing that next week."

"Feels good, eh?"

Good is an understatement. "Mmm . . . hmm."

"I need to tell you something, Peach. It's been on my mind for a couple days."

My pulse speeds. Nothing good ever follows when a person says they have something to tell you. "The last time I heard those words, my husband confessed he'd been seeing someone else."

He laughs. "I'm not cheating on you."

I laugh, too. "Well, that's good to know."

He's silent for a moment. That makes me think he's struggling to say whatever's on his mind. "I told you a lie the night we met. It's been bugging me ever since."

"Oh?"

"I told you I didn't know if I wanted the baby or not. That's not the truth. I wanted that child very much."

I'm not at all surprised to hear this. "I suspected as much."

"How could you possibly know?"

"I heard the pain in your voice."

"Erin wasn't ready to leave poly behind for motherhood by any means but her real reason for aborting the baby was because she was afraid it would be like Ashlyn."

Oh, God. That must have been a horrible thing to hear. "I'm so sorry."

What a bitch.

"I wouldn't have cared if it was. I'd have loved that child unconditionally, just as I do Ashlyn, and would have raised him or her without Erin."

Shit. I just choked up a little. I clear my throat but nothing comes out. I don't know what to say to that.

"I know that's more baggage than you signed on for but I just needed to get that off my chest."

I twist around and place a light kiss on his lips. "Thank you for sharing that with me."

Beau has opened a part of himself I wasn't expecting. I'm not yet sure how I feel about that.

"Want me to get your back now?" I ask.

"Please."

I squirt a large quantity of sunscreen in my hands and rub it together so I don't slap cold lotion on his back. "Just warming it up a little."

I place my hands on his skin and begin rubbing. I work his shoulders first. He's so tense. Full of knots. "Feel good?"

He nods. "Mmm hmm."

I'm glad. I want to make him feel good.

"Peach. Look out there in the water. What is that moving up and down?"

I lean over his shoulder to see what he's talking about. "Where?"

He points toward a general vicinity. "Right there. What is that?"

It takes a few seconds but I finally see what he's talking about when a child's blond head quickly bobs out of the water and then back down again. We simultaneously dash from the lounger toward the water, but he's much faster.

"Get a lifeguard." His voice is saturated with panic.

I stop in my tracks and turn to run toward the lifeguard tower. "Help! Help! There's a child drowning."

The man blows his whistle and jumps from the stand, running

toward the water, but Beau is already emerging with the boy. The child's conscious, his arms wrapped tightly around Beau's neck.

The boy's mother races to Beau. "Oh my God, Nelson! Are you all right?" She's hysterical. "I don't know how he got out there. He was standing right next to me."

"Mama." He puts his arms out for his mother to take him.

She clutches the boy and kisses his face. "Thank you so much, sir. You saved my son's life."

"Glad he's okay." Beau's voice is trembling, as are his hands.

My heart is pounding so hard I can hear it thumping in my ears. "Omigod. You just saved a kid's life. You're a freakin' hero."

Beau drops to his knees in the sand, looking out over the ocean. He's silent except for the puffing as he regains his breath.

He rubs his hand on his swim trunks before wiping away the tears pooling in his eyes. I drop to my knees behind him and wrap my arms around his body. I prop my chin on his shoulder. I hold him, not saying a word, while telling him all the things he needs to hear.

～

MEREDITH HAS TEXTED me umpteen times since we sat down at the restaurant. Her interest in my relationship with Beau is starting to get on my nerves a little. "Sorry. Meredith won't leave me alone."

Beau wrinkles his forehead as though confused. "I thought she was cool with this."

"A little too cool. She's reading a lot into it."

"Why do you say that?"

I'm embarrassed to tell him what she said. I don't want him to think I'm suggesting anything. "She hinted this morning that we could continue whatever this is after we get home."

I hit send on the message telling Meredith to chill because she's interrupting my date.

"You sound opposed to seeing me after we get back." I think I may hear regret in his voice. Or am I imagining it because I want him to want me?

I *want* to see Beau at home but he scares the shit out of me. He has the power to hurt me. And I'm not sure my heart can survive another heartbreak. "I'd love to see you after we're home, but I don't feel like

I'd ever be enough to please you. And I won't be half of a female duo it would take to keep you happy. That would make me miserable, and I deserve better than that."

"Of course, you deserve better. The best."

"I won't ask you to be someone you're not." That would make him miserable.

Beau closes his eyes and lifts his face to the ceiling. His sighs loudly when he shakes his head.

I don't know what all of that means.

When he finishes what appears to be an inner self-consultation, he lowers his face so we're looking eye to eye. He reaches across the table and takes my hand. He brings it to his mouth and kisses the inside of my wrist. "I've been with one woman before. I know what it's like. Maybe I'd like to give it another whirl if that woman was you."

I don't answer because I'm so taken aback.

"I like what we have, Peach."

Three days isn't long but I already know how much I enjoy being around Beau. We felt like good friends from the first night we met.

"Think it over. That's all I'm saying."

Is that what I want? I've just gotten out of a marriage. Am I ready to do another relationship?

Now I have two things to mull over.

I look out the window. It's dark and we have a ninety-minute drive ahead of us. "It'll be ten o'clock by the time we make it back."

"Need to turn in early because you have somewhere to be in the mornin'?"

"Nope. Can't think of a single place I'm expected." Except maybe breakfast with Meredith and Grayson. I'm sure she can't wait to drill me about Beau.

"Will you stay with me tonight?"

I don't say so, but I was sort of already planning to. "I will if it's what you want."

"I'm asking . . . because it's what I want."

"Then I'm accepting . . . because it's what I want."

We cover the top of the Jeep and its doors for the ride back since the sun has gone down. Although we changed into dry clothes, I'm concerned about getting cold.

The drive along the coastline is peaceful tonight. There's very little traffic on the road. "I love night driving, or riding, since I'm not the one behind the wheel." I'm completely relaxed with my hand stretched toward Beau, twirling a piece of hair at the back of his neck.

"You're turning me on, Peach, playing with my hair like that."

"Really?" I lean over and kiss the side of his neck before whispering in his ear. "I'd rip your clothes off and do dirty things to you if you weren't driving."

"You should watch what you say. There's a beast inside me." He thinks I don't already know that?

"I'm completely capable of pulling over to ravish you." I think he's serious.

"That'll only prolong us getting back to the resort." And I think we know what's going to happen there.

"We've already established we're in no hurry."

He slides his hand beneath my dress between my legs until he's rubbing my panties over my most sensitive spot. His fingers feel exquisite, and I'm certain he can feel the dampness collecting there. "I don't think I'm the only one getting turned on."

"It's possible you're right."

"Possible, my ass. Definite is more like it, according to how wet your panties are. Do I need to pull over?" He wags his eyebrows at me.

Is he completely nuts? "You want to pull over on the side of the road for sex?"

"Hell, yeah."

He uses his finger to push the crotch of my panties to the side. He slides his fingers up and down through the slickness pooling there. "I think someone else wants to pull over too."

"Is it safe?"

"I have condoms." Smartass knows that's not what I mean.

I put my hand over the tent in his pants and rub his cock. "I'm taking that as a yes."

Beau pulls into a picnic area across the road from the beach and slams the Jeep into park. He gets out and races around to my side. He opens my door and grabs my panties, pulling them down my legs and over my shoes. "Out. Now."

He grabs my hands and helps me out before leading me over to a table. He puts his hands around my waist and hoists me up.

Great. We're going to fuck on a table where a family will picnic and have sandwiches tomorrow.

He slips my flip-flops off and places my feet on the edge before he pushes my knees apart. He pops his button and unzips. "Lie back."

I hear the rattle of a plastic wrapper. He's at my entrance one moment and then inside me the next. It all happens so quickly.

I bring my legs up to encompass his waist while he wraps his hands around my hips. He holds me firm as he slides in and out. Once we establish a rhythm, one hand moves to my crotch to rub my clit. "That feels so good."

"I like making you feel good."

My legs are trembling as his fingers circle my clit slowly with the perfect amount of pressure. Tingling waves of pleasure grow in my pelvis. "I can feel my orgasm starting."

"Right there with you."

I stare at the stars above as my body does its own magical thing. I have no control over it, and it's sensational when I feel those rhythmic contractions deep inside. "Ohh . . . I'm coming."

"Ohh . . ." His body convulses with mine as we achieve our climaxes together. Perfect timing. *Fuck, this man is a sex god!*

He relaxes and lowers himself to press a soft kiss against my lips. "You're sort of kinky for a vanilla girl."

He pulls out and removes the rubber, tossing it into the nearby trash. "I despise those things."

I'm inclined to think he's accustomed to skin on skin. I assume he didn't wear them with his fiancée since she became pregnant.

I didn't use them with Drake; he was my husband so there shouldn't have been a reason to. I was sick to my stomach to learn he'd been unsheathed inside me while he was screwing another woman. That's a mistake I won't make again. "A necessity, I'm afraid."

"Agreed."

He slips my flip-flops back onto my feet before helping me down from the table. "Just so you know, I liked that a lot."

"I did too. Immensely."

Beau reaches for my hand, holding it on the walk back to the Jeep. He opens the door and takes my panties from where he tossed them on the seat. I'm a little taken back when he bends down to hold them out so I can step in. "Such the gentleman."

He pats my bottom when they're put back into place. "I hope you'll allow me to take those off again later."

"I'd be terribly disappointed if you didn't." Terribly disappointed, and despite the fact I've been given more orgasms by this man in the last two days than by any other man in my lifetime, I'd certainly like some more.

CHAPTER 7
ANNA JAMES BENNETT

Ping! I'm awakened this morning to the alert of a text message. I lift my head to look over Beau's body at the clock. Six-fucking-thirty, way too early for someone to be messaging me. I will be pissed off beyond all recognition if it's Meredith bugging me about Beau again.

I grab my phone from the nightstand, and my irritation instantly melts. It's one of my star students.

Hey, Mrs. Langston. It's Emery Whitworth. I'm in big trouble. I really need someone to talk to.

Mrs. Langston. I'm certain it's going to be an ordeal retraining the students, and maybe even faculty, to call me Miss Bennett.

I sit up on the edge of the bed and unplug my phone from the charger. Beau's bedroom is dark, so I fumble around, clumsily knocking the lamp over. My hands jolt forward and catch it before it crashes but not without sending my phone into the floor.

"Shit." I hope I didn't shatter the screen; it's brand new. My cell provider is going to think I caught my husband cheating again if I show up with another busted phone.

"What are you doing, Peach?" Beau's voice is gravelly.

"Apparently being a klutz. Sorry to wake you."

"It's awful early in the morning to be a klutz. Something wrong?"

"I don't know. One of my favorite students just messaged me saying she was in a lot of trouble and needs to talk."

Beau rolls over to look at the clock. "At six thirty in the morning?"

"In her defense, it's seven thirty in Buford. But I'm still very concerned. I fear it could be bad." Emery would never reach out to me over the summer if something wasn't terribly wrong.

I grab Beau's T-shirt from the floor and slip it over my head. "I'll go into the living room so I don't disturb you."

"You don't have to do that. This is my usual wakeup time; I'm not going back to sleep." He gets up to visit the bathroom. "You can call her from the bed."

"Mrs. Langston." Emery answers on the first ring, saying my former name in a hushed whisper.

"Emery. What is wrong?"

"I'm in trouble. I don't know what I'm going to do." She's crying so hard I can barely make out what she's saying.

"Okay. First, I need you to calm down so I can understand you." The crying combined with her low tone makes it nearly impossible to hear.

The other end goes nearly silent. "Emery? You there?"

"I'm here."

"Honey, you have to tell me what's happening if I'm going to be able to help you."

She clears her voice. "I'm pregnant."

Sheez. I was sort of afraid of that. "How far along?"

"I don't know. Maybe around five months."

"You've not been to see a doctor?" I try to not sound judgmental but Emery knows better than this.

"No. I can't. My parents will find out."

"Sweetheart, your parents are going to know very soon whether you tell them or not."

"I know, but I'm scared."

I can already guess who the father is but I ask anyway.

"Ryan Shepherd." Yup. Just as I suspected.

That's too bad because Ryan is an immature little prick who prides himself on getting into girls' pants. I noticed him giving Emery a lot of attention mid-semester but I never, not for one second, thought she'd fall for his bullshit. "Have you told him about the pregnancy?"

"Yeah. He says it's not his."

Of course, he denies it. Little shit did the same thing with Cameron's pregnancy last year. She miscarried, but I still remember the way he celebrated.

Beau returns to bed and crawls in next to me. He traces his fingertip up my thigh until it disappears beneath his T-shirt I'm wearing. I push his hand away and mouth, "Stop. This is important."

"Ryan is lying, Mrs. Langston. He knows it's his."

Looks like this baby isn't going away. "Don't worry about that. It only takes a DNA test to prove otherwise."

"I have to tell my mom and dad and I don't know how to do that. They're going to hate me."

I know the history behind Emery's parents. They divorced a couple years ago, and it was nas-ty. Both are selfish human beings, thinking only of themselves, rather than the well-being of their children. I know that's why Emery went in search of affection. Ryan Shepherd used his pecker to take advantage of the problems she was having at home. And look where it landed her.

I'd love to put my foot in that little bastard's ass. Or chop off his overactive pecker.

"I'm scared."

"Do you want me to be with you when you tell them?"

"Yes. Please." I figure this was the reason for the call to begin with. But that's fine. I will always be there for my kids.

"I'm out of town, but I'll be back next week. I want you to call me on Monday night, and we'll set up a day and time to meet with your parents."

"Thank you, Mrs. Langston. I'm really grateful."

"You're welcome, sweetie. Everything will work out. You'll see."

I end my call with Emery and toss my phone on the bed; I'm disgusted. "Ugh! It's just as bad as I imagined."

"Pregnant girl, I gather."

"Yes. And she's one of my brightest pupils. The most expressive kid I have in my creative writing class. Breaks my heart, especially since the boy who has knocked her up is a twittlefuck. And it's not his first time to do something like this."

"Having a baby at a young age is definitely a life-changing event, but it's not the end of this girl's world."

"How old was Caroline when she got pregnant?"

"Seventeen, but she turned eighteen before she delivered."

"Is she in college now?"

"Yeah. She wanted to quit school, but my parents insisted she graduate and go on to the local community college. She's a smart girl. Got a three point eight so she's transferring to UGA for the fall semester."

"Good for her. Who takes care of Ashlyn while she's busy with school?"

"We all pitch in. Whoever's able to get freed up will take her."

"You mean you and your brothers take care of a baby?" By themselves?

"All the time. Took some getting used to, but we do all right."

It sounds like Beau's family is unusually close. I wonder if they know he's poly.

"Caroline's lucky to have the love and support of your family. I'm not sure Emery's will be as helpful. But that's something for me to deal with next week."

"Right. Because you have me to deal with right now." He moves over me and kisses the side of my neck when I won't open my mouth. I smell mint, meaning he brushed his teeth while he was in the bathroom. No way I'm having ass breath while he's minty fresh.

I pat him on the shoulder. "Let me up."

"No. I want you right where you are." He pushes up the hem of the shirt until I'm exposed all the way up to my waist. He moves downward until his face meets my groin. "God, I love the way you smell."

"You'll love it more after I brush my teeth." I made sure I brought my toothbrush when I packed my overnight bag last night.

"Nope. Won't effect this down here one bit."

One lick of his tongue is all it takes to turn my legs to mush. No way I'm able to leave this bed now. "Oh, God."

He gets on his knees and pushes my legs back and apart. I arch, staring at the mirror above me in anticipation of his touch. I watch his head dip between my legs as I feel the second upward swipe of his soft, wet tongue through my center. The next sends another jolt of pleasure straight to my groin.

"Ohh . . ." I clench the sheet tightly in each of my fists. I'm lost to all senses but one, the feel of Beau Emerson's mouth on me.

"Mmm," he groans. "I love the way you taste. So fucking sweet."

He licks me one last time before sucking my clit into his mouth. Sometimes soft tugs, alternating with a firmer pull. As much as I'd love this to go on forever, it can't because I'm unable to last any longer. He's taken me to that place—the one where a little is too much, yet never enough. I'm coming undone.

"Ahh . . . Ohh." Once the rush of pure pleasure starts, I can't stifle the incoherent garble escaping my mouth. I fist his hair and pull his mouth harder against me.

I recognize that new sensation I've only experienced with Beau—tiny quivers deep in my pelvis as I spiral down from the place he's taken me. I come to my senses and release his hair when I realize I'm fisting it tightly. "Sorry."

"It's okay. I like it. Means I'm doing something right."

"It means you're doing everything right."

He kisses my belly and breasts on the way up. "You are so damn beautiful."

Beau's the beautiful one—soft and hard in all the right places. *And he chose me.*

This man wastes no time grabbing a condom from the box in the nightstand and returning to nestle between my legs; he's anxious to fuck me. And I'm anxious to be fucked.

He enters me quickly. We find our rhythm, and my hips meet his stroke for stroke. There's nothing gentle about what's happening. This is hard-core fucking. And I love it.

Using my legs, I coax him to move faster. "Fuck me harder."

I know he has beaten me to the finish line when he slows and thrusts deeply those last few times while groaning against my ear. "Uh . . . uh!"

His body burrows between my legs, his head resting on my chest. "I really enjoyed that."

"Good, because I really enjoyed you doing it."

That's the last thing I remember before drifting back to sleep.

~

MY EYES POP open when I'm startled awake. No fucking way. That did not just happen . . . except it did.

I just sleep farted.

I turn to look at Beau to see if he heard me. "Yeah. You did it so you might as well claim it."

"Shut up!"

I'm. Fucking. Mortified. Someone kill me now.

"Chill. Peach. We all fart." He doesn't even look in my direction.

He's working on his laptop. "Come here. I want to ask you about something."

I sit up and slide over to take a gander. Looks like real estate listings on the web. "You remember I told you I flip houses with my brothers? My job is to find and negotiate the prices. Wilder takes care of the financing. Judd and Hutch contract it, sometimes doing a lot of the work themselves. That all depends on the job and how sideways the budget becomes. The problem is the price of Buckhead real estate is astronomical. You have to use the best materials in a reno because it's what residents of Buckhead expect and demand. While upscale furnishings will help sell a house, it doesn't always bring a higher appraisal since they're based on dollars per square foot. Spending more and getting no return cuts into profit."

"That makes sense."

"We're thinking of branching out to middle-class suburbs. It's far less a gamble to have three hundred thousand tied up in a reno rather than one and a half million."

Whoa, Nelly. That's a shit ton of money even if they divide it four ways.

"I'm looking at some properties in Buford, and I'm curious to know what you think."

"Buford is a great place to locate if you don't want to live in the middle of all the chaos in Atlanta. It's quiet. Family-oriented."

"I've found six short sales I'm interested in."

"What's that?"

"An alternative to foreclosure. Basically the property is sold for less than the home owners owe."

Beau's cursor hovers over one of the houses. *Click!* "This one looks really good. Doesn't appear to need a lot of extensive work but of course that's basing it completely on the listing, which can be deceiving. Do you know this neighborhood?"

It takes a minute for me to get my bearings. "Yeah. I know someone who lives in that subdivision. Nice neighborhood but it's close to a busy highway. It's really loud."

"Those are definitely things you have to consider on a flip.

Variables like that will prevent a house from selling, and each day it's on the market is money coming out of our pockets."

I think he values my input. It feels good to have my opinion considered.

He closes his laptop. "Enough about that. What do you want to do today?"

We did a lot of driving yesterday. I'd prefer we didn't do that again. "How would you feel about something low-key?"

"I'm up for that."

Beau's the one who's familiar with Montego Bay. "Any suggestions?"

"I want to take you to Luminous Lagoon in Falmouth, about a thirty-minute drive. It's a night tour so we could hang in Montego Bay today, have lunch with the locals, and do a little shopping."

Totally carefree day with Beau. I love it. "That sounds perfect."

I peek at the clock. "What time you want me to be back?"

"Where are you going?"

"To my room to get ready."

"Why do you need to go to your room? You brought your stuff over last night."

I laugh. Silly boy thinks that duffle holds everything I brought. "This is an overnight bag to do me until the morning when I can go back to my room. All of my things are in my suite."

"You aren't going to be sleeping there. I'll arrange for a bellman to bring all of your things here while we're out today."

That's a little dominating. "Do I get a say?"

"You already did when you agreed to be with me this week."

I consider showing my ass until I see the logic in what he's suggesting. I won't be sleeping in my suite this week and running back and forth is going to become a hassle. "I'll be back when I'm finished getting ready. And done with packing."

I look over at Beau and he's grinning. It's the sideways one so only one dimple shows. *Gah, I love that smile. It sends goosebumps up and down my skin.*

He uses his finger to motion me closer. I step within his reach, and he pulls me onto his lap. He kisses my mouth hard and deep, taking my breath away.

He pulls back and looks at my eyes. "Thank you for moving your things over." *Oh, this delightful man.*

"We'll see how thankful you are when you see everything I have."

I get up and he smacks my ass. "Oww."

"Don't be gone long or there will be more of that when you get back." Is it bad that I hope so?

I call my mom before getting into the shower. She puts me on speakerphone so I can talk to her and Willa at the same time. "Tell us everything."

Umm . . . no. I won't be doing that.

No one but Meredith and Grayson knows I'm at a hedonism resort. That would not go over well with my mom or sister. And I can't imagine what the school or parents of my students would say if word got out. There would be more rampant rumors than already exist after the shit Drake pulled.

People love to talk shit.

"It's breathtaking. The beaches are white. The water is the bluest and clearest I've ever seen. And I got to swim with dolphins."

"You finally got to do that. I'm so proud, honey."

"Meet any handsome men?" Willa asks.

Before I left, she bet I'd meet a man while in Jamaica. She's trying to find out if she's in the red or fifty bucks richer.

"You've won, Willa. I owe you fifty dollars when I get back."

"Yes," she yells. "Tell us about him."

"His name's Beau, and he's from Buckhead."

"Shit. You went all the way to Jamaica to meet a man who lives in Fulton county?"

"I know. Sort of funny."

"Do you *like him* like him?" I like fucking him.

"I've known Beau four days, but I like what I know so far." Except that he enjoys having two women at the same time. "We've discussed seeing one another after we get home, so we'll wait and see how it goes."

"Be cautious, Anna. Don't allow yourself to be swept away because you're on the rebound."

I had been incredibly cautious with Drake. I'd done everything right and still got screwed. Now I'm in a place where I just don't feel like being guarded all the time. I'm ready to take a leap. But I won't tell that to my mom. "You know I'm always careful."

"I'm so grateful you're with Meredith and Grayson. I know they'll take care of you." She'd shit a golden egg if she knew those two brought me to a hedonism resort and dropped me to fend for myself.

"I gotta run. Beau is waiting to take me shopping."

I'm rather proud of myself. I'm ready and back at Beau's suite in record time, considering I packed all my things as well.

I knock and wait. He needs to give me a keycard since I'm calling this suite mine the rest of my stay.

Beau opens the door, looking very much like a deer in headlights. "Don't be upset, Peach."

"I'm not." But those big eyes are scaring me. "Unless you're giving me a reason to be."

"I didn't invite these girls over." I peek around Beau and see a pair of brunettes on his couch.

"Then why did they come to *our* suite?" If I'm staying here then I get a say about who comes and goes.

"Why do you think they came?" Right. Sex. Why else does anyone come to your room at Indulge?

"Do you know them?"

"I briefly met them during another stay."

"Well, do you still want to spend the next six days with me or would you rather fuck them?" I'm pretty confident he isn't interested in these chicks, but I need confirmation. If for some reason the pendulum is going to swing back in the poly direction then I want to know now, before I move my shit.

"I want you, Peach. Just you." Good. We're still on the same page.

"Then let's put 'em out on their asses." I brush past Beau. "Hello, ladies. Your interest is appreciated, but no thank you."

They look at one another and laugh. "We didn't come here for you."

I cross my arms and turn to Beau. He must be the one to turn down these two sausage jockeys.

"Thank you for your interest, but no thank you." The pair doesn't move. It's as though they didn't hear what he said.

For fuck's sake.

I go to the door and open it wide. "It was lovely meeting you, but Beau and I have plans for the day. We really should be going."

I let go of the door as they exit, and it's possible it hit the second one in the ass.

"Please don't be angry."

"I'm not." Beau didn't do this. There's no reason to quarrel over something he has no control over.

He comes to me and cradles my face. "I want to be with you. I've moved you into my suite. I want you to be the first thing I touch in the morning and the last thing I taste at night. Only you." A huge grins spreads across his face. "Even if you do fart in your sleep."

I slap him on the chest. "You, sir, are not a gentleman."

"Never claimed to be."

THE SHOPPING CENTER is crawling with tourists, along with locals ready to take advantage of their fat wallets. The peddlers border on harassment. Many don't like to take no for an answer.

Beau is patient but eventually becomes annoyed with the aggressive vendors, so we move toward the upscale stores.

His hold on me is firm and possessive; I think it's because he's concerned for my safety in this horde of people. Whatever the reason, I like it.

We enter a nice boutique selling a variety of items, including lingerie. I didn't bring any with me. I had no reason to but I wish I had some to wear for Beau.

I remove a black lingerie set with fishnet stockings from a rack to take a better look. I study it in the mirror while holding it in place to get an idea of how the sexy ensemble might look on me.

"Hot damn. You'd look dynamite in that, Peach."

"You think?"

"I don't need to think. I'm going to find out tonight because I'm buying it for you."

I'm not arguing because this lingerie is really all about him. "You won't regret it. I'll make sure you get your money's worth."

I join him at the counter and notice he's buying three lingerie sets. "Whatcha got there, Beauregard?"

"You'll find out later."

I've never been wealthy and have always had to save my pennies, so this lavish spending is a little difficult to swallow. But, what the hell? We're in Jamaica and this gorgeous man wants to buy me lingerie. I'm in.

"I look forward to it." And I look forward to how he takes it off too.

What a dirty girl I have become. Sigh.

I pick up all kinds of Jamaican goodies on our shopping trip: rum, jerk spices, coffee. And I find a variety of hand-woven straw items. "You tried to buy them out, Peach. We'll have to take this stuff back to the suite before we go to Falmouth."

I probably overdid it. I may have trouble finding a place to pack this stuff to get it home. "Sorry. But I'm done if you're ready to go."

We find my bags in Beau's living room when we walk in. "You may regret moving me in with you. Girls take up a lot of room with their stuff."

"I know. I've lived with two at one time."

I don't know why but I hadn't considered he cohabited day in and day out with a pair of women. Dumb me.

I wonder what their sleeping arrangements were. Did they all sleep together, or is it like polygamy stuff where they rotate beds? Not sure I really want to know.

I open one of the bags and see the special gift I purchased—a hand-carved wooden bunny on wheels. "I bought this for Ashlyn. She can play with it during tummy time. I thought it might be helpful with her motor development." I demonstrate what I mean. "It has a string so she can pull it when she begins to walk."

Beau stares at me, saying nothing. Have I offended him? Or bought something unsafe for his niece. "I'm sorry. Was the bunny a bad idea?"

He comes to me, taking the toy from my hand. He looks it over and smiles before placing it on the cocktail table.

I'm confused. I can't read what's happening here. "You don't have to give it to her if you think it's unsafe."

He cradles my face, searching my eyes for a moment, before pulling me in for a kiss. It's deep and passionate while warm and cherishing. Different from our other fervent kisses.

I'm nearly breathless when he releases me. "Wow. You must really like bunnies."

"I'm fond of this one because it represents your kind and

thoughtful heart. It's a nice reminder that everyone in the world isn't cruel and prejudiced against those they consider less than perfect. Thank you."

I didn't really know I was doing anything special when I bought that toy. That's why I'm so surprised by Beau's reaction. I had no idea something so simple could mean so much to him. This side of him delights me each time I see it.

I love the way he loves his family. And isn't afraid to show it. And especially Ashlyn. *There's something incredibly sexy about a man who loves a child, even one who is not his own.*

Beau's so different from Drake.

Selfish. Thoughtless. Hateful. Those three words come to mind when I think of my ex-husband.

I cried myself to sleep more nights than I like to recall because I thought something was wrong with me. Maybe I was unlovable? Or unattractive?

Turns out I wasn't the problem at all. I just married a son of a bitch.

Beau kisses my forehead. "Ready to go?"

I love being kissed on the forehead. It's so . . . intimate. "Yeah."

Beau got the rental Jeep for the week, but we choose to catch a taxi to Falmouth. It's a thirty-minute drive, which will be costly, but he wants to have drinks. We are like-minded regarding drinking and driving. I'm glad; I could never be with someone who is under the disbelief it's okay.

"They say the tour is best after the sun goes down so we should probably have dinner first."

"Fine by me. I'm starving."

We're seated at an outdoor table beneath the covered patio next to the water. I can't help but notice all the couples sitting around us. "I think they put us in the romantic section."

"I would agree."

"Have you been here before?"

"No. I've rarely left Indulge during my visits." Right. Because you don't really frequent the honeymooning and family establishments when you come to a hede resort.

"I think this is only one of four or five places in the world you can see this kind of phenomenon. It's said to be the brightest here because of the consistent weather."

I only know this place is called a luminous lagoon. "What is it, exactly?"

"From what I understand, there's a glowing organism that thrives where fresh water meets the salt-water ocean. It illuminates because the microorganism emits a flash of light when disturbed by movement."

"Organisms sound a little scary." There I go being cautious again.

"It's safe."

"Are you getting in?"

"Hell, yeah."

The thought of going into the water at night frightens me. "I don't know if I will."

"Come on, Peach. When else will you get to swim in glowing ocean water?"

I shrug. "I'm excited to see it, just not get in it."

"You're going in. Might as well prepare yourself for it."

Beau doesn't know me. If I decide I'm not doing it, I won't be forced. A Brahma bull isn't more stubborn than me. "We'll see."

Our meal arrives and I'm in heaven. "Dear, Lord. This curried shrimp is delicious." I peek at Beau's plate. It sounded disgusting when he ordered but it looks appetizing. "Is your oxtail good?"

"The best I've ever had. So tender. Want to taste it?"

"I've never tried anything like that but I think I would like to."

He forks a bite and holds it over the table for me. "Mmm . . . wow. That is good."

A mischievous grin spreads and those dimples make their presence known. "See? You're capable of enjoying things you've never tried before."

That statement can mean a lot of things. "Are we talking food or something else?"

"What do you think I mean?"

I suspect he's referring to our discussion about trying anal sex but he isn't going to get me to say so. "I can't possibly guess what you mean. It could be anything."

Our server appears, interrupting our conversation. "Could I interest you in dessert?"

"None for me," Beau says.

I shake my head. "Me either."

Beau waits until the waiter walks away to add, "I have my own plans for dessert when we get back to the resort."

"Something you want to devour?"

"Yeah. And I'm feeling especially hungry tonight."

I clench my inner muscles in anticipation. "Then let's get this show on the road."

Beau won. He got me into the water. And it was one of the most awesome experiences of my life. It would have been a shame to have missed it. Another experience over too quickly.

I get out of the car while Beau is paying the taxi driver. Not sure what's going on but there seems to be some negotiations happening between them.

I've heard the cabbies charge two prices: one for locals and another for tourists. I guess Beau is trying to arbitrate a better price for our ride.

"Want to sit on the balcony and have some drinks?"

I'd love that; I can listen to my favorite sound in the world. "Definitely."

Beau rings room service and has them bring six bottles of Stella. It's probably not what I would have chosen for an after-dinner drink, but I'm not a fan of mixing liquor and beer.

We move to the balcony with our Stellas. I prop my feet on the railing and listen to the waves. Complete euphony.

"I got a little something for us." Beau holds up what I believe is a joint. "I haven't smoked pot in fifteen years but I thought why not? We're here to have a good time."

"Is that what you were doing in the taxi?"

"Sure was."

"I knew something was going on." I grin and bite my lip. "I've never smoked pot. Always been too scared."

"We don't have to. I just thought it might be fun to get high together."

"What's it like?"

"For starters, you get a euphoria."

A lot of people achieve those with painkillers but not me. Most narcotics make me barf up my toenails. "I've never experienced a chemically induced euphoria." But a sexually induced one is *now* a different story.

"I don't know how to explain it except it just feels good."

"I need more to go on than that."

"Your sensations are heightened, especially taste and hearing. Music sounds better. Food is almost unbearable because it tastes so good. You want to eat everything."

I'm full as a tick right now. "We'd want to eat even though we just had dinner?"

"Definitely. And most people say it makes sex better." Shit. Sex with Beau is already hotter than the hinges of hell.

"It won't hurt us?"

"No, but we'll probably act silly."

Silly, I can handle. "Okay. I'll do it with you."

"I'm ordering food now so it'll be here when we get hungry."

I can't imagine eating anything else. "Don't get me anything."

"Trust me. You might not think so right now but you'll want food." He looks over the menu. "We'll get cheeseburgers and fries. And chocolate cake."

He seems to know an awful lot about this. "Were you a pothead?"

"Nah. I enjoyed a little combustible herbage while I was in college but never more than once a month or something like that. It's not addicting."

"I don't guess I had too much fun in college. I was dating my ex-husband then, and all he wanted to do was play Xbox."

"I partied my ass off. I probably had a little too much fun."

We swap UGA stories while waiting for room service. It arrives unusually fast. I had expected to wait at least thirty minutes.

"All set."

He puts the joint to his mouth and inhales while lighting the end. He sucks in and holds his breath before releasing the smoke. "That little shit charged me ten bucks for this lighter. The joints didn't even cost that much." He said joints, meaning he got more than one.

He takes another drag on it and holds his breath while passing it my way.

He exhales and the scent invades my nose. Stinky. "Inhale the smoke like you would a cigarette, but hold it in your lungs before releasing. You'll get a stronger effect."

I sputter and cough with the first inhale. There's no filter so you're basically puffing straight weed. "That's fucking horrible."

"You don't do it for the pleasure of the smoke in your lungs. It's what happens afterward that's magical." I make a second attempt and do a little better but I still hack.

"How long does it take for this stuff to work?"

"You'll feel something soon but it peaks in around fifteen to thirty minutes."

I suddenly feel . . . sort of . . . really good.

"We need music," Beau says before disappearing from the balcony.

It seems like he's gone a long time. "Where did you go?"

"To the living room to turn on the music."

"Where else did you go?"

"Nowhere. I walked straight there and back." Oh. Feels like he was gone much longer.

I don't think I've ever been more relaxed in my life. "I like this stuff."

"Give it a few minutes, and you'll love it."

"That music is so intense. What band is that?"

"Arctic Monkeys."

"Oh. My. God. I love this song." He wasn't joking. You can hear and understand music better when you're high.

"'Do I Wanna Know?'"

"Do you want to know what?"

"No. That's the name of the song. It's 'Do I Wanna Know?' by the Arctic Monkeys."

"Oh." I burst into laughter. "That's so funny."

"You're already tripping, Peach."

"Beauregard, I believe you are correct." My mind is flooded with a ton of thoughts at once. "Is your name really Beauregard? Because I think it is."

"Even high, you aren't going to get that information out of me."

I have no sense of time. I can't recall if we've been on the balcony for fifteen minutes or fifteen hours. I can barely complete a thought in my head, so there's very little hope of verbalizing much. But I'm happy.

CHAPTER 8

ANNA JAMES BENNETT

I OPEN MY EYES AND ASSESS THE FUCKING DISASTER HOVERING IN THE MIRROR above me. I reach into my tangled hair and find something gooey and mushy. "What the hell is that?"

I pinch it with my fingers and pull it down through the strands it's stuck to. Shit. It's a fucking squashed French fry.

I lift my head to look beneath the sheet. Looks like a massacre happened in this bed; ketchup is everywhere. And chocolate. Housekeeping is going to love us today.

Bits and pieces of the night ping pong back and forth in my head. Then I remember. Beau and I got high together.

It was a freakin' circus, and we were the clowns. So much fun.

Oddly I'm not hung over, but I feel out of sorts. Not bad, just . . . weird.

I have a memory, maybe, of Beau smearing chocolate frosting down my stomach and then licking it off. I'm not sure if it was a hallucination or a dream so I check my tummy. I find remnants of chocolate in my belly button so yeah, that happened.

I sit up and look over at Beau. He has chocolate smeared from one side of his face to the other. Priceless. I need a picture of that before he wakes, but I don't have a clue where my phone is.

I look at the clock. I can't believe my eyes when I see that it's almost noon. I'm not sure when we went to bed but I'm guessing we've slept at least ten or eleven hours.

Knock! Knock! "Housekeeping." I hope that door is bolted, so she doesn't come barging in.

I find Beau's shirt on the floor and slip it on. I dash to the living room and crack the door minimally. "Housekeeping. Do you need services today?"

God yes, do we ever. "Yes, but it'll be a couple hours before we leave. Can you come back?"

"Of course. No hurry. I'll come back after three." Good. I don't think either of us could be in much of a hurry right now.

I go back to the bedroom and find Beau sitting on the edge of the bed. "Who was that?"

"Housekeeping. She's coming back in a few hours."

"Good." Beau looks at me, I'm sure assessing my disheveled appearance. "What's in your hair?"

"French fries and ketchup. I think." I lift his shirt and point to my belly. "And I'm identifying this as chocolate frosting."

"Fuck!" Beau laughs as he falls back on the bed. "What did we do last night?"

"I was hoping you could tell me."

"Only the mirror knows for certain because I sure don't. But I know we fucked. I can recall that much."

I clench the inner muscles in my pelvis. I'm sore so we definitely had sex—a lot of it. I'll check it out fully when I go to the bathroom but I think my stuff is swollen.

"We're filthy. Why don't you come to the shower with me?"

I feel gross so I want to bathe as soon as possible, but I have something I want to investigate first. "Get in and I'll be there in a minute. I need to grab my body wash and razor out of my bag."

I hear the shower turn on but I wait until Beau has had time to get in before I snoop in the nightstand drawer.

Before last night, Beau and I had been together four times. He used condoms from his wallet on two of those occasions. The other two came from the box inside the nightstand. Simple math tells me there should be a minimum of three gone from the box, depending on how many times we did it last night. That's anyone's guess.

I count the remaining latex squares. Twenty-two of the twenty-four remains.

Shit. We had unprotected sex. And I don't think he even realizes it.

I feel sick to my stomach. I swore that would never happen again.

I was just tested for all those sexually transmitted diseases, and now I have to worry about it again . . . plus a potential pregnancy.

I'm so stupid. I shouldn't have stopped my birth control just because my marriage ended. I knew I'd eventually have sex again. I just didn't expect it to be this soon after my divorce. I had every intention of avoiding something like this for a long while.

Neither of us can really be sure of what happened last night. We may not have even had sex, although his memory and my body say otherwise. It's possible he didn't come inside me. Or at all.

I do the math. I started my period two weeks ago. That puts me in prime ovulation time.

Shit. This is bad. Very, very bad.

I have to make a pharmacy run for a morning-after pill. No way around it.

Beau doesn't need to know. I'm afraid it'll remind him of the situation with Erin.

I step into the shower with Beau. Everything I do feels like slow motion. I'm certain it's the aftereffect of the weed we smoked last night. "How do you feel about keeping it low-key again today?"

Beau's scrubbing his hair, suds flying in all directions. "Can't lie, Peach. I was hoping you'd want to stay local. And out of the sun."

"Do you feel hung over?"

"Hung over isn't the right word, but I don't feel normal."

"I feel out of sorts myself. I wouldn't mind making a run to a pharmacy. I've been feeling a little fatigued anyway. It's probably just the sun but a little dose of vitamin B12 always perks me up."

"Maybe it's all the hot sex wearing you down." Laughter rumbles deep in his chest.

"Probably."

"I don't remember this post-smoking sensation from years ago. I guess the pot could have been laced with something. Or maybe I'm too damn old to be doing that shit."

"It was a lot of fun, but I don't want any more."

"You'll get no argument out of me. And I'm sorry about squashing French fries into your hair. I'm sure that was my fault."

"It's okay. I figure it's my fault you had chocolate frosting smeared in your facial scruff."

I feel better after the shower, but I'm still in slow motion.

I grab my laptop and do a search for top things to do in Montego Bay. Most of it looks hot and exhausting. "What do you think of going to a reggae club? We can chill and have some cold beer."

"You're talking my language, Peach."

"Then I guess we should roll since housekeeping will be back any minute. I can't be here to face them when they come in and see what we did to the bed."

"I'm sure they've seen worse."

"I don't know. Those brown and red stains could be mistaken for something else." The things they'll think make me cringe. I almost feel the need to stay to explain.

There's a knock at the door right before we open it. "Shit. They're here." I want to die of mortification.

"Only one thing we can do. Face them."

Beau opens the door, and I'm grateful to see Meredith and Grayson on the other side. "Go! Go! We've got to get out of here."

"What are you talking about?" Meredith asks as I shove her.

"No questions. Just go and I'll explain in a minute."

We successfully make it to the elevator without coming face to face with the woman who is going to want to kill us.

"What have you done?" Meredith asks when we're in the clear.

Beau and I look at one another and burst into giggles. "We got high last night and apparently had a munchie explosion in the bed. It's bad."

"You, Anna James Bennett, got high?" Meredith shakes her head. "I'm jealous. I wanna get high too."

Beau removes the extra joints from his pocket and passes them to Grayson. "You're welcome."

"Thanks?" Grayson says.

"We're going to a reggae bar in town. Y'all want to go with us?"

"Yes! I could use a break from this place and one of the people in it." Meredith's nose flares when she rolls her eyes. "What about it, Grayson? Think you can leave her for a little while?"

I cringe at Meredith's use and tone of the word her. That can't be good.

"You know I'll do anything you want, babe. Anything," Grayson pleads.

Oh, shit. G's in the doghouse.

"Well, I want out of here so we're going." Yikes. Something unharmonious is happening between them. I'm sure I'll get the lowdown later.

"Nearest pharmacy," I tell the cab driver.

Meredith's head spins in my direction. "Are you not feeling well?"

I give her my *big-eyed, go-along-with-me* look. "You know how I get when I've not had B12 in a while."

She looks at Beau, who isn't paying any attention, and gives me her *what-the-hell shrug.* "Oh, yeah. Right."

Meredith and I aren't in the door of the pharmacy when I freak out. "We had a huge fuck-up last night."

"What are you talking about?"

I look up at the aisle labels and lead Mere toward the feminine products. "We got stoned last night and had unprotected sex. Or at least I think so. I can't be positive because we were high as kites, but I was sore when I woke up."

"Oh. Shit." She knows I got off birth control pills after the divorce. *You're so dumb, Anna James.*

"That's why I'm here, to get a morning-after pill."

"Well, yeah. But where are you in your cycle? You know those things aren't as effective toward the end of ovulation."

"I'm in the middle so I should be fine."

"God, let's hope."

I pay the cashier and take the pill before leaving the store, tossing the box in the receptacle by the door.

Done. Over. It'll be fine. Beau will never know we had a blunder. *So why do I feel so guilty about not telling him?*

THE CLUB IS SO CROWDED we're lucky to find a free table.

"Hey, guys. I'm Iggy. I'll be your server. Drink specials are on the board. The apricot cider is fantastic if you like something sweet." He places a laminated menu on the table. "Here's a list of domestics and what we have on tap. I'll give you a minute to look it over and be back to get your orders."

I don't have to look. "I'm going with the apricot cider."

"Me too," Meredith says.

Beau and Grayson go with dark stouts. Maybe it's a man thing but I can't stand that stuff. The color alone turns me off, but oddly, I love the way it tastes on a man's breath. Weird but total turn-on.

We finish round one, and Meredith insists I go to the bathroom with her. The door doesn't lock so she leans against it to keep unwanted bathroom companions away. "I'm going to kill Grayson."

Uh-oh. I knew something was up. "What did he do?"

"I'm so pissed off." She sighs. "He was with someone a couple of nights ago, which is fine. I was with someone too, but he fucked her again last night. He didn't even ask. He just did it."

I shrug, totally lost. I thought that's what they did. "I don't know what that means."

"We have boundaries, very strict ones, that we don't cross. They're in place for a reason. Rule number two says we never sleep with the same people twice. It's one of our strictest rules because anything beyond once can become a basis for a connection. And a connection steps into the land of infidelity."

"Have you talked to him about it?"

"Yes, but after the fact. He snuck behind my back to do it, AJ. I'm not sure he was even going to tell me about it. I know we swing, but in our books, that's as good as cheating. I feel betrayed."

She's clearly hurt, but I don't know what to say since having sex with someone else, period, would be considered cheating in my book.

The door pushes in and Meredith slams it shut. "Occupied."

A voice on the other side calls out, "Hurry up. I gotta piss." Nice. So ladylike.

"Fuck off. We'll be out in a minute."

This is sort of a sketchy place we're in. "You shouldn't say things like that down here, Mere. A bitch'll cut you."

"Let 'em try. I'm not scared; I'm fueled by fury." Meredith is like a chihuahua with a pit bull's bark.

We're given the stink eye on the way out of the bathroom. Frankly, I'm happy to escape unscathed. Those women were scary looking.

There's another round of apricot ciders waiting for Mere and me when we return to the table. "Another cider is okay?"

"Absolutely."

Beau leans in so Meredith and Grayson can hear him over the music. "Have you been enjoying Wicked Week?"

Oh God. He could have said anything but that.

"Why don't you tell us about that, Grayson? How much have you enjoyed your time at Indulge?"

"Beau, my wife isn't pleased with me in case you didn't gather that from her tone."

"Beau practices polyamory so he understands about rules. Tell him about the one you broke and see if he thinks it's okay."

No. I do not want either of us in the middle of this.

I grab Beau's hand beneath the table. "Dance with me."

"Gladly."

We move to the dance floor. It's a fast song, J Boog's "Let's Do It Again."

"I love this song."

"You know reggae?"

"A little more this month than last. I brushed up when I found out I was coming here. I'm a big J Boog fan now."

"Mishka is my favorite."

"Love them, too. Favorite song?"

"'Above The Bones.' Yours?"

"That's a great one but for me it's a toss up between 'Another Like You' and 'Give You All The Love.'"

"Let's Do It Again" ends and "Before You Go" by Common Kings comes on. "Love this one, too. They're playing awesome music in this club."

I look over at Mere and G. "I don't understand all that swinging stuff, so I don't know how to advise her."

"What did he do?"

"They never sleep with people more than once. It's their rule; it's only about sex and never a connection. He went behind her back and fucked a woman a second time. She isn't sure he was going to tell her about it either."

"Shit."

"That's a big deal, right?"

"Huge, because it's a trust issue. You can't really screw up worse than that." Breaking trust. I understand the toll that can take.

"They're my best friends. I don't want to see them like this."

I look over at the table; Meredith looks ready to walk. "I'm sorry. I need to check on them."

Meredith's purse is on her shoulder. "I'm sorry to have intruded on your time with Beau and then bail, but I can't look at this cunt grabber right now."

"Baby," Grayson says as he grabs her arm, "don't be like that."

She jerks her arm from his grasp. "I'm going back to the resort. Do what you want but don't even think about riding in the same taxi."

"What are you going to do?"

She stares him down. "What do you think I'm going to do, Grayson?"

He shakes his head as he pleads, "Don't. Please."

I'm in the dark but his reaction makes me suspect he already knows what she's referring to.

Meredith leaves her seat. "I admire your confidence in assuming I give a shit about what you want right now."

"Don't go." This is painful to watch.

"You threw one of our biggest rules out the window. Now, I'm going to do the same thing. Hope you enjoy the way it feels." It's frightening how much Meredith sounds like her mother.

She walks away, waving at Grayson over her shoulder. "See you in the morning. Or not."

I punch Grayson in the arm as hard as I can. "Douche nozzle! Why did you do that? You know she has huge issues with trust." Meredith never had faith in a man . . . until Grayson. Now, he's ruined that. "You may have literally just ended your marriage over one fuck."

"I know. It was so fucking stupid. I don't know what I was thinking." He wasn't thinking.

Meredith can go a little bat-shit crazy when she's angry. She doesn't always make the best decisions. "You know how vindictive she can be when she's hurt. Get your ass up and go after your wife before she does something stupid that your marriage can't bounce back from."

Grayson runs his hand through the top of his hair. "Fuck, AJ."

She's going to get away if he doesn't move fast. "Go. Now."

Grayson dashes toward the exit without a word.

Meredith and Grayson don't fight. Ever. This is new to me, and I don't know what to think. "Not their finest moment. I'm sorry you had to see that."

"Been there. I know how ugly it can get."

He doesn't know Meredith's history. "You can't begin to imagine how much she has feared this happening in her marriage. Grayson knows that, and now he's wrecked her. I want to put my foot in his ass." And I may yet.

Meredith's parents messed up her perception of marriage. She grew up in the middle of a battle zone. Her father was forever cheating. Her mother always retaliated. Poor Mere didn't know husbands and wives could get along until she met my parents.

I want to go after her, to make sure she's okay, but she and Grayson need privacy to work this out. They don't need me in the middle.

I'm not sure how Grayson will manage to make this right with her. Once the trust is gone, it's gone.

Been there. Done that. It's a sickening feeling.

Beau pulls me to stand between his legs and puts his arms around me. "I know he messed up, but swinging is what they've chosen to do within the confines of their marriage. This isn't unfamiliar territory. They'll work it out."

Beau's right. This isn't the same thing as cheating within a monogamous marriage, although I'm certain it's still hurtful.

"Don't let it ruin your good time." He puts his hands on my hips and sways my hips. "Bob Marley is playing. Want to dance with me?"

I listen for a moment. It's "Is This Love," one of my all-time favorites, so I can't resist the invitation. I nod, taking his hand and moving to the crowded dance floor.

Everyone hit the floor when Bob Marley came on, and we're squished like sardines. Fine by me. Means I can get as close as I like without unwelcome attention.

I turn my back on Beau and grab his hands. I put them on my hips and back up until my whole body is rubbing against him as we dance.

He puts his mouth to my ear. "You're making me hard."

"I know. I feel it pushing against my ass."

"Not the way I'd like it to push against your ass."

I haven't had time to talk to Meredith about backdoor action, and I sure won't get to now, but I've made my decision. "I've decided I want to."

Everything Beau has done to me thus far has been amazing. If anyone can make it feel good, it'll be him.

Beau twists me around so we're facing one another. "You're sure?"

I nod.

He cradles my face and kisses my mouth. He grabs my bottom and squeezes. "I'm paying our tab now; I don't want to wait any longer than necessary to get in that ass."

I'm inwardly cringing. "You have a filthy mouth."

"Yes, I do."

We're in the back of the taxi on the way back to the resort, and I'm as nervous as a fox at a hound convention. "You're quiet."

"I'm thinking about it." Psyching myself up.

He puts his arm around me and pulls me close. "I can tell. You're trembling."

"I'm afraid it'll hurt." I know a lot of people do it, but I can't stop thinking about why the other part of the population doesn't.

"I'll get you ready for it. You'll even want me to put it in when I'm finished warming you up."

I have mixed feelings right now. Fearful. Excited. Aroused.

"Will you wear the black lingerie set with the fishnet stockings for me?" Good. That means he plans to give me plenty of time to prepare myself.

"I would love to wear that for you."

The suite is spotless. It's as though last night never happened. Except it did, and I pray it isn't followed by disastrous repercussions.

I go to the bag and take out the black bra, G-string, and stockings. "I need a few minutes."

"No problem."

I slip into the sexy outfit and fluff my hair. I finish myself off with body spray as I inspect the final product in the mirror. I'm not a vain person but there's no question—I look hot in this.

I feel every beat of my heart in my flushed face; I'm on edge, but I want this man and everything he has planned for me.

I come out of the bathroom and stop just inside the doorway. I don't go to him right away. Instead, I put my hand on my hip and lean into the doorframe, supporting myself with a raised hand. He says nothing, but the hunger I see in his eyes tells me everything his mouth doesn't. He's dying to have me. *And fuck if that doesn't turn me on.*

He watches as I walk to where he's standing by the bed. When I reach him, he twirls his finger in a circle. "Turn for me."

I make a full spin before he drops to his knees in front of me. He kisses my stomach before he drags his tongue over my belly button.

I put my hand on top of his head and run my fingers through his thick, dark hair as he kisses each of my hipbones above the elastic waist of my G-string. No man has ever gone to his knees before me and explored my body like this. On one hand, it's unnerving. On the other, it's hot as hell and has me drenching wet.

I guess it's all part of getting me ready for what's to come.

He hooks his fingers in the black lace and drags them down my legs. I have to use his shoulders to balance myself and step out of them because my head is spinning so hard from everything he's doing to me.

He tosses them aside and runs his hands up the back of my legs, starting at my ankles until he cups my cheeks and pulls my groin to his face. His mouth is almost right where I crave it most. I'm ashamed to admit how badly I yearn for his tongue.

He gazes up at me through long, dark lashes. He smiles when his eyes meet mine but we break contact when he leans forward to lick me in one long stroke. I'm stunned, but not by the feel of his tongue. It's the sight of seeing him do that to me.

"Sit on the bed." His voice is gruff. And demanding.

I sit farther back than he wants me to, so he grabs my legs behind my bent knees and pulls me until I'm barely on the edge. He takes my feet and places them on the rails before pushing my legs apart. "I want to eat you first."

I've never had anyone say such crude things to me. I love it.

I tremble with an impatient desire to be touched. I'm considering begging when I feel the first flutter of his tongue.

Just as I grow accustomed to one motion and rhythm, he stops and changes to a completely different speed and direction. It's a guessing game as to what he'll do next and how it will feel.

Beau inserts his fingers and slides them in and out while he uses his mouth to stimulate my clit. I instinctively lift my hips from the bed in a rhythmic, rocking motion.

His fingers leave me, and he glides them toward the back. He touches me there, rubbing in a circular motion while he continues licking my clitoris.

I can't help it. Instinct forces me to tense. "It's okay. I'm only touching right now; you can relax."

I catch my breath and loosen up, surprised to see how different his touch is from what I expected. It's actually pleasurable, which puts me more at ease.

"I'm going to push one finger inside, Peach. It's slick from being inside you already. It might feel strange but it won't hurt."

"Okay."

He resumes licking me, and I feel the insertion of his finger. Again, I tense, but only for a second. "Good girl."

He thrusts in and out slowly. I'm surprised a second time when I realize I'm rocking with him.

"You're doing so good, baby. I'm going to give you two now."

He just called me baby. But I don't have time to think about it because his second finger enters me. Same reaction. Tense. Relax.

He repeats the same procedure, thrusting in and out slowly. "Does that feel good?"

"Yes."

"Good. Now I'm going to make you come."

I'm looking in the mirror above, watching his head bob between my legs, while he thrusts his fingers in and out of my bottom. It's an entirely different type of sensation and arousal. It feels dirty and wrong. Taboo. Maybe that's why I like it so much.

My back arches and I tense when the quivering begins in my pelvis. He sucks harder and thrusts faster. It's almost more than I can stand. "Ohh . . . uhh."

My body shudders and my womb flutters rhythmically for several seconds before it's finished. Pulsating warmth spreads through my body. My face, hands, and feet tingle.

Beau comes up and kisses my mouth quickly. "I think someone liked their sample of anal play."

"Guilty."

He moves to the nightstand to fetch a condom and bottle of lube. It's the first time I've seen that. We've not needed it before tonight. "I'm glad because there's so much more to come."

I prop on my elbows and watch him roll the latex sheath over his cock. I take note how much wider and longer it is. His fingers were pleasurable. This I'm not so sure of. His cock's an impressive size.

"Don't worry, Peach. I'm going to make it good for you."

I've squirmed my way up the bed, so he grasps the back of my lower thighs and pulls my bottom to the edge just like when he went down. Not what I was expecting. "I thought you'd put me on my hands and knees."

He slaps my butt cheek. "I will next time."

He squirts a generous amount of lubricant in his hand before rubbing it on my bottom. "Gotta have it nice and slick so it'll feel good."

He kisses the top of my knee. "Ready?"

"Yes." It sort of comes out sounding like a croaking frog. Not very convincing.

"I'll tell you everything before I do it so there are no surprises." That makes me feel minimally better.

"Okay."

"I'm going to position myself at your entrance." I'd call it an exit, not an entrance.

"I won't thrust like usual. This'll be more like a rocking motion with shorter strokes. It'll go in easier like that."

I inhale deeply and exhale. "I'm ready."

"Tell me if anything hurts."

Beau informs me of every move he makes beforehand. It's reassuring and helps me to trust he won't hurt me.

Pushing through the muscle inside me wasn't the most pleasurable experience ever but things greatly improve after that. I feel like I'm ready for the full experience now.

"You're okay?"

"Mmm hmm." I can't believe he's giving it to me in the ass. And I like it.

Beau pushes my legs back and moves a little faster, although it doesn't come close to matching what he usually does. "I love being inside you."

I rock my hips in counteraction with Beau's. "You like my cock in your ass, don't you?"

The filth that comes out of his mouth! I can't believe I let him kiss me with it. "I do."

He pushes my legs apart, rubbing my clit. "I want to feel you come."

I want to have an orgasm while he's inside me, there; I want every kind of pleasure he's willing to give me.

It isn't long before I recognize the peak of my arousal approaching. "Omigod. It's starting."

My body rocks with the motion of Beau's faster thrusts. The waves of pleasure in my pelvis explode. Everything in my groin buzzes with delight. A moment later, the sweet torture begins—the pulsation of contractions, mixing with the warm euphoria spreading throughout my entire body all the way to the tips of my curled toes. *Bliss*.

Complete and utter ecstasy—that's what he gives me every time we're together.

Beau's face is so tense. I can tell he's holding back because he doesn't want to hurt me. "I'm fine. You can do it harder."

"You're sure?"

I reach out to touch his handsome face. "I'm positive."

I've had my pleasure, twice, but now I get a third dose by watching him come undone.

He closes his eyes and moves faster. Deeper. I clench around him, making it a tighter fit.

I do it for him because I want this to be the best piece of ass he's ever had.

"Oh, fuck," he hisses through his teeth while thrusting into me three final times. Hard. Deep.

Beau pulls out of me and releases my legs. He collapses over me, chest to chest, heart to heart.

After a minute or two of intense breathing, he whispers, "I'm the only man who's had that part of you. I'm glad I was your first."

I wrap my arm around him, lacing my fingers through the back of his hair. "Me, too."

CHAPTER 9

ANNA JAMES BENNETT

THERE'S A TICKLE ON THE TIP OF MY NOSE. I SWAT AT THE ANNOYING PEST AND scratch the itchy spot left in its wake. "Peach."

Oh. Beau is the annoying pest. "Hmm?"

"Let's get up and go down for breakfast. I'm starvin' like Marvin."

I grin. "I'm snoozin' like Suzan."

"Aren't you the clever one?"

He pokes me in the rib with his fingertip and wiggles it back and forth. I instantly spasm, and my body contorts into a bizarre position. I despise being tickled.

We were planning to go out for dinner last night, but that was put on hiatus when I told Beau I was ready to let him have some backdoor action. "Funny how a little bum fun can make you forget to eat."

"Are you up for having breakfast at the resort, or do we need to go into town?"

Beau has been such a good sport about taking me away from this place, so I should cut him some slack, especially since mornings around here have proven to be a normal experience. "I'm fine with eating here."

He slaps my butt cheek. "Then get this fine ass up and get ready."

I twist my hair into a bun to keep it from getting wet while I speed shower. I try to hurry because I know Beau is dying of starvation. I'd hate for him to perish since I'm certain there's plenty of hot sex in store for us the next four days.

The countdown is on. More than half of my time with Beau Emerson is behind me, instead of ahead. The closer our last day comes, the more I consider what it would be like to go back to Buford and never see him again. The thought creates feelings of heaviness in my heart.

"The breakfast crowd is drastically smaller this morning."

"Last night was the huge pool party. The attendees stayed up fucking 'til the crack of dawn therefore they're sleeping in." He has no idea how much that grosses me out.

"I guess we're the prudes in the bunch since we stayed in to have sex privately."

He wags his brows at me. "Baby, there's nothing prudish about what happened in our bed last night."

He called me baby again. I can't stop the smile spreading over my face as I duck behind my menu. "Whatcha gonna have this morning?"

"The quiche."

"It's good but I'm going with the sweet potato pudding this time." I'll have coffee to counter the sweetness.

"Never tried that but I like sweet potatoes."

"Then you'll love this. You can have some of mine. No way I can eat all of it." The bowl it's served in is as big as my head.

I didn't realize how hungry I was until our food was arrived. "Want a bite?"

He nods.

I spoon a sample and hold it out over the table, pulling it back each time he tries to put it in his mouth. "You little tease."

Ping!

I hear the sound of a new message, and I give him the bite so I can see if it's Meredith.

"Finally, she responds. I must have called her at least a dozen times last night. I was worried because it went straight to voicemail every time."

I need to see you

I'm not sure I like the tone of that message.

Swoosh!

I'm at Devour.

Ping!

Be right there.

Swoosh!

K

"Meredith says she needs to see me so she's coming by."

Beau grimaces. "That doesn't sound good."

"I agree." I'm worried about what she did last night.

I wave my hand when I see her standing at the restaurant entrance. "Shit. Grayson isn't with her. That isn't a good sign."

"Did you really think he would be?"

"I guess not but I had hopes."

Meredith pulls one of the empty seats from the table and joins us. "I'm happy you finally saw fit to contact me. I was worried all night."

"I'm fine but I wanted to come by in person to let you know I'm going home today."

"With Grayson?"

"No. He didn't come to the room last night. I haven't seen him since I left the reggae club. I'm sure he spent last night with *her*."

Something is terribly wrong. She's wearing huge Audrey Hepburn sunglasses instead of her usual Ray-Bans. "Take off your glasses."

"No. I've been crying and my eyes are puffy."

I see the edge of the purple bruise she's tried to cover with foundation. "Take them off now."

She doesn't so I reach to do it for her. She slinks away, slapping at my hand. "Stop, Anna James."

"Don't make me cause a scene in the middle of this restaurant. Because I damn sure will."

She removes her glasses and glares at me. "Happy?"

Her left eye is purple and swollen shut. "Oh, Mere. What happened?"

"The wrong guy—that's what happened." Her voice breaks on the last word.

The fucker didn't blacken her eye in public, which means she was behind a closed door with him. "Did he do anything else?"

She pulls the neck of her shirt away. "He tried to choke me while we were having sex. I thought he was going to kill me."

I can make out the partial outline of a handprint on her skin. His fingertips have left deep purple bruises on the front and each side of her neck.

She points to her face. "When I fought back, he did this to me."

Grayson insisted she learn how to protect herself in case something like this ever happened. The defense skills he taught her may have saved her life. "Does Grayson know?"

She shakes her head. "No, and he's not going to."

She can't keep this from him. "He's your husband. You have to tell him."

"I don't have to tell him anything. He lost that privilege when he betrayed me."

"Who did this to you?" Beau's voice is alpha and commanding.

"Linc Michaels." That son of a bitch. He's the one who crawled into the booth with us at the private couples lounge and propositioned us for a poly relationship.

Beau curses beneath his breath.

"This is a very serious matter. Grayson needs to know his wife's been violated."

"I'm leaving because I don't want him to see me like this. It's humiliating."

"This is a criminal offense. Did you report it?"

Meredith scoffs. "We're in another country. What are the authorities going to do to him?"

"Maybe nothing but there should be a police report."

"Don't have time for all of that. I've changed my flight, and I'm leaving for the airport now. I came by because I couldn't go without seeing you first."

Meredith doesn't need to be under the impression I'm going to keep this secret from Grayson. "If you don't tell him, I will."

She gets up to leave, and I stand to hug her. "Good luck finding him. He was out all night. If he's still between her legs, he won't resurface for a while."

Is he stupid? Would he really throw away their marriage for a fuck?

I know he messed up, but I don't think he'd do it again after seeing the way he hurt Meredith.

"Call me the minute you're home. I need to know you made it back safely."

"Will do."

She replaces her sunglasses and points her finger at Beau. "You! Be good to my girl or I will drive to Buckhead and personally take it out on your ass. Despite what I look like right now, I'm a pretty good brawler."

"You got it."

My stomach drops to my feet as she walks away. "I feel sick." All of that sweet potato pudding I just ate is threatening to make a reappearance.

"You have to call Grayson." No doubt.

"Doing it now." I choose Grayson's contact and hit call. "That fucking Linc. I knew he was screwy, but who would have imagined he would be a choker and hitter?"

The phone rings several times and goes to voicemail. "I don't want to tell him about this through text, but I'm afraid he won't call if I don't give him a heads-up something went wrong."

Swoosh!

Call me immediately. Something bad happened to Mere last night.

Grayson immediately calls me back. "What's wrong? What happened?"

I'm not having this conversation over the phone. "Where are you?"

"The suite. All of Meredith's things are gone. What is going on?" He must have just missed her.

"We're leaving Devour right now. It'll take us about five minutes to get back to Beau's suite. Meet us there."

"AJ! Is Meredith okay?" That's a subjective opinion.

Physically, she's going to be okay, but I think it's highly probably she will experience some emotional repercussions from this.

She was assaulted. It has to be a reminder of the violence she witnessed between her parents. If I know Meredith, she's going to equate this to her becoming like them. Her worst nightmare.

"It's complicated."

"That's not an answer."

"It isn't a clear-cut yes or no. Come to our suite and I'll tell you everything."

Grayson's standing outside our door when we arrive. His shirt and face are sopping wet with sweat. He must have run all the way here. "Will you please tell me what the fuck is going on?"

Beau opens the door and we file in. "Meredith was attacked by a man last night. He choked her hard enough to leave purple handprints and finger imprints around her neck. She fought back and was able to get free but he did a number on her face. One of her eyes is purple and swollen shut." I leave off the part about Meredith having sex with him. Grayson can probably insert that part for himself but that's for them to sort out.

"Who was it?"

"Linc Michaels," Beau says.

"You know him?"

Beau nods. "He's from Alpharetta."

"Will you help me find him?"

"Gladly."

Grayson is an experienced kick-boxer. He has the ability to do more than hurt someone. "What are you going to do?"

Grayson punches his fist into this palm. "He attacked my wife so I'm going to show him what it's like to have his ass kicked."

Assault in a foreign country. That's a recipe for disaster. "Please don't do anything that could get you detained by the police. You don't need to land yourself in a Jamaican jail."

Grayson takes his phone from his pocket. I assume he's trying Meredith. "I'm kicking this guy's ass and getting the fuck out of here so I can go home to my wife."

"She's not taking my call. Fuck." He takes the phone away from his ear. "You ready, Beau?"

"I'm ready."

He comes to me and kisses the side of my face. "Listen, Beau. Grayson works out with a professional kick-boxer. He has the ability to hurt this guy bad. Please don't let him take it too far."

"I'll keep him in check."

It feels like Beau's gone too long. I'm a wreck, but I hate to call or text since I already know he'll be back as soon as they're done with Linc.

I decide it's a good idea to sit on the balcony and watch for him. Or an ambulance.

I listen to the ocean's waves. The sound normally brings me peace, but it's a bust today. Too much has happened.

The curtains are sucked into the open doorway by the draft when Beau comes into the suite. "Out here."

He comes the doorway, his shirt saturated with blood. "Not mine."

"I take that as a sign you found Linc."

"Yeah, but it took a while." Coward was probably hiding since that's what cowards do.

"Grayson opened a can of whoop ass on him?"

"I don't want to piss that man off. He's a beast."

"Told ya. You didn't have to moderate?"

Beau shakes his head, appearing to be in disbelief. "Dude never lost control. Every move he made was calculated."

"He's been training for a while. I think focus is one of the first things they're taught."

"He's yet to see what his wife looks like. He's going to regret not killing Linc Michaels when he gets home and figures out how brutally he attacked her." Alpharetta isn't far from Buford. Linc might want to consider lying low for a while.

"I'm glad he didn't know. He might has done something very bad."

"I'm not sure how much control I'd have if your face and neck looked like Meredith's." I don't know what that means. Would he go after Linc to right a wrong or would some form of affection for me drive him to go after my attacker?

I have no idea.

"I need to check in with Grayson."

I call his cell and he answers on the first ring. "Tell me you've heard from her."

"I haven't. Sorry."

"My calls go straight to voicemail."

"Her phone's probably turned off because she's on her flight." Or she's blocking him. Meredith wouldn't hesitate to do something like that.

"I can't live without her, AJ." His voice is gritty with raw emotion. Good. He needs to feel the pain and consequence of his actions.

"Where were you last night while Meredith was getting the shit beat out of her?" I need to know he wasn't with that woman if I'm going to give him my support.

"I got drunk with some buddies and then slept it off in your suite. I knew she wouldn't let me go to our room, and frankly I didn't want to walk in on something I could never unsee."

My room was booked under his name, so he wouldn't have had a problem getting a key.

"I swear I was not with her, AJ. I'm not stupid enough to go down that path again."

"I believe you." But I'm not the one he has to convince. "You have your work cut out for you. What are you going to do?"

"I'm going home to try and save my marriage. My flight leaves in two hours." Good. That's the first step toward a reconciliation.

He has to get moving if he's going to catch that flight. "Call me as soon as you can. I need to know everything is okay."

"I will. Love you, AJ."

"Love you, too, G."

I'm gutted when I end my call. "I don't think I feel like going out today."

"That's fine. We can stay in, watch television, and order room service. Anything you want."

"Thank you for being understanding."

"No problem. I need to make a few phone calls anyway. Plus, my brother emailed me about a new listing in Buford. I should probably check it out now in case I need to move fast to secure it."

Wow. He's serious about moving his gig to Buford. "I'm happy to take a look if you need me to."

"Thanks, Peach. I may have to hire you on as a business consultant."

"I wouldn't turn down the extra income."

He looks away from his computer, all his focus on me. "Are you having financial difficulties after your divorce?"

"I do okay, but teachers don't make a ton of money. I enjoy nice things, so I usually have a second job for supplemental income. I call it my fun money since I use it to splurge on things I can't afford."

"What's your second job?"

"I work in one of Meredith and Grayson's restaurants doing whatever they need me to for the night."

"You're a fill-in for whoever calls in sick?"

"Yeah. I float. I started out as a hostess, but they were short-staffed on servers one night so I filled in. One time I helped cook. I'm a jack of all trades."

"That must work out well for them since you're dependable."

"Except when I take ten-day vacations to go to a hedonism club." Where I meet the most fantastic guy who's perfect for me.

Beau's phone rings. "This is business. I need to take it."

I nod. "Sure."

"Hey, man. Give me just a minute to get to the listing."

I don't want to intrude on Beau's call, so I put my earbuds in and listen to my writing playlist while I try to jot down a few words for the book I've been working on.

Yes. I'm a creative writing teacher who dreams of publishing a novel. And no one knows. Not a single soul.

I'm listening to "Sorry" by Ross Copperman. If I could choose only one song to describe the plot of my story, that would be it.

I busy myself channeling the day's emotions into words. Before I know it, I'm a thousand in. That's good progress for me; I tend to write slowly.

I get up to take a bathroom break and stretch my legs. I become restless so easily. It often prevents me from making more progress in one sitting.

I finish in the bathroom and Beau waves his hand to gain my attention. I take the earbuds from my ears. "Huh?"

"Come here. I want to show you something."

I go to the computer and sit in his lap, putting my arm around his shoulders. Oh, my. I'm shocked to see the faces of a woman and a baby staring at me. "I was FaceTiming with Caroline and Ashlyn. Caro saw you walk by and threw a hissy to meet you."

Thank God I showered and got ready earlier or I'd be mortified.

Beau adjusts the computer so we're centered. I hold up my hand and wave. "Hi. I'm Anna James. And I know that little cutie must be Ashlyn."

Caroline uses Ashlyn's arm to wave at me. "Nice to meet you. I guess Beau told you I'm his sister, Caroline."

"He did."

"Did he also tell you that his niece is the apple of his eye?"

"He might have mentioned something like that."

"He couldn't stay away the whole week without seeing his girl. She misses him, too." Caroline bounces Ashlyn on her lap when she whines. "See Uncle Beau, Ashlyn? He's right there."

Ashlyn's face fills the screen when she leans in to bite the device they're using to FaceTime. "Sorry, girl. Can't have that."

"She's beautiful," I say. Her hair is the exact color of Beau's, but I can't tell if she has hazel eyes like his or not.

"Thank you. She can be a handful sometimes."

"Yes, she can be," Beau says.

"We've gotta run, Beau. Anderson is supposed to be coming by to see her in a few minutes."

Beau tenses. "Okay. Love you. Kiss my girl for me."

He closes his computer. "That son of a bitch, Anderson, gets their hopes up and then won't show. Happens at least once a month. Caroline's a mess for days when he stands them up."

"That's so sad."

"Shitty and lowdown. But what do you expect from a guy who'll take advantage of a seventeen-year-old kid when he knows better?" Beau rubs my back in a circular motion. "What have you been working on so diligently while I was making my calls?"

"Just a little project to keep me busy."

"What kind of project?"

"I'm writing a novel." I don't know why I tell him but it feels right.

"Writing a book? Like a real book?"

"Yeah, not a fake one. 'Cause that would just be silly, right?"

"Smartass. I want to know everything about it." I like that he has an interest in my passion.

"Let's see. There's no title because I'm too indecisive. It's a teen/young adult romance about two neighbors, a boy and girl, who were friends their entire lives until they entered high school. The boy becomes too cool for school and begins bullying the girl. Somewhere over the course of their four years in high school, he falls in love with her. During their senior year, he has to figure out how to convince her he has changed so he can win her heart."

"I want to read it."

"It's not finished. Or edited."

"So?"

"I'm not at all comfortable with that." The thought of him reading my private words makes me panic a little.

"You weren't at all comfortable with me fucking you in the ass either, but you got okay with it real fast."

That mouth.

"The antagonist's name is Michael, but I've decided I'm changing it to Beauregard."

Beau scowls. "You must hate that character."

"I love that name."

"If you want to keep it realistic, you'd better include kids making fun of it."

I was right. "Your name is Beauregard. I knew it."

"I'm only saying that because I know I would have made fun of a kid called that. It's stupid."

What is the big deal with his name? It's cool. "You're so full of shit."

"Come on, Peach. Let me read it."

I pretend to think it over although I already know I'm going to let him. He has a way of talking me into things.

But it's not only his ability to persuade. I feel safe with Beau. Less guarded. More open.

"Okay."

I get my laptop and take it to him. "You have to be honest, even if you think it stinks.

"Promise."

Beau's an hour into my manuscript and has said nothing. Aside from the occasional grin, he's motionless, except for his eyes moving from left to right before darting to the left again for a new line. I'm not sure he's blinked the last fifteen minutes. "What part are you on?"

He waves his hand at me. "Shh . . . don't bug me. Can't you see I'm reading?"

"Smartass. Seriously, what part are you reading?"

"She's just gone into the store where he's working for the summer."

"Love that chapter." Michael becomes infatuated with her from across the store and nearly pisses himself when he figures out who she is.

"You really make teenage boys out to be dicks."

That's because they are. "Am I far off the mark?"

Beau laughs. "Absolutely not. I haven't been a teenage boy in over sixteen years, but you seem to have it pretty accurate by what I remember. Incidentally, this Michael character in your book reminds me of the little bastard who got my sister pregnant."

Ashlyn's father must be a huge asshole. Poor kid.

I stretch out on the sofa, opposite him, and close my eyes. When I open them again, He's closing my laptop. "Wow. I guess I fell asleep."

"Yeah."

I push myself up to a sitting position. "So, what did you think?"

"I thought you were smart before, but I had no idea you were that intelligent and creative. I don't give a shit about teenagers in love, but that held my attention from the very beginning. You made me hate that little prick."

"And I'll make you love him before it's over."

"It's brilliant, Peach. My sister reads stuff like that all the time. She took a lot of shit for being pregnant in high school. It was embarrassing for her so she spent most of her senior year in her room. Reading became her passion. Caroline would love your book."

"Then I'll make sure she gets an advance copy." I giggle.

"I have an amazing idea for the book you should write next."

This should be entertaining. "Tell me about it."

"Beautiful, sexy, heartbroken woman goes to hede resort where she meets an older stud, and they have hot sex for nine days before going home to Georgia to make a go of a normal, vanilla relationship. Just him and her. No one else."

I could read a lot into that but I'm afraid to.

"That, sir, sounds like a bestseller to me."

"I'm serious, Peach." I can tell he is by his solemn expression. "I want to give us a try."

Shit. He may have just knocked the breath out of me with those seven words.

Jumping into a new relationship, especially one with a man of Beau's tastes, so soon after my divorce is crazy. *But what if this is right, and I miss out because it was all wrong before?*

Beau could be the one for me. Can I chance letting him slip away?

I have so many concerns but my biggest is he'll want to bring another woman into our relationship because I'm not enough to satisfy him. *That would destroy me.*

"Be very specific about what you want, so I know we're on the same page."

"I'm not ready for us to end. We've not known one another long, but I already know I want to try a monogamous relationship with you."

I want that too but I'm terrified. "This story you think I should write. Tell me how it ends."

"I don't know, but I sure want to find out."

"Me, too."

CHAPTER 10

MAYBE IT'S ALL IN MY HEAD BUT I SWEAR THE SEX WE HAD LAST NIGHT WAS different. Beau's touch was tenderer. His words, sweeter. Our connection, deeper. It was more intimate, less like fucking.

Our situation has changed. We're going to try dating, monogamously, to see what happens. No promises. Only potential. And lots of hot sex. I'm okay with that since the leery side of my heart isn't ready to commit to anything more.

I'm excited to find out where this relationship could go. I'd be lying if I claimed I was confident. I feel like I've made a truly good friend, with some spectacular benefits, but I'm terrified of being let down again. That's why I must proceed with extreme caution. History has a strange way of repeating itself.

I don't know what time it is, but the sun is bright on the other side of the closed drapes, as evidenced by its luminosity. I lie perfectly still with my back to Beau, only the wheels inside my head turning. I'm trying to not disturb him after the long night we had. He needs his rest so we can do it again tonight.

We met at a tropical paradise and every activity we've experienced together has been amazing. For me, some of them have been once-in-a-lifetime. That sets a high bar for our future. I hope our relationship doesn't wither when we return to the ins and outs of everyday life.

The mattress dips behind me, and Beau's hand creeps around my waist. His lips press against the back of my neck. "Good mornin', Peach."

I lace my fingers through his. "Good mornin', Beauregard."

"Been awake long?" he says between nibbles on my neck.

"How did you know I was awake?"

"You were doing a weird twitching thing with your shoulders."

I move them a little to see if I can replicate what he's talking about. "Probably because I was talking to myself in my head and answering back."

"About?"

"Us."

"What did you and yourself discuss regarding us?"

No way. He's not privy to my private thoughts. "We were trying to decide what we should do during our last two days."

Beau chuckles. "Good topic. What did the two of you decide?"

"When I spoke to Meredith last night, she told me she and Grayson were supposed to attend a couples' cooking class today at a local culinary institute. They were planning to explore Jamaican cuisine so they could introduce some dishes at one of the restaurants. She said we could take their places if we wanted to."

"You cook?" He sounds a little surprised.

Cooking was my responsibility during my marriage to Drake. And cleaning. And the laundry. And the lawn work. I pretty much managed our home without any help.

"I'm not a chef but I do pretty well." My real goal is hoping I might be able to learn something basic to share with Meredith and Grayson for the restaurants."

"Sure. Sounds fun. What time?" Beau couldn't be more different from Drake. So accommodating. Pleasant. How did I get so lucky?

"Ten o'clock but it's a six-hour class. Your first entrée serves as your lunch so we're covered there. It'll be a long day, but we'll have plenty of time to do something tonight."

"I saw a poster at the reggae club promoting movie night at the beach."

"That sounds cool. What movie's playing?"

"Don't remember. Seems like it was one from the eighties. Maybe something with Richard Gere in it."

"Anything Richard Gere will be just fine, but I think the experience will be better than the movie itself."

"The flyer said they'd be selling cocktails and beer so if it sucks, we can get a buzz."

"I almost wish you hadn't given that pot to Grayson. It would be fun to do that after smoking a little."

"We're in Jamaica. There's plenty more weed around here."

I recall what happened last time we went to bed high. I do not need a repeat of that. "Nah, we should probably leave it alone."

Beau twists around to look at the clock. "Eight thirty. Gotta get up so we can get out of here at a decent time."

He kisses the back of my neck, just a peck. "I'm glad we're doing this. It'll be fun."

~

COOKING CLASS IS NOT FUN; it's hard work. Meredith and Grayson would probably rock this, but Beau and I . . . not so much.

We're learning to make gizzadas, a Jamaican pastry filled with butter, fresh sweetened coconut, ginger, and nutmeg. Mmm. Sounds absolutely delicious. But I don't have a lot of faith in what's before me. It's more like one of those #nailedit moments when you see something cool on Pinterest but your version is a royal screw-up.

I evaluate my tough ball of dough lying on the cold, marble countertop. "This can't be right."

"How do you know? Just looks like dough to me."

I pick it up and drop it on the marble. Sounds like a brickbat. "It's going to be too tough. Pastry crust is supposed to be light and flaky. This is going to cook up as hard as a rock."

I lift my hand to gain the attention of Athena, our instructor. She's all smiles when she notices me. Thank God she isn't easily annoyed. "I've messed up, again."

"Just a moment, dear."

"We are the worst culinary students in the history of this establishment. We're going to get expelled, Peach."

"I know. She's probably thinking we are the dumbest American cooks she's ever encountered." I'm typically successful at most things I try, so this is sort of a kick in the ass.

Six hours later, I can admit that attending this class was mostly a mistake with two exceptions: I learned how to make a decent jerk chicken and to properly cook plantains. "I'm sorry I had us waste half a day doing this."

"I'm glad we did it. It's better I learn now to never ask you to cook for me."

I punch Beau's arm. "Jackhole! I can cook plenty of things. I'm quite a good one, as a matter of fact."

"You could have fooled me back there." *Not* my finest moment for sure.

"I've never been great at pastries or ethnic food but I'm great at anything southern. My mom and grandmother taught me."

"Good. Because I enjoy eating. I'd love for you to invite me over for dinner sometime. Or come to my place; I have a great kitchen. It deserves a good cook to give it a spin every now and then and that wouldn't be me."

"I look forward to it." I need to redeem myself after this disaster.

We return to the suite and change into casual wear for our movie night at the beach. We opt for a taxi for this excursion so we can have as many drinks as we want.

Good thing we arrive early because we grab the last two loungers. "I'll go for drinks. Whatcha want?"

I'd like to have more apricot cider, but I don't guess I'll get that here. "Rum punch."

Beau returns a moment later and parks himself in the empty lounger beside me. He holds out his beer. "Let's make a toast. Here's to life's little wonders." He wags his brows at me. "And small hours."

I have to add something heartfelt. "And twists and turns of fate we don't see coming . . . because if we did, we'd probably run and hide. And look at all we'd have missed."

We tap drinks. "That's the damn truth, Peach. And it would have been a shame to have missed you."

I don't know what to say to that. "Find out what's playing?"

"The guy at the drink stand says *An Officer and a Gentleman*."

"Ah, classic romance. Love it."

"You love it because of Richard Gere."

This movie may be more than thirty years old but Zack Mayo is still one of the hottest movie heroes to date. "Zack can put a little of his mayo on my sandwich anytime."

"Did you mean that the way it sounded?"

"Sure did."

Beau laughs. "You talk about the filth that rolls off my tongue but you have your own little case of dirty mouth."

"And you love it."

He nods. "Yes, I do."

"When we get back to the suite, I'm going to show you how filthy my mouth can be."

He sits up on the side of his lounger. "We can go now."

I shake my head. "Nope. Need my dose of Zack Mayo first."

Beau crawls onto my lounger behind me and snuggles. It's sweet. Intimate. Feels like we've known each other for years rather than under a week.

The days we've spent together have been so pleasant. I feel like I am finding myself again, becoming the Anna James Bennett I want to be, and I'm thankful. I don't like to consider what this getaway would have been like had I not met him.

Beau was so sweet about the cooking class being a bust. Drake would still be bitching at me next week about my dumb decision to go.

Every minute I've spent with Beau has brought me closer to reality. Drake's affair wasn't an injustice. Instead, he did me a favor by ruining our marriage. Our divorce opened a new door for me. One where Beau is standing on the other side.

BEAU STOPS at the suite's door before inserting the keycard and kisses me. No, that word's too simple to describe it. His mouth makes love to mine. When he releases me, I'm dizzy.

Our kiss was arousing so neither of us pretend to do anything other than make a beeline for the bedroom.

I push him so he's walking backward to the bed. He stops when the back of his legs hit the mattress. He's wearing linen, elastic-waist shorts, so they're easily shoved down. He multitasks, kicking out of his sandals, and pulling his T-shirt over his head as his shorts drop to his feet.

I step back and slowly pull my dress up and over my head, followed by my bandeau. Next, I wiggle out of my panties, like a new butterfly emerging from its cocoon. "You are so fucking sexy."

I place my hands on his chest and shove hard so he falls backward.

He scoots to the middle of the bed, and I climb up to kneel between his legs. "I'm about to make you happier than a rooster in a hen house."

I put my palms on his thighs and glide them upward until my fingertips brush his balls. I tease him for a moment, lightly sweeping my fingers back and forth. He clasps his hands behind his head and strains to watch what I'm doing.

I move my hand up and grasp the base of his cock before circling my tongue around the head. The stiff tip flicks several times when I lick that sensitive area just below the crown. I alternate licking his length and circling my tongue around the head's edge before taking him fully into my mouth. "That feels so fucking good."

He puts his hands in my hair, pulling all of it into a high ponytail. "I love watching my dick slide in and out of your mouth. I could almost come just by the sight of it alone."

I take him out of my mouth and tilt my head so I can lick his balls. I drag my tongue up, beginning at the base, and I follow the seam connecting the two. I suck the loose skin into my mouth and lightly suck. I've always heard it brings blood and pleasure receptors to the surface. "Fuck!" he groans.

Seems it could be true. "You like that, huh?"

"Yeah. I'm all kinds of loving that. You can suck me anytime you want."

"Not done yet."

I suck his cock back into my mouth and massage his balls for a moment before slipping my finger against the skin beneath his sac. I press while rotating in a circular motion. Slow, and then fast. Soft, and then hard. I adjust according to how loudly he moans.

"Can't fucking believe . . . about to come." I brace for it, ready to swallow quickly. And I do.

"Holy shit, Peach. That was . . . I can't even think of a fitting word to describe it."

"Good?"

"I'm pretty sure that calling that good would be an insult of the worst kind. Astonishing is a better description, but even that doesn't do it justice."

"I wanted to make you feel good."

"Again, good doesn't come close to covering it. You give

remarkable head. I've never experienced anything like that."

I'm surprised to hear him say that after his vast experience.

"You completely emptied my tank, baby. I'm bone dry. I'm gonna need a minute." I love hearing his praise.

"We have all night."

I move up the bed to lie next to Beau while we wait for the next round. He reaches for my hand and brings it to his mouth for a kiss. It's endearing. "I want to introduce you to my family when we get back to Georgia."

Wow. Meeting his family is sort of like . . . a declaration of intent. You don't take temporary people in your life to meet permanent ones.

I've already met Caroline and Ashlyn via FaceTime, and liked them very much, so I'm okay with this. In fact, it feels right. The Emersons sound so wonderful, and if Beau is an example of the people they produce, I'm in.

I'm instantly curious if they'll think I'm his girlfriend or a new partner. "Does your family know you practice hedonism or polyamory?"

"My brothers know. All three bug the shit out of me about coming to Indulge. I've been meaning to get them down here for a couple of years but Erin always vetoed that. She didn't want them ruining our good time."

"So they met Erin and Jenna. And Heath?"

"Erin and I were engaged so the whole family knew her. My parents and Caroline know nothing about my lifestyle choices so Jenna played the part of Erin's best friend who always tagged along. I never told my brothers about Heath. You can't imagine the hell I would have caught from them about another dude in my bed."

"But they thought having two women was okay?"

"They envied me, but they wouldn't have gone for Erin, Heath, and me."

Erin is stupid but that works in my favor. "What she did to you sucks, but if she hadn't, we wouldn't be hanging out now."

"And we wouldn't be doing this." Beau puts his hand on my hip and pushes. "Get on your stomach."

I roll so I'm face down. Beau gets up and his body stretches over mine, pressing my front into the mattress. He kisses my neck while caressing my body. Goosebumps erupt on the top of my head and spread downward. My back arches, and his hand rubs my ass.

His mouth covers my ear and he pats my left cheek. "Lift up."

He shoves two large pillows beneath my stomach and pushes me down with a firm palm between my shoulder blades. Ass up. Face down.

Beau starts at my shoulders, raining kisses down my back until he reaches my bottom. "Hope you're comfortable because I'm about to fuck you like this."

The bed dips as he grasps the backs of my thighs and pushes them up and apart. He licks my clit and drags his tongue through my center. I roll my hips, rubbing myself against his facial scruff. Feels so fucking good.

His tongue abandons me but two fingers are there to replace it. "You make me want to fuck you hard."

"Then do." My voice is breathless.

"I think I shall, sweet Peach." I hear the crinkling of a condom wrapper before he puts a knee between my thighs and pushes them apart.

I push my head into the bed so my bottom is where he wants it. He presses his tip against my entrance. I push backward, forcing him to enter me a little. He pulls away and slaps my cheek. I yelp, mostly because I wasn't expecting it. "Like that?"

Weird, but I do. "Yes."

I'm finding all kinds of new things I didn't know I liked. Smacking my ass is added to the growing list.

He glides his cock up and down my slit, teasing me. "Tell me what you want."

"You inside me right now." He continues teasing me so I say the magic words. "Please, Beau."

He burrows into me hard and fast, shoving my head against the headboard, so I brace myself with outstretched arms. He rocks against me, thrusting in and out, while holding my hips so firmly I'll likely wear the evidence for days.

I can't help but move in counteraction. It's pure carnal instinct. "Harder, Beau."

He does as I say. And he doesn't disappoint.

I hear his prelude-to-an-orgasm groan. He's going to come any minute. And I am as well because he's hittin' it in all the right spots.

He pushes inside me one last time. "Ahh . . . oh."

A moment later he collapses on top of me. He kisses my neck before leaving me to lie on his back. "I enjoyed the fuck out of that."

I push up and roll over so I can lie next to Beau. And I smile. Because I'm happy.

Lost in him. It's a lovely place to find myself.

CHAPTER 11

ANNA JAMES BENNETT

YESTERDAY MIGHT HAVE SEEMED A BUST FOR A LOT OF PEOPLE BUT IT WAS PERFECT for me. *Seriously. One of the best days of my life.*

We spent the day in the suite doing nothing. We lay on the couch watching rented movies and pigged out on room service. I'm glad; the downtime gave me the opportunity I needed to talk to Meredith.

Geez, I'm scared for Meredith and Grayson. They are in a fucking mess. I'm not sure they're going to recover from this.

I'm worried about them, but I can't dwell on their problems. Beau and I are down to our last day in Jamaica, and I want it to be special.

I'm not sad. No reason to be. Our departure home tomorrow isn't the end of us. It's the beginning.

I'm standing in front of the mirror with a towel wrapped around my wet hair. I need to know what's on today's agenda so I can choose how I'll fix it. "What are we doing today?"

"I was thinking I want to take you back to Consume for lunch since it's where we first met." That's sort of sweet.

Beau isn't saying it but we both know this is the only chance we'll ever have to revisit the place we met. I'll never return to this resort and if he does, it won't be with me.

"And what shall we do with the rest of the day?"

"There's a cool bar on the beach. You can drink, dance . . . and cliff dive."

I turn from the mirror to look at Beau. "No way I'm jumping off a cliff."

"You haven't even seen it."

"Don't need to. I don't like heights." I'm not really even a huge fan of going out on the balcony.

"You don't have to jump, but would you consider going with me so I can?"

It's easy to see he really wants to, and I don't want to rain on his parade. "Of course, I will."

"I have to take the rental back by two o'clock, so I guess I'll do that between lunch and the beach. Probably be gone about an hour and a half. Maybe two. Want to go with me?"

I look at my clothes all over the room. It looks like my closet threw up. "I have an early flight; I'd rather not wait until in the morning to pack. I can work on getting my stuff together while you're gone then I won't be so rushed in the morning."

"Sounds like a good plan." He comes to me and snakes his arms around my waist. "Because I'll want to send you off properly in the morning."

"What time is your flight?"

"Two." He'll be in Atlanta by five. Six, our time.

I want to ask him to come over. Maybe even stay the night. *But is it too soon? Maybe we need a little breathing room after nine days together.*

I'll see what he says and play it by ear. If he seems eager to be together soon then I'll roll with it.

Consume isn't that crowded for lunch today, but I bet you don't have a chance in hell at getting a table for dinner tonight without a reservation. It's nearing the end of Wicked Week.

The hostess breaks into a smile when she sees Beau. "Welcome back, Mr. Emerson."

She knows him by name. I'm surprised by how bothered I am about that.

I can't help but notice the way she touches his shoulder when we're seated. "Navaro will be your server, but don't hesitate to let me know if you need anything."

I wait until she's gone to comment. "She certainly delivers service with a smile."

Beau laughs. "In case you've not noticed, that's a huge part of the mission statement at this resort."

Mission statement, my ass. "She didn't smile at me like that."

He's wearing a huge grin. "If I didn't know better, I'd say you're jealous."

I roll my eyes before lifting my menu to serve as a divider between us. "You wish, Beauregard."

I search the chef's specialties section for the perfect Jamaican dish. "I think I'm going with the Jamaican patty. That's one I've not tried yet."

"Beau-mother-fucking-Emerson!"

I lower my menu to see the owner of the rude mouth who just called out to Beau.

Beau gets up from the table and greets an attractive older man with a sweet young thing on his arm. "Carl-mother-fucking-Dennison."

They shake hands and do the half man-hug thing. "Have you been here all week?"

"Eight days."

"How have we managed to miss each other?"

Beau gestures to me. "She's a fucking nymph. I met her on night one, and she's barely let me leave the bed."

He wants to play, I'm game. "Those Viagra pills came in handy."

Carl bursts into laughter. "She's a feisty one."

Beau wags his brows at me. "You have no idea."

"Mind if we join you?" Carl asks.

No. No. No. I want this time with Beau. I have things I want to talk about.

Beau looks at me and shrugs. "Sure. You don't mind, do you?"

I deflate all at once. "Of course not."

Proper introductions are made, and I learn Beau and Carl have been friends for years. Hailey, the sweet young thing, is the arm candy he meets at Indulge for a bi-yearly fling.

"You and Anna James should come back to our place and have some drinks." I don't need to be fluent in hedonism to know what kind of invitation that is.

"Sorry, Carl. We've already made plans."

"Plans often change around here. You know that."

"No can do. I've gotta get our rental car back by two and Anna James has to pack so we can do one last thing this evening before we fly home in the morning."

"Okay, but let me know if anything changes. We'd love to get some alone time with the two of you." Gross. Just . . . fucking gross.

"Will do, man."

Is this what being with Beau back home will be like? People propositioning us for threesomes and *whateversomes*. I hope not.

"I gotta roll if I'm going to get the car back on time." That's my cue to run. Fast. No way I'm hanging out with these weirdos.

"And I have a ton of packing to do. It was very nice to meet you."

Beau stops at the door. "I'll be back as soon as I can, but I'm working on a surprise for you. May take me a little bit longer."

I hate knowing there's a surprise coming. I rather just find out it when it happens. "Tell me."

"Nope. You'll find out."

He leans in to kiss the side of my face. "Think about doing the dive with me. I'd love to jump together." Geez. Holding hands on the way down. That could be romantic.

"I'll think about it." *I'll think about it? What's with that, Anna James?* Damn. This man has a way of talking me into things I wouldn't normally do.

We part ways at the restaurant and I have three things on my mind. One, I dread packing. Two, it would be amazing to share an experience like cliff diving with Beau. And three, what kind of surprise does he have for me?

I'm undecided about cliff diving, but I'm wearing my swimsuit just in case. I'll make my decision after I see how far down the water is.

I change into my bikini and cover-up. I'm sure my attire will be fine considering the type of bar it is. Besides, no one in town dresses up.

I set my outfit for tomorrow aside and toss my big bag on the bed. I work on stuffing it with dirty clothes. I have a ton so catching up the washing should be fun.

"Shit!" I scream at the exact moment my heart takes off like a speed rocket. Carl-mother-fucking-Dennison is standing in our bedroom.

I put my hand to my chest. "You scared the hell out of me."

How did he get in here? The door locks automatically, and I know Beau isn't here to open the door.

This isn't right.

Carl twirls a keycard between his fingers. It looks like Beau's; it has the image of a topless woman on it just like the one he's been using all week. The keycard he gave me is different.

"Beau gave this to me. Said I should come over and get you warmed up while we wait on him to get back."

Fucking liar. "He did not tell you that."

Carl laughs. "If he didn't send me over then how did I get his key to your room?"

I don't know but I have the heebie-jeebies. Every hair on my body is standing on end.

"Come on, Anna James. It'll be fun."

"No."

"I'm here because Beau asked me to be. He wants to have a threesome before you leave."

"Get out."

Carl moves toward me. "Sweetheart, this is what Beau does. He chooses a newbie and spends the week grooming her so she'll agree to have her first threesome with him and another man. Those are the dynamics he likes. Watching gets him off. This is what he's wanted from you since day one. And he chose me to participate because I'm damn good at what I do. He wanted to surprised you."

I dash to the phone. "I'm calling security."

Carl holds up his hands. "Whoa. There'll be no need for that. I know where the door is."

I secure the deadbolt after he's gone and return to the bedroom, collapsing onto the mattress. I'm not sure how my legs carried me to the door and back. They're like gelatin.

That jerk's lying. He has to be; Beau wouldn't do this to me.

But how did he get Beau's room key if it wasn't given to him? It's not like he could show up at the front desk and request a keycard for our suite. And how did he know our room number?

This was Beau's surprise for me? Clever trick.

I want to introduce you to my family when we get back to Georgia.

I want to give us a try.

I'm not ready for us to end.

How could I have been so gullible?

Trying to deny the possibility is useless; it's clear. I've been played. And it's breaking my heart.

I can't stay.

I change out of my swimsuit into the outfit I laid aside for tomorrow. I toss all my things into my suitcase with no regard for organization. If it won't fit, I'll leave it behind; I have to be out of here before Beau returns.

An hour later I'm passing my ID to the airline employee behind the counter. "I'm on a flight scheduled for tomorrow morning but I want to see if you can get me on one departing for Atlanta today."

"Let's have a look and see what's available." She studies her computer screen for a moment. "I have a 6:05 flight to Atlanta arriving at 9:55 Eastern."

"Thank, God. I'll take it."

I check my bags and do the airport shuffle. I have ninety minutes until departure. I want to call Meredith so bad I can hardly stand it. She's the only person in the world I can talk to, but she has a shitstorm of her own going on right now. She doesn't need me dumping my problems on her.

Anna James. It's just you and me, babe.

~

It's five in the morning when I hear the doorbell and beating on my door. "Open up, Peach!"

Obviously, Beau got an earlier flight home since he's here but how in the world did he find me? I never told him my physical address.

"Open this door, Peach!" The pounding becomes louder and more insistent.

I'm not going to the door. I'll take one look at those beautiful hazel eyes and . . . I don't know. Probably cave to whatever he says.

I get out of bed and move down the hall. I stand behind the wall so he can't see me through the glass of my front door. "Please." *Bang!* "Please." *Bang! Bang! Bang!* "I have to talk to you."

He's a magnet; I'm steel. I feel a pull to go to him. But I can't. He's already proven he has the power to bend me to his will.

My cheeks are damp from the tears slipping down them. I wrap my arms tightly around myself and lean against the wall for support. *Please give me the strength to not open that door.*

Ring! Ring! He presses the doorbell over and over. It's driving me mad, but I'm sure that's his intention. "Don't do this, Peach."

More than an hour passes when I notice all noise has ceased. I dash across the living room and peek out the window just in time to see a black Hummer backing out of my drive. Good. He's given up.

Why did he come to find me? Jamaica is over.

I get seven hours of peace before he's back doing the same thing. Again, I pretend no one is home although I'm certain he's seen my car in the drive. He'll eventually give up. He did last time.

Two hours later, the black Hummer leaves a second time. I'm not sure I can take a third round so I call Meredith. "I'm coming over."

"You don't have to. I know you're tired from flying, and I'm fine. Really." Sorry, Mere. This isn't about you.

"I'm the one who isn't fine. I need to get out of my house for a while. Can I use your guest room for a couple of days?"

"Sure, but what's going on?"

"I'll explain everything when I get there."

I throw my essentials in a bag and make a run for it. I don't want to be caught during my escape.

There's a combination of mouth gaping, a blank stare, and a shaking head as I tell Mere how things went down between Beau and me yesterday. "That fucking asshole! I can't believe he manipulated you like that."

"He did a nice job of it. He completely pulled the wool over my eyes."

"Mine, too. I thought he was a good guy. And so perfect for you. That's so damn disappointing."

"I've been burned again. I'm not sure I'll ever want to make another go at a relationship." I'm such a stupid woman.

"It'll get better in time. You'll see."

I think my memory must be failing. For the life of me I can't recall my heart ever aching this dreadfully after my breakup with Drake. How can that be? I was with him for four years. I only had a mere nine, no eight, days with Beau.

I don't want this to get better in time. I want the pain to go away now. Tonight.

I survived one broken heart. Surely, I can do it again.

"HELLO AND WELCOME TO FUSION. How many in your party?"

"Four. Two adults. Two children."

I look at the server assignments. I find two open tables and choose to seat this family with Natasha since she's so much more patient with children. Marcus can be a real ass about kids, especially the ones in highchairs who throw food on the floor.

I reach to grab menus from the cubby on the wall and our eyes meet.

Fuck. Fuck. Fuck. Beau's sitting in the bar area, staring directly at me.

My heart takes off like a Kentucky Derby racehorse leaving its gate.

It's been two weeks since his last visit to my house. I thought I was rid of him. I thought he'd probably moved on to his next sucker.

But I've yet to move on from my anger and hurt.

I'm trembling as I lead the family of four to their table. "Natasha will be your server tonight. Enjoy your dinner."

Shit. What do I do? I can't see him. I won't.

I don't feel well at all. "Hey, Jackie. Can you cover me at my station for a few minutes? I need to visit the bathroom."

"No problem."

I can't have Beau thrown out of the restaurant. He hasn't done anything to warrant that since all he's doing is having a drink at the bar. It isn't a crime to watch me. Unsettling? Definitely, but not illegal.

I hunch over the sink while pondering what I should do. I have no idea so I go into a bathroom stall to call Meredith. Not sure why. It won't gain me any privacy. "Beau's in the restaurant. I don't know what to do."

"Shit. Is Grayson still there?"

"Maybe. I'm not sure. I've been busy at the front; he may have left already."

"If he has, it couldn't have been long ago because he hasn't made it home. Check, and if he's gone, call him to come back. Let Grayson handle that jackhole."

She's right. I need zero contact with him.

Beau's aware of Grayson's ability to kick his ass so it's definitely best to let him handle this situation. He'll happily take care of the jerk for me. He's not been pleased about the way things ended. "Okay. I'm going to find him now."

I yank the door open and come face to face with Beau. Shit.

I attempt to pass but he catches my arm. "We have to talk, Peach."

"That's where you're wrong because you have nothing to say that I want to hear."

"Why did you take off on me?"

I look around and notice we're gaining unwanted attention. "People are looking at us."

"I don't give a fuck. Let 'em look." An older woman standing by the bathrooms gasps.

"This is my job. You can't come in here and harass me."

"I just want to talk."

"And I don't. Did you not get the hint when I didn't answer the door after two hours of beating on it and ringing my bell?"

"I don't understand what happened." I turned his surprise for me into a surprise goodbye for him. That's what happened.

He's going to keep coming back as long as he believes he has a chance at persuading me to do what he wants. It's time I snuff out that bit of hope. "My husband called and asked me to come home. We're working things out." Those words taste disgusting on my tongue.

"Why would you go back to that asshole after he cheated and left you for another woman?"

"We were together for four years, most of our adult lives. We decided it was worth another try."

He stares at me blankly. "Then I guess there's nothing I can say to change your mind?"

I shake my head. "Not a thing."

He nods slowly. "Then I guess this is it."

I need to shut this down immediately. "No. Two weeks ago was it."

He leans forward, maybe for a hug, but I put my hands up to stop him. I step out of his reach because I can't bear to feel his hands on me. I fear I'll fall into his embrace with the simplest touch of his skin against mine. "Don't."

His forehead wrinkles as he studies me through narrowed eyes. He looks pained. *Good. I want him to hurt the way I do.*

He swallows hard and stiffens as he inhales deeply. He looks away briefly and closes his eyes before turning back to speak to me again. "I want you to be happy, Peach. If this is it, then I wish you the best."

I can only nod, as my throat has tightened to the point if I attempt to speak, I'll most likely burst into tears. *I miss him. But he's not what I need.*

I watch him walk out of the restaurant and all I can think is how badly I wish he could leave my heart behind. But he doesn't. It goes right out the door with him.

~

BEAU'S APPEARANCE at the restaurant only makes the task before me harder. It's been on my mind all day, penetrating every moment. But I'm scared. Scared shitless.

Three minutes. My anxious eyes won't leave that stupid, fucking stick for a second.

No. No. Fucking hell, no. This can't be happening. Except I'm looking at a home test that says otherwise. A second line. Pregnant. *I took the morning-after pill. This wasn't supposed to happen.*

Worst. Fucking. Luck. Ever.

I can't believe this. I have unprotected sex with Beau *one time*, not even by choice, and I get pregnant.

I'm experiencing a case of disbelief. "This isn't happening. It could be wrong. False positives occur."

Except I already know in my heart this is real.

What am I going to do? I can't have a baby with Beau Emerson. He is not the kind of man I'd want as a father for my child.

So many things to consider. Keeping this baby means I'm tied to him the rest of my life. Forever. I'll never be rid of him. Him and his forever revolving harem. *Bastard.*

What kind of mother would I be to let him in this child's life? Beau's fucked up in a serious way so I have to consider how he might screw up my kid. It could be more harmful than beneficial to have him in his or her life.

But look at how he is with Ashlyn. He adores her. And he said he desperately wanted the child he lost. *Could I really take a second child from him?*

But that pregnancy was with his fiancée, the woman he loved and wanted to marry. Not a woman he met and spent eight days with.

I need to take a step back. I don't even know if I want this kid. I need to make that decision before I can even consider this other stuff.

I collapse on the bed and succumb to the tears. I ugly cry like never before. I kick and scream, yelling at the top of my lungs. No one's around to hear me, so I throw one hell of a hissy fit.

I give in to the exhaustion and close my eyes. Beau's all I see behind my lids. And I hate it. *Hate. It.*

I want to forget how handsome he is.

I want to forget how good he smells.

I want to forget how good he felt inside me.

I want to forget how considerate he was.

I want to forget how cherished I felt.

I want to forget how he manipulated me.

Fucker.

That's the last coherent thought I have before surrendering to sleep.

CHAPTER 12

BEAU EMERSON

CAROLINE STANDS IN THE LIVING ROOM DOORWAY, HER HANDS PROPPED UPON her hips. "This is so classic."

My sister isn't wrong. This is typical Emerson behavior she's observing.

Georgia is playing their first football game of the season today in Texas, hence the reason we're gathered around the television at my parents' house instead of watching from our box at Sanford Stadium. This family bleeds red and black. Caroline knows we never miss a game. Ever. I'm not sure why she's acting surprised by our enthusiasm.

"I apologize for giving birth during football season but it's time for cake. Do you think it's possible to tear yourselves away from the game long enough to sing Happy Birthday to Ashlyn?"

I'm not annoyed because Caroline scheduled this party during the football game, but I am pissed off because she arranged the entire thing around Anderson's schedule. We're the ones who take care of Ashlyn while he shows up whenever it suits him.

Caroline is still in love with him. It's apparent in everything she does. And it makes me sick. I wish she would wise up and move on. *I bet he has.*

Anderson's standing in the corner with a sullen face, his arms crossed. He can't even get excited about watching his daughter delight in her cake. Asshole.

"You silly girl. You have frosting all over your face." My mom grabs her camera and snaps a bazillion pictures. She fancies herself a photographer, and poor Ashlyn is always her subject since she's the only grandchild.

All the Emerson men put the football game on hold and fulfill our duties: singing, cake and ice cream, and gifts. But when it's all over, we're itching to get back to the television.

"Your time is served so get your butts back in there and see what's happening with the game."

We file into the living room. Last quarter just started. "Georgia is up by fourteen," my dad calls out. *Hell yeah. Go Dogs.*

Caroline comes into the living room and puts Ashlyn on the floor with a new toy before sitting on the arm of the chair next to our dad.

Sweet Ash. She has taken a few steps, but still prefers crawling.

"Who are we playing next week, Dad?" Caroline asks.

"Vandy."

"Good. We'll smoke them. I want to bring Hilary, if the jerkfaces haven't claimed all the extra tickets."

"Nope. Still have three."

Caroline points at our brothers and me. "I'm calling dibs on one of them right now. Got it?"

"Depends. Is Hilary hot?" Wilder chuckles.

"Yeah, but she's smart, too, so that means she won't give you the time of day."

Wilder shoots Caroline the finger, and she returns the gesture. "Back at cha, buddy."

"Look at that, Beau. Ashlyn just crawled away from her new toy to go after that bunny you brought from Jamaica. I don't think we'll ever find anything that competes with it."

Ashlyn rarely lets go of that damn bunny. I almost wish I hadn't given it to her. I can't look at the thing without thinking of Peach.

Angry yelling, and maybe a little mild cursing, erupts when Texas scores a touchdown. And I miss it because my mind has wondered off to thoughts about a vanilla girl. *I miss her. So fucking much.*

Ashlyn immediately wails. Shit. Their shouting scared her.

"Ugh!" Caroline picks up Ash. Even frightened, she never releases the bunny. "Papa and those loud boys hurt our ears, don't they?"

The rest of the last quarter is uneventful, and it ends with Georgia up by seven. Not the win I was hoping for but it's still a victory. Can't complain.

I go into the kitchen where Caroline is hanging out with her friends. "Where's Anderson?"

"He left." Bastard couldn't even spend more than an hour with his daughter on her birthday. I'd like to ask why, but I don't want to make Caroline feel worse than she already does.

"Don't, Beau." Her eyes are pleading.

"I didn't say a word, Caro."

"But you want to."

I shrug. "Not my business."

There are two of the same paperback books on the table and a couple of e-readers. Seems a good way to change the subject since I don't want to have this conversation again, the one where she tries to convince me Anderson loves her and Ashlyn and things are getting better. *Such bullshit.*

"What do we have going on here? Having a book club meeting?" I pick up one of the paperbacks and flip it over to read the back.

"No, Beau." My sister grabs it from my hand, so I snatch the second book from the table.

"What's up with you?" I study the sexy couple on the cover. "You've moved up to mommy porn?"

"This is none of your concern." She makes an attempt to get the book but I'm faster.

"I'm not concerned. I'm just being nosy to annoy the shit out of you." God knows she does enough to bug me.

"Caroline is making all of us read this book."

My sister flings her hands up. "Thanks for throwing me under the bus."

"I don't mean that the way it sounds. It's a really great book. Well written, while hot and sexy."

My sister is barely twenty but I can't think of her reading this kind of stuff.

I flip to a random page in the book and begin reading.

He's into poly relationships. I'm not sure about the ins and outs of what they do, but I know it's the big time. Miranda and Grant won't even consider going there. Two women at once. I hear that's every guy's fantasy.

Holy shit. Why is my sister reading a hot and sexy book about polyamory?

"Two women at once?" Caroline has turned a bright shade of red. "Caro, what the hell are you reading?"

"A book, purely fictional, and I'm enjoying it."

I don't like this worth a damn.

"The book is not really about that stuff. You just happened to have gone straight to that part." I have my doubts.

"Then what is it about?"

Caroline looks at her friends. "Can I get some help here?"

Emily steps up the plate. "The hero of the story practices hedonism and polyamory. Do you know what those things are?"

This is almost laughable. "Yeah."

"Okay. Well, he goes to one of those sex resorts in Jamaica and meets a girl who doesn't do all those things. They sort of start out being friends but things get heated. I'm only a third in so that's all I know right now."

Macy giggles. "I'm further along and I can tell you that things go from heated to hot, hot, hot."

I know what that means. "This is a dirty book."

"It's sexy but the focus is on their relationship, not the sex, so that makes it romance."

"I think he's going to turn her kinky," Emily says.

"Or try to make her one of his new threesome partners," Macy adds.

This story sounds a little too familiar. "Why would a vanilla woman be at a sex resort?"

Emily doesn't mind answering any of my questions. "She's freshly divorced and heartbroken. Her best friends brought her as a getaway. But I want to know the friends' story, too. I think that would be hot."

Caroline is shaking her head. "Not me. I don't want to read about swingers."

No fucking way. Peach did not write and publish a book about us.

I study the front cover.

Hede by A.J. Clark.

Never heard of this person but it's a little difficult for me to believe those initials are coincidence.

I'm sure this happens all the time—an author writes a fictitious story that parallels with someone's real life. Except our story isn't a simple one. It's not the kind of stuff people can randomly make up without knowing something about it.

"When was this book released?" I ask.

"Why so many questions, Beau? You want to get in on our book club? If so, you're bringing the cookies next week."

I guess my interest does seem peculiar. "I think Phoebe is reading this," I lie. And they probably know. She's not exactly a book-reading kind of girl.

"You wish Phoebe was reading this." Emily makes a show of fanning her face.

Caroline takes her copy of the book from me. "It's a very popular book so she probably is. Or maybe re-reading because the installment from the guy's point of view comes out next month."

"Speaking of Phoebe . . . where is she?"

"Busy with work." Truth is I didn't want her here so I didn't tell her, or Zoey, about the party. It's always a problem when Phoebe participates in family functions and Zoey can't.

I have two women in my life, and bed, and it's never enough to make me stop thinking of Peach. Even when Anna James isn't in the forefront, she's lingering, always threatening to intrude.

It's been more than a year since we shared the best nine days of my life. I still remember everything about her—the way she smelled, how she tasted, the way it felt to be inside her. But most importantly, how much she made me want to change into the man she needed me to be. I was prepared to do that for her.

I could live to a hundred and never forget those things. Peach was, and is, the best thing that has happened to me. No doubt. And I'll never stop wanting her. Not for one fucking second. Doesn't matter how many women come and go through my bed.

When I met Phoebe and Zoey, it had been almost six months since Peach turned her back on me. Half of a fucking year without her. I knew it was over. I finally accepted she wasn't coming back to me.

What do you do when the love of your life moves on without you? You fake it. Because it's easier to pretend you don't care than to admit it's killing you.

And it's easier to slip back into old habits.

I hadn't been keen to start up another poly relationship, but I didn't have Peach. Wasn't ever going to have her again. Nothing was stopping me, so I went along with it. But they're not who I want.

Simply a means for sex and getting off.

More than a year later I'm still pissed. And hurt. I told her I wanted her to be happy, but fuck if I didn't want her to be happy with me. *Why would she return to someone she knew would cheat on her?*

Fuck. I'm a wreck now. She's all I can think about. And now that fucking book, too. *Hede*.

I slink away to the bathroom to electronically stalk A.J. Clark on my phone. I find nothing personal. The only photos are of the book covers and an avatar for social media. She's secretive. That makes my suspicions even stronger.

Phoebe, Zoey, and I have plans for tonight but I call to cancel. I lie, telling them Judd needs my help at one of the flips. I send them on without me; they don't mind. The two of them do not have problems partying without me. I sometimes think they could function just fine if I weren't in the picture. And I don't give a fuck.

I'm not sure at what point I made the decision to go to the bookstore. It's a little bit like my Hummer drove itself there.

I find the book on the local author's shelf and immediately flip to the back to see the author's photo. Nothing. Just like the Internet. Not a single photo of this author exists anywhere that I'm able to find. It's almost as though she doesn't exist.

I scan the paragraph about her biography. Very generic and straightforward. Lives in Georgia with her cat. No mention of a husband or children.

I read the description of the book. When I finish, I'm certain there is something to this. No one could write fiction so near the truth without having experienced it.

Fuck it. I'm buying this book. I have to know if this is our story. Because if it is, maybe I'll finally get the answers I need about what happened the day Peach left me in Jamaica. Because I don't believe for a second she was stupid enough to go back to a man who fucked her over the way her ex did. She's way smarter than that.

I thought what we had was real.

The first thing I do when I get home is change. I grab a Stella and fall onto my leather sectional, novel in hand. I thumb through to see how many pages are in this big bastard. Three hundred sixty-nine. And the print is small. It's at least an inch and a half thick. I haven't read a book that size since . . . ever.

I'm stalling. I don't want to start reading this book because I'm chickenshit. I'm afraid A.J. Clark is really Anna James Bennett. I'm terrified this story is actually mine with Anna James. It could mean finding out things better left unknown.

Stop being a pussy, Beau.

I crack open the book and start at the beginning, the credit stuff before you ever reach the story.

We were together in July 2014. The copyright for this book is 2015 so the book was published after we met. That much of the timeline fits.

I turn the title page, coming to the dedication.

For Beauregard.
Thank you for the precious gift you gave me.
I will treasure it always.

Beauregard. She loved that fucking name. I hate it. Always have, always will. I've taken a lot of shit over the years because it.

My heart is slamming against the inside of my chest; there's no doubt in my mind now. Regardless of what this story is about, these words belong to Peach.

I flip to chapter one and settle into the corner of the sectional, blanket covering my legs. Time to find out if *Hede* is a retelling of the best nine days of my life when I came to know something true and beautiful.

CHAPTER 13

BEAU EMERSON

THE MORNING AFTER I FINISHED READING *HEDE*, I MADE A BEELINE TO PEACH'S house, but she no longer lives there. I could spend time and money hunting her down, however I don't see the need when she'll be within my reach soon.

Excited for tomorrow, I check in at the NYC hotel and settle into my suite. Fourteen fucking months. I finally get to see my sweet Peach. *Will she be as cold as last time? Or open her arms with a warm embrace?*

Sleep didn't come easily. By the time the clock flashes a decent hour to rise, I've had breakfast via room service and three cups of coffee.

I fear I'll climb the walls before this signing begins.

I'm standing in a line a mile long, definitely sticking out like a sore thumb. I must be among a thousand women. And most of them are giving me more attention than I'd like. One even asked if I were a cover model. That's not good for my plan.

The doors open and we file into a banquet room. It's fucking chaotic. Women, with books in hand, are scampering in every direction. Reminds me of a freshly kicked ant bed.

Huge posters and tables piled high with books line the walls. Pairs of women, with a few exceptions, sit behind each table while attendees holding armfuls of books stand in line on the opposite side.

I'm grateful for the hoards of people. It's the concealment I desire.

The map of the authors' tables shows me A.J. Clark is in the far corner to the right.

I hang back, careful to not be seen. I don't want to spook Peach and let her get away again.

I still can't believe she'd have gone back to that douche. But if she did, surely she isn't still with him.

My heart is slamming against my chest. I feel my heartbeat in my face and hear the throb of my pulse in my ears. I wouldn't be surprised to learn my blood pressure is stroke-level high. I'm nervous.

I hang back about fifteen feet, waiting for the crowd to part so I can catch a glimpse of A.J. Clark at a distance. The crowd is thick so that doesn't happen quickly enough to suit me. I'm impatient so I move closer.

Ahh. My sweet Peach.

I haven't laid eyes on her for fourteen months, and I think she may have grown more beautiful while we were apart. Looking at her, I fall further in love. *Fuck, I've missed her.*

I've tried to convince myself I'm fine without her, but it's a fucking lie. She's in my veins. My bones. I ache for her.

What I've been doing is called existing, not living.

I move about the room for three hours, careful to remain undiscovered. Longest three hours of my life. Seeing her from afar and not being able to go to her is brutal.

The end of the signing is approaching, meaning it's time to put my plan into action. Finally, I'm able to get into her line so we can come face to face. And she can't run.

The woman in front of me is gushing over the main character in *Hede*. She's going on and on about how much she loves him and his alpha ways. I nearly choke when she asks if his character is based on someone Peach knows.

"Ben's personality is very similar to a man I once knew."

"I knew it. You wrote his character too well to have been making all of that up. You lucky, lucky lady."

Ben is very much like me but he got his happy ending with Emma Jane. I didn't.

Peach and the woman sitting next to her are cackling when I approach. Her laughter quickly dissipates, her expression turning to stone.

This isn't her happy face.

I hold out my book, waiting for her to take it. "I'm undecided if I want you to sign it for Beau or Ben since apparently I'm both."

The woman by her side appears confused but takes the book from me and places it in front of Peach.

"I think we both know who I should make this out to." She signs the book and then holds it out for me to take. I think it's my dismissal.

"Want a picture with AJ?" her assistant asks.

"Yes. I would love that." I'll take any opportunity to touch her.

She stands and adjusts her dress before walking to me. I put my arm around her and inhale her fragrance. "Smile, Peach."

The assistant snaps several pictures. "I took several so maybe one will turn out okay. I'm not the best photographer."

She passes my phone back. "I bet you did a fine job."

"Do you mind if I step away for a minute since no one else is in line? I have a few books I need to get signed. I promise I'll be back to help break everything down."

"It's okay. I have someone who'll be coming down to pack everything."

The woman takes forever to gather her things. I need her to go away five minutes ago. "Be right back."

Peach looks around as though she's checking to see if anyone is watching us.

Why does she look so nervous? "Come to my suite when you're finished here. Thirty-three sixty-nine."

She closes her eyes and shakes her head. "That's not a good idea. And I can't anyway. I have an engagement after this."

"Find a way to come." I don't want to threaten her but I will if I must. "We can talk about this in private, or we can do it in a very public manner. Your choice."

She sighs. "It may take me a little while to get away. I'm having cocktails with some people and then I have personal business to tend to."

I reach out to caress her face, but she steps out of my reach. "Don't do that."

I lower my hand. "Come as soon as you can. I've waited long enough."

THIRTY MINUTES PASS. Then an hour. Now, three, and no Peach.

Fuck.

Reality sinks in. She's stood me up. I don't know why I'm surprised. She doesn't like being *told* what to do. Shit.

I open the book she signed to me.

Beauregard,
I see your face every day.
Peach

I'm working on the third small bottle of liquor from the minibar when the tap on my door finally comes.

Fuck. She's here. And I'm buzzed. This is not the way I planned this.

I waited more than three hours. I had given up and gotten comfortable. That includes being shirtless.

Her eyes roam my chest before looking away. "Really, Beau?"

"Sorry, but it's been hours since I saw you. I had decided you weren't coming."

"I considered it but I'm here."

I open the door, taking a step back so she can enter. When she's inside, I embrace her. "It's so good to see you."

I've never missed anyone the way I've missed her.

She embraces me back and my soul jumps for joy. "I'm happy to see you."

I release her and look at her face. "Could have fooled me."

"You shocked the hell out of me. I was dumbfounded."

"Come in. I'm not standing by the door to talk." I grasp her hand to lead her into the living room of the suite.

"I can't stay long. I have a very early flight, and I'm not packed."

"I've heard that one before." She doesn't get to bail on me until she hears what I have to say. She owes me more than a moment of her time. I'm not letting her out of here until I say everything that's been burning me alive for the last year.

I gesture toward the couch and sit beside her. The chair is too far away. "It's been a long time. How have you been?"

"Fine." One fucking generic word is all I get?

"I think you're more than fine. You're quite a success."

She shrugs. "The book has done well."

"*Hede* is clearly our story . . . except they get a happily ever after. We didn't."

Peach sighs. "I don't know what you want from me."

"I need to know if Emma Jane's feelings are hers or yours?"

She looks away, shaking her head.

"You're shaking your head but I don't know what that means."

"You don't get to come here and ask me that after what you did to me."

I'm clueless. "What did I do?"

"You sent Carl into our suite while you were gone to get me ready for a threesome."

What the fuck?

I'm stunned. "I have no idea what you're talking about."

"He told me everything—how you'd groomed me all week to get me ready for it."

I'm going to kill that bastard. "Carl Dennison is a fucking liar. I did not send him."

"He had your keycard and used it to come into the room."

"I lost my key. I had to go down to the front desk and get another one. That fucker must have swiped it off the table at lunch." I move closer and cover her hand with mine. "There's no way I would've shared you with anyone. I told you that."

"I know you said that, but he told me you wanted to watch us, that you liked it that way. That it was my *surprise.*"

"Carl was trying to fuck you. I swear what he said was a lie. Your surprise wasn't him. I changed my flight so we could fly home together."

"All lies?" she whispers so softly it's barely audible.

I grasp her face with my hands. "I told you a year ago I wanted to try. I still do."

She places her hands on top of mine and pulls them away. "You live in a world where you chase pleasure in multiple women. I can't be a part of that."

"I don't want that life anymore. I want it to be just the two of us."

She smiles, but it isn't a happy one. "It's too late for that."

She couldn't be more wrong. "It's not too late for us. I don't believe that for a second."

I kneel in front of her. "I will beg you from my knees if it's what you want."

Her eyes close, and she shakes her head. "Please don't, Beau."

She moves to get up but I stop her, my hands holding her in place, my face pressed against her thighs. "I'll do whatever you want. I'll be whoever you need me to be."

She caresses her hand down the back of my head. "I would never want you to try to be anyone but yourself."

I push her dress up and kiss her bare legs. "I love you. I want you. Only you."

She doesn't stop me so I push a little farther. "With all of my heart."

I love her not only for who she is, but also for who I am when I'm with her.

"Beau." My name's a whimper on her lips. I don't know if it's intended to stop or encourage me, but I go with the latter.

I push her dress higher. And she lets me. "I've missed you so fucking much. You have no idea how bad."

"Oh, God. What am I doing?" I'm barely able to decipher her words.

I put my hands on the insides of her knees and push them apart. I kiss up her inner thighs. I inhale deeply. "It's been too long since I've smelled or tasted you." *Her scent has been a ghost in my haunted mind.*

She's panting when she pushes her fingertips into my hair. "We can't do this."

Her words say one thing while her actions say another. "Yes, we can."

She's trembling. "But we shouldn't. It's wrong."

For me, it couldn't be more right. "You want me to. I know you do."

I pull her down onto the cushion and push her legs apart. I graze my fingers up and down the crotch of her panties over the outer edges of her lips. The fabric is already wet. And it's all for me. "You want me to lick your pussy until you come in my mouth, don't you?"

Anna James writhes beneath my touch. She turns her head, hooks her arm over her face, and growls, "Yes."

It's all the permission I need.

I grasp the sides of her panties and drag them down her legs. I toss them aside and spread kisses up her inner thighs. I move to her groin and the bend of her leg. My mouth caresses her everywhere from the waist down except her pussy. I want her ready to explode when I finally make it there.

She moans loudly when I lick her the first time. Feeling her. Tasting her. Hearing her. It's almost too much. I fear my plan could backfire and I'll be the one to detonate.

While flicking my tongue over her clit, I plunge two fingers in and out. She fists my hair, pulling lightly. "More."

I add a third finger, giving her what she wants. "Omigod. That feels so good. It's been so long." *Been so long since she's had this done or done by me?*

I alternate between sucking and licking Peach; I still remember what sends her over the moon. She tenses and trembles, a sure sign her orgasm is approaching. She grabs the back of my head and presses my face into her. I suck harder and release, doing it over and over to finish her off with a bang.

"Oh. Oh. Uh." She says those words over and over while she's coming.

She's finished coming when her body goes limp, her legs shaking almost violently. Heavy panting is the only sound filling the room.

I move to my feet and take her hands in mine, pulling her from the couch. I cradle her face and study it. "It's been too long since I've seen these beautiful blue eyes."

I take possession of her mouth with my own, claiming it as mine, and then doing the same with her neck. Her shoulder. I want every part of her to belong to me. "I can't wait another minute to have you."

My hands grasp her ass and hoist her up so her legs are wrapped around me. She holds my shoulders, kissing my neck as I move into the bedroom.

We tumble to the bed, me on top. She spreads her knees wide, and I nestle between. My hips thrust between her legs as she rocks against me. We're humping like teenagers.

I push her dress up. "I want this off you."

She lifts her bottom so I can drag her dress up. She's left only in her bra. But not for long. "This too. I need to see all of you."

I press my palms to the sides of her tits and push them together. They feel so full. *Are they bigger?*

"Still fucking gorgeous."

She reaches behind my neck and pulls me down for a kiss, cutting my time with her tits short.

Her kiss is hungry. She devours my mouth. My neck. My chest. "I think you want this as much as I do."

She reaches for the button on my pants, yanking it open with one tug. "Probably more."

No fucking way that's possible.

I pull my shirt over my head and toss across the room. Pants and underwear next. Don't know. Don't care where they land.

We're both naked, the tip of my cock rubbing her entrance. One thrust. That's all it would take to be inside her, skin on skin with nothing between. I want that so badly. But I can't. Not right now. I have things to get in order before that can happen.

"Be right back." She whimpers when I pull away. It's sexy as fuck.

I go to my suitcase to grab the box of rubbers I brought with me in case our reunion went well. I tear one off and toss the remaining ones on the nightstand. I'll be needing more later; one won't be enough. *It never was with us.*

I move over her after my cock is clad in latex. "I want to be inside you without one of these. I'm going to do that one day very soon."

"You already have. You just don't remember it," she whispers so softly I barely hear.

"We've never fucked without a condom. I would remember that." It would be etched on my brain.

She bites her lip, trying to disguise a smile threatening to spread. "Yeah, okay."

She grabs me behind my neck, pulling me down for another kiss. Her legs are spread wide, ready to take me inside. "I'm giving myself to you tonight. Take any part of me you want. I'm all yours."

I want to fuck her mouth. Her pussy. Her ass. I want to claim it all for myself again but first I just want to love her. "Let's start with making love."

She puts her hands on my forehead, pushing my hair away, and spreading kisses all over my face. "I've imagined this so many times, but the real thing is so much better."

My cock is positioned at her entrance when I lower myself. I want our bodies pressed together when I enter her. Closer than close with nothing between.

She's drenched, and I slip in easily. I thrust deep, closing my eyes and relishing in the squeeze of her body around my cock. I want to savor her for a minute before I start moving.

My arms are framing her head inside the pillow. I kiss the side of her neck, moving upward until my mouth hovers over her ear. "We belong together, Peach. I hope you know that."

She wraps her legs around me and squeezes. "Fuck me, Beau. Hard. Please. It's what I need."

No way I can deny her, so I guess we'll save making love for later.

I rise to my knees and grasp her around her thighs. "I'll do anything you ask of me, Peach."

While holding her in place, I thrust hard. I do it several times, each plunge causing her to loudly gasp. "Is that what you want?"

"Harder!"

I grasp her ankles and move them to my shoulders. "You like it deep, too, don't you?"

"Yes."

She wants intense, she's getting it. I hold on to her thighs, sinking hard and deep. It feels fantastic but it's tiring as fuck so I take her legs down and move over her again. *I don't stop when I'm tired. I stop when I'm done.*

She's holding me tightly so we're chest to chest. Heart to heart.

God, I'm in love with this woman. I need her in my life forever.

I wonder if she'll ever understand just how much of me belongs to her.

I trail kisses up her neck until my mouth hovers over her ear. "I'm so in love with you, Peach."

I slow my thrusts because I want this to go on forever and ever. My hands find hers, and I bring them above her head where I lace our fingers together tightly. She is my everything, and I'm never letting her get away again.

She opens her eyes and watches mine as I move above her.

I thrust the last few times before I'm about to come. She brings her legs up around my waist and crosses her ankles behind my back. She uses the strength in her legs to bring me closer until there's not a bit of space between us. I groan as I squeeze her hands and drive into her one last time, climaxing.

I'm panting when I pull out, completely emptied and satiated. I roll to my back and pull Peach to lie against my chest. I'm still catching my breath as I kiss the top of her head and hold her tightly. This is where I want to be—next to Anna James Bennett. Not sandwiched between two women I don't give two shits about.

"You'll never know how sorry I am that you slipped through my fingers. But it won't happen again because I'm never letting you go. Ever. I'm not letting our story end. There's much more needing to be written." That's the last thing I remember before falling into a dream world where Anna James is mine.

~

I WAKE to the sound of the toilet flushing. I can't believe I fell asleep. But I always did in Anna James's arms. She's soothing to my body and soul.

She comes out of the bathroom, dressed, and my heart plummets. "Please, don't go. Stay with me."

"Can't. I have things to take care of."

She disappears through the bedroom door into the living room so I get up, pull on my underwear, and follow her. "You still have plenty of time to pack."

She's looking for something. Panties? "They're under the couch."

She steps into the black lace garment and pulls it up her legs. Not the direction I like.

I go to Peach, wrapping my arms around her from behind. "I'm not done with you."

"I can't stay, Beau."

"Go pack and then come back so you can spend the night with me."

She sighs. "I can't do that."

I'm not taking no for an answer. "You can and you are."

"You don't understand." She presses her palms to each side of her head and groans. "Someone is waiting for me. And I'm going to owe him an explanation about where I've been."

Okay. She has someone. I have two someones. We can ditch all of them. "Fine. Get rid of him."

"I can't just get *rid* of him. I have commitments."

"What is it? Are you married or something?" Please say no.

She exhales loudly. "I'm engaged." Not what I wanted to hear.

This isn't happening. I just found a way back into Anna James's life, and she's yanking it out from under me. "Fuck, no. You cannot marry someone else."

She lowers her head. "I am. And I just fucked you. Oh, God, that's horrible."

Engaged isn't married. It's not too late. "You can call it off and we can be together."

She's shaking her head. "It's far more complicated than you know."

"You're not legally bound to this clown; how complicated could it be?"

"Very." She crosses her arms. "And I already know you're involved in another poly threesome. And have been for a while." *Bam. A ton of bricks just landed on top of me.*

There's only one way she would know that, but I want to hear her admit it. "How would you know that?"

"I came to Buckhead. I saw you with them." *She came for me?*

"Why did you come?" I want to hear her say it. Please say it. *That you came to work things out.*

"I needed to talk to you." *About us?*

"But you changed your mind when you saw them?" Fuck. Fuck. Fuck.

"Of course I did. I knew any chance for us no longer existed." Her face is pained as she says the words. I need to hold her.

She tries to turn away, but I stop her by grasping her arms. "That's not true."

"Which part isn't true? That you're not in another threesome with two women or that our chance at being together isn't forever gone?"

She thought I'd lied to her, set her up. *Betrayed* her.

"I will end my relationship with them for you. Right now. They can be out of my house before I make it home."

She shakes her head vehemently. "We won't work."

I don't understand why she's so unwilling to make a go of this. We are perfect together. "We'll never know if we don't try. And I desperately want to."

"You haven't had a one-on-one relationship in years. How do you know you could be fulfilled by one person?"

"The best nine days of my life were spent with the only woman in this world who's ever completed me." That's a fact.

"I'll always wonder if I'm enough for you. I won't live like that; too much is at stake." I have to change her mind.

I go to Anna James and wrap my arms around her. I stroke my hand down the back of her long blonde hair. "What do I have to say to make you see I'm willing to do whatever it takes to make us work?"

I can feel her shaking her head against my chest. "I can't chance it."

I step back and cradle her face before kissing her softly. "I want you. I want us."

She pushes me away. "But for how long? Until you decide you want to bring another woman into our lives? Our bed?"

I grasp her upper arms. "Dammit, Peach! I don't know another way to say it. I don't need anyone else if I have you."

"I won't put us through that." She closes her eyes and peels my hands from her arms. "Damn you. I finally had it together again. Why did you have to show up and ruin everything?"

She may not realize it, but she just confessed her true feelings. "You love me. Otherwise, I wouldn't have the power to ruin anything."

I already have the answer I need.

"I have to go. He'll be wondering where I am."

She tries to pass but I step in her path. "So, that's it? You're with me, and then you go back to him with my smell all over you?"

"That's it, exactly. Just like you were with me, and you'll go back to that pair at home and pretend nothing happened while you were out of town."

"Does he fuck you the way I do? Does he make you come so hard you scream?"

She stares at me. Silent.

"I didn't think so. That's why you wanted it hard and dirty. You said you needed it, and I'd bet that's because you're not getting what you need from him."

"Faithfulness. Respect. Security. That's what he gives me."

"You left off true and beautiful." I haven't forgotten the words she used because they were powerful.

She doesn't have a reply for that.

I follow her to the door. "Please don't do this, Peach. I'm begging."

She steps forward, cradling my face as she kisses me softly. "I will always carry a part of you with me."

"You must mean my heart. Because it will always belong only to you."

She doesn't reply before walking out the door and out of my life.

And it breaks my fucking heart. Again.

CHAPTER 14

BEAU EMERSON

I GO TO BED, BUT IT'S A JOKE TO THINK I'LL SLEEP. I LIE THERE SEEING ANNA James behind my lids every time I close them. I hear the echo of her voice telling me we won't work. But she's wrong. We belong together.

Lust. Intrigue. Ecstasy. Love. It happened in that order.

Peach sat down at my table at the restaurant at Indulge, and my dick came to full attention. One look. That's all it took for me to know I wanted to bend her over and screw her brains out.

I wanted to make her my first fuck at Indulge. Planned on it. Had every intention.

But then the craziest thing happened. I spent time with this Georgia peach and figured out there was more to her beneath that thin white dress proudly displaying her nipples than what I was fantasizing about.

Vanilla. A fucking beautiful vanilla girl at a hedonism resort. What kind of cruel joke was that? *Don't we always want what we can't, or shouldn't, have?*

I knew I'd never be with her, but she was so intoxicating. Fucking addictive. I just wanted to breathe the same air as her. *Because when I'm with her, the only place I want to be is closer.*

We talked that first night, and she had the power to make me tell her things I had planned on taking to my grave. All she had to do was threaten to withdraw her presence. And bam. I bent to her will just like that. Had she told me the only way she'd stay was if I walked on water, I'd have found a way. That's how much I craved her company.

I nearly fucked it all up that first night when I teased her, asking if she'd help me choose my first fuck. She didn't catch on to the part about it being her, so I pulled back and did something I've not done in years. Flirt. Made me feel like a teenager instead of a thirty-five-year-old man. But I liked it.

She made me do something else I've not done near enough. Laugh. That, too, can be highly addictive. *I'd been so full of anger and resentment.*

Anna James Bennett. The sound of her name, alone, has the power to silence my demons.

I found a friend in her, and it would have been enough had it been all she was willing to give, but I couldn't resist pursuing her. I had to give it another shot; I wanted her too badly to give up. *I felt like I was beginning to breathe again.*

I can identify the exact moment I fell. It was the day we went to the market, and she gave me the bunny she'd bought for Ash. In that moment, I saw into her heart. And damn. It was a beautiful heart. Sweet. Caring. Loving. That's when I knew I wanted her in my life beyond the nine days we agreed upon. *I don't want to exist without that heart.*

A strange, powerful force took hold of me, its root weaving itself around my heart, body, and soul. And there it grew because she kissed my heart awake when her soul whispered to mine.

Last night she told me about her fears. That she wouldn't be enough for me because of my past. Legitimate concern. I get it. But there's something she's failing to see. I didn't ask for the threesome. Didn't need it to be happy. Erin did. *I don't think I ever explained that. Fuck.*

As far as Phoebe and Zoey go, they mean nothing to me. A total mistake. Just a means of trying to get over the sting of losing the woman I truly love. A way to get my dick wet.

Will I be able to escape the consequence of that error in judgment?

I hug the pillow Peach's head rested upon three hours ago. Her scent lingers; I press my nose against it and inhale deeply.

I know we'd be together now if Carl hadn't fucked me over, trying to get between her legs. She wouldn't have left me or said she was back with her ex. And I wouldn't be with Phoebe and Zoey.

Having those kind of fuckers in my life has ruined what I could have had with Peach. But no more.

She came to Buckhead to talk. *There's hope yet.*

Why the hell did I take on Phoebe and Zoey? Shit. I fucked everything up by being with them.

I take my phone off the charger and call Phoebe. "Hey, baby," she yells.

It's three in the morning but I hear people talking in the background. They're probably throwing a damn party at my house, trashing my place, providing everyone with alcohol I've bought. "Put me on speaker so I can talk to you and Zoey."

"Come 'ere, Zoey. Beau's on the phone and wants to talk to us."

"Heeeyy, Beau," she slurs. Totally wasted.

"Can you both hear me?"

"Yeah," they shout in unison.

"Good. I want both of you, and all your shit, out of my place when I get home Monday. I'll put you up in a hotel for a week. That's plenty of time to go apartment hunting."

There's a rustling noise. I think Phoebe just took me off speaker. "I don't understand."

"The only thing you need to understand is that you and Zoey have to go; our threesome is done."

"Whatever, Beau."

I end the call, glad neither of them tried to plead for me to change my mind. Not that I really expected either to do so.

I feel good about this. Ending my relationship with Phoebe and Zoey is the first right step in winning Peach back, but I have to formulate a plan; I'm on a deadline.

Peach wants true and beautiful. That's what I have to give her.

I'm pumped about where this thing is going. So much so that I have an adrenalin rush. To burn off some of this pent-up energy, I need a run. Not something I've done in a long time but I feel good enough to jump right back in.

I alternate running and walking for an hour, spending the entire time thinking of Peach and how good our lives will be after we're together. This is the first time I've felt encouraged in more than a year.

I enter the hotel and spot Peach in the lobby. I see her from behind but know it's her because I recognize her long blonde locks. No one has hair as beautiful as hers.

She's sitting alone on the couch, surrounded by suitcases, and I can't resist the opportunity to see her again before she leaves.

I've ended things with Phoebe and Zoey. I want Peach leaving here knowing I did that for her. Because I love her, and I'm going to do whatever it takes to turn this around.

"Anna James," I call out.

She turns at the sound of her name. Her eyes grow large when she sees me approaching. And so do mine when I see the baby sitting in her lap. "Beau . . ."

I'm dumbfounded. Speechless. *She has a baby?*

I do the math, counting the months on my fingers. We were together last July. If she became pregnant, she would have likely given birth in March. Maybe April. This is September. This baby would have to be around five months old to have a possibility of being mine.

I shouldn't jump to conclusions. He could belong to her fiancé. This could be the complication she was referring to.

"You didn't mention a baby."

"I didn't know how to."

He's a beautiful boy, sitting so big in her lap. "How old is he?"

She avoids answering. "I'm sorry, Beau."

"Sorry for what?"

The baby bucks and twists in her lap. His tiny fists rub his hazel eyes surrounded by thick, dark lashes. My eyes. *Oh, shit.* "He's mine, isn't he?"

Her eyes dart toward the elevator doors and back to me. "Please don't do this now. And not here. Please."

"You've not answered me. Is he mine?"

She nods. "Yes."

"How?" I mean I know how. But . . . how?

"I think he happened on ketchup and chocolate night. We didn't use a condom." Oh. That explains what she meant when she said I'd already been skin on skin with her. He's the proof.

"I took a morning-after pill when I realized what we'd done." She shrugs and shakes her head. "Didn't work."

It isn't possible to label the many different emotions running through me at once but a few are front runners.

Happiness.

Love.

Anger.

"You've kept him from me." Again, my choice has been taken from me in regards to my child.

"I'm sorry, Beau, but we have a plane to catch, and our car will be here any minute."

"Fuck making your flight. I'll get you another one."

She's still staring at those damn elevator doors. "You're watching for *him*, aren't you?"

"He had to go up to the room but will be back any minute."

Fuck him and the horse he rode in on. "I want to hold my son."

She's fidgety, looking around like a thief about to be caught. I don't care. It's nothing to me if her fiancé comes off that elevator and catches us together. In fact, it'll only help me get him out of my way faster.

"Peach. Wouldn't you want to hold him if someone had kept him from you his entire life?"

She looks thoughtful for a moment before holding him out for me to take. "Just for a minute."

A minute, my ass.

I take him into my arms and all I can do is stare at him. "He has my eyes."

"He has your everything, Beau. Except the chin. I get credit for that."

She's right. I wish I had one of my baby pictures to show her. We're clones.

I can't believe I'm holding my son for the first time. "He's perfect. And amazing."

He grasps my thumb in his tiny hand, bringing it to his mouth. "Hey, little guy. I'm your dad."

I hug him, kissing the top of his head. His skin is soft. And he smells so good. Reminds me of Ashlyn when she was smaller.

"What is his name?"

"I need him back." She's already reaching for him.

"Come on, Peach. I've only held him ten seconds, and you already want to take him away from me?"

I take my phone from the case clipped on my shorts. "I want a picture."

She doesn't take the phone. "I deserve a picture."

She nibbles her lip. "All right. Quickly."

"Look at Mommy." Anna James is smiling as she takes the pictures.

"Found it." The preppy prick who just appeared at my side is holding up a pacifier. "It was on the floor under the table."

I turn away. Looking at him pisses me off.

She didn't tell me our son's name. "What's his name, Peach?"

"Clark, after my daddy, and Beauregard, after his father. But we call him Clark."

My heart melts. I can't believe she named our son after me. But his last name should be Emerson. And it will be.

I tickle him under his chin, making him smile. Ashlyn always loved that, too. "That's a great name, little guy."

"I wanted to name him Clark Preston, but she insisted on Clark *Beauregard*." He chuckles as he says my son's name. My name.

This dickhead has a bigger place in my son's life than me. Infuriating.

I hate this douche nozzle. I want him out of our son's life. And Anna James's. I will make that happen.

I offer my hand to this jackass, but not as a friendly gesture. I want him to know whom he's dealing with. "I'm Beauregard Emerson, Clark Beauregard's father." This may be the first time I've ever voluntarily introduced myself using that name.

He looks from me to Peach and back again, clearly confused by what's happening. But maybe he'll put his thinking cap on and figure it out.

That's right. Keep pondering about it, pal, and you'll figure out whose bed she was in last night while she disappeared for hours.

"Preston Mitchell, Anna's fiancé." He tries to play it cool, but his poker face is shit. The bastard is scared. And he should be; I'm taking back what belongs to me.

Anna James reaches for Clark. "We have to go now."

I relinquish my hold on Clark. And it kills me. I don't want to let him go.

His hold is tight on my thumb so Peach must break his grip. "Bye, little buddy. I will see you again, soon."

I lean in for a hug while Preston is gathering their bags. I whisper in Peach's ear. "We are unfinished business."

She looks at me wide-eyed.

"We have to talk about this. And him. There are a lot of important decisions to make concerning this little guy."

"This is going to be a busy week for me, but I'll call so we can make arrangements to get together."

Under no circumstances was I ready to see her walk out on me last night, but watching the woman I love *and* our son disappear out the door with another man is brutal. It's taking everything in me to keep my feet planted and not go after them.

When I'm back in my suite, I fall onto the bed and stare at the ceiling in pure wonder. I'm hugely pissed off at Anna James for keeping our son from me, but my anger is masked by delight.

I take out my phone and flip through the pictures of me holding little Clark. Now, I understand the dedication in the book when she thanked me for the gift I gave her. She was talking about Clark.

And the inscription in the book. *I see your face every day.* She was referencing seeing my face in our son's.

He's true and beautiful. *So, will she still have a place for me in her life?*

I loved her before I knew about our son, but now he changes everything. I'm twice as vested because the stakes have doubled.

Mistakes have been made through misunderstandings, but Clark isn't a mistake.

IT'S BEEN the longest seven days of my life, and watching my girl and my son walk out of that hotel was soul destroying. But today, I see them. Alone.

I'm happy, but nerves and excitement battle inside my stomach for dominance. Right now, nerves are winning.

She wants to talk about Clark. Of course I want that, too. We have a ton of decisions to make, but I also plan to address our relationship beyond parenting.

Peach greets me at the door. She's courteous but standoffish. I bet Preston's here.

"Nice house."

"Thanks. Have any problems finding it?"

"Nope. Navigation brought me straight here."

I follow her through the foyer to the living room. I'm a real estate agent. I evaluate everyone's home, whether I intend to or not. The things I know by looking at Peach's home are these: One, she, or someone on staff, keeps her house more organized than she kept our suite in Jamaica. Two, her book has been successful; this isn't a cheap house.

"Want something to drink?"

"I'm fine, thank you."

I immediately spot Clark on a quilt on the floor. "We were having tummy time."

I sit on the pallet's edge. "Hey, little guy. How are you?"

"Cranky," I hear a man call out from another room.

Damnit. Dickhead is here. That throws all kinds of wrenches in my plans for today. *I thought we'd be alone.*

But I can't say I blame him. If my fiancée's hot and sexy ex was coming over, I wouldn't leave either. I have baby-daddy status. He'll probably want to ensure that doesn't happen again.

"Thank you for letting me see him today." I want her to know I'm grateful. I realize she doesn't have to voluntarily do this. She could be forcing me to drag her into court.

"It'll need to be a short visit. Anna has plans," the asshole, again, calls out from another room where I can't see him. It's like he's wants me to know he's eavesdropping.

A streak of brown and gold rubs up next to me. "What is that thing? A baby leopard?"

Peach laughs. "That's Kermit. He's a Bengal."

"As in tiger?"

"No. As in domesticated house cat."

I lift Clark from the floor and lie on my back, placing him on my chest. "I think he's grown since I saw him a week ago."

"He's about to nurse me dry; he's in the middle of a growth spurt. I had to buy him twelve months clothes this week because he's outgrowing everything he has."

"He probably gets that from me. I was always big for my age."

"Pff," echoes from the other room. Asshole.

"When was he born?"

"April ninth. He just turned five months."

No way. "You've got to be kidding, Peach."

"I'm not."

Of course, she'd have no way of knowing since we never talked about it. "Clark was born on my birthday."

Her eyes light up as a smile spreads widely. "That's exceptionally cool since he was three days overdue, and I had to push forever. They thought I was going to need a C-section, but then he finally popped out two minutes after midnight. On your birthday. I can't believe that."

The best gift ever, even if I wasn't there.

"It's like he was waiting to be born the same day as his dad." The more I learn about him, the more I realize he's more and more like me. I love that.

There's a sudden crash from the mysterious room, followed by a rustling. Preston appears out of nowhere. "I have to go to work. Walk me to the door?"

"Sure."

I use Clark's hand to wave at Mr. Fiancé. "See ya later, Preston." Too bad you have to leave me here alone with Peach.

"We're teaching him to call me Dad. Not Preston."

Bull-fucking-shit. My son will not be calling any other man anything remotely close to that.

Peach goes to the front door with the asshole. I can't make out what they're saying, but I'm guessing he kissed the fuck out of her since her mouth is glossy and slightly reddened when she returns.

I'm here to talk parenting, so the first thing on my agenda is bringing up what they're teaching Clark. "You have to know it's not okay with me for my son to call him Dad."

"Preston's been in Clark's life since before he was born. You showed up last week."

"Because you didn't give me a fucking choice!" I realize I'm raising my voice so I look at Clark to see if I've upset him. Little buddy is fast asleep. That was fast.

I get up from the floor. "He's out. Where's his nursery?"

He's only five months old, but I don't want him in the room while we're talking in case things get heated.

She points to a doorway. "Second one on the left."

I take him into his bedroom and place him in his crib. His thumb instantly goes into his mouth. I laugh because I was a thumb-sucker, too.

I go back to the living room and sit on the sofa next to Peach. I've calmed down a little.

"Does Preston live here?" The thought of him spending as much time as he likes with my son, while I've not been given the option, irritates the fuck out of me.

"No."

"But he spends a lot of time here?"

"Yes." That means he gets to be with Clark while I'm left to fuck off.

"You know I wasn't in his life because you kept him from me. You can't imagine how it makes me feel to know I've missed the first five months of his life while some other man got to have that time with him. It hurts like hell, Peach. Why did you do that to me?" I told her how I felt when Erin stole my choice from me. I don't understand how she could do the same.

"I wasn't trying to hurt you, but what kind of mother would I be if I brought a baby into this?"

"What are you referring to when you say *this*?"

"Your lifestyle. Polyamory. It's no place to raise a baby, even if it's only on a part-time basis. I don't want Clark growing up around that kind of life."

Polyamory living may not be ideal for raising a child, but she doesn't get to be the judge, deciding I don't get to be part of Clark's life. "He's mine, too. You had no right to keep him from me."

"I was protecting him. That's what a good mother does."

I'm picking up what she's laying down. "You were protecting him from me? Because you think I'm unfit?"

"I don't think you're unfit. I'm sure you'd make an excellent father. But I do consider poly life unsuitable for my child."

I interrupt to correct her. "*Our* child."

"Yes. *Our* child is going to grow up, see the way you live, and ask questions. I don't want to have to explain why Daddy sleeps with two girlfriends." No. I don't want that either.

I already love my son, and one of the greatest gifts I'll ever give him is to love his mother. And I do. Wholeheartedly.

"They're gone. Both of them. I ended it for you and Clark."

"Until the next two come along."

"There's never going to be another two. But I am hoping for one.

You, Peach."

She's silent. Does that mean she's thinking it over? Or coming up with a way to tell me to fuck off? I can't tell.

"Erin wanted it, not me. And the girls you saw . . . they meant nothing. I met them at a club; they were a package deal. I missed you like fucking crazy but couldn't move on to a relationship with one woman. I didn't have it in me to care enough when you owned my heart. I'm done with poly relationships. Forever." I mean that.

"You shouldn't make promises you might not keep."

I've thought about this all week and there's no confusion. "I know which life I want—and it's the one with you and Clark."

"Clark is your son. I'm his mother, but that doesn't make us a couple."

"I think we can make it work, Peach. We are incredible together. You know we are. And I want to raise our son together."

"We were incredible for nine days in Jamaica. Anyone could be great in a vacation setting without responsibilities. But this is real life. Totally different scenario. We have no idea if we'd even tolerate one another in this environment."

"I damn sure want to find out."

"I'm engaged to Preston."

That's fixable. "You can get unengaged."

"I spent eight days with you. Preston has been around for a while."

"A while? As in you started dating him while you were pregnant with my child?" Fucking stunned. I can't believe she was over me so quickly, that she could move on like we never happened. *Did our week together mean so little?*

"No. Preston and I were just friends while I was pregnant. I couldn't even consider being with a man. We didn't begin dating until after Clark was born."

"And you're already engaged?" That's too fast.

"He proposed two weeks ago; we're newly engaged. I know it must sound like it happened really fast, but we were very close friends before. It's not as though we didn't know one another." It's a reminder she knows him better than she knows me.

"Do you love him?" I ask the question, knowing all along her affirmation will kill me.

"Of course I do. I'm marrying him." Not if I have anything to do with it.

"Tell me one thing. What have you thought or fantasized about every night this week in the moments before you fell asleep?"

She looks down at her hands in her lap and doesn't reply. I'm noticing she usually doesn't answer the hard questions. *Can't even look me in the eyes to deny it.*

"You don't have to answer that. I already know." Her chest rises a little higher and falls harder. Her mouth is slightly open, her breathing louder. "You're thinking about us right now."

"I'm not." She's blushing. Gives her away every time.

"I bet you're picturing yourself on your hands and knees and I'm pounding into you from behind. Tell me, Peach. Am I fucking your pussy or your ass?"

"Stop, Beau."

"I bet you're soaking wet right now." What I wouldn't give to touch her and confirm what I already know is true.

She sucks her bottom lip into her mouth and closes her eyes. She shakes her head. "No."

Clark's asleep and probably won't be waking anytime soon, so I'm going to take full advantage. I scoot closer. I trace her lips with my fingertips, imagining them going down on me.

I kiss the side of her neck beneath her earlobe. She lets me, but I won't push too hard. I need her to see she wants this. Us.

I rub her thigh, moving it up her leg slowly. "Tell me what you want. You know I'll give you anything you ask for."

She's shaking her head again. "I'm no better than Drake if I let you keep going. I can't do it."

"I think you can. In fact, we both know you already have."

My hand is at her mid-thigh. Climbing higher. "Do you want me to touch you?"

"We shouldn't do this. It's wrong." She drops her head against the back of her sofa and covers her face with both hands. "Shit. I didn't have you come over for this. We're supposed to be deciding on a parenting plan."

"We will. Later."

That's right, baby. Keep squeezing those thighs together and releasing them. Not because you're locking me out; I know what you're doing. Work that seam in your shorts against your clit.

I suck her earlobe into my mouth. "Tell me everything you want."

She stops writhing and grabs my face. Her eyes lock on mine. "Touch me. Lick me. Fuck me. All of the above." *Now, that's what I'm talking about.*

I crush my mouth against hers. "I love . . . how greedy . . . you are."

I move my hand to her crotch and rub her through her shorts. "God, Beau. This is wrong on so many levels."

"Let's pretend it isn't." *Because it feels so very right to me.*

I don't want her to think. Only to feel.

I take my hand from her crotch and slip it down the front of her shorts. My fingers find her slick slit. "I guessed right. You were definitely thinking about us."

I flick my finger back and forth over her clit, but my hand is a tight fit inside her shorts. It's not very conducive for rubbing her off so I take my hand out. I yank the button of her shorts open, push down the zipper, and put my hand back inside her panties. A much better fit.

She wraps her hand around my wrist and rides my hand. "Make me come, Beau. I need it so bad."

"I'm going to take care of you, baby. I always do."

It may kill me, but I have to know. "Have you been with him since you fucked me?" *Please say no.*

She grasps the back of my neck and brings me forward so our foreheads are pressed together. "No. I couldn't."

She releases me and extends her hand over her head, grabbing the back of the sofa. She thrusts her pelvis upward. "Omigod. Right there, Beau. Don't stop." *This is mine. She's mine. Not his. I own her orgasms. Not him.*

Anna James has always been incredibly responsive to my touch. "You love it when I rub you off, don't you?"

I pull back. I have to watch her come.

"Yes!" Her eyes are shut tightly, and she's biting her bottom lip as her head thrashes from side to side. Panting. "It's starting."

She's squeezing my wrist tight and arching higher. I have to stand up and reposition so she doesn't hyperextend my hand. Or break it. "Oh. Oh. Uhh."

She turns her face into her arm to stifle the scream threatening to escape. I'm afraid she'll shout and wake Clark so I lean down. "Kiss me."

After she turns to face me, my mouth possesses hers. I swallow every one of her moans of pleasure.

She suddenly jolts. "Shit. What was that?"

"What was what?"

"I heard a car door slamming." She dashes off the sofa and fastens her shorts only moments before Preston comes through the front door.

"Forgot the papers . . . I was grading." He stops short when he sees Peach looking like a deer in headlights. "Is something going on here?"

"You startled me. I wasn't expecting you." She definitely looks freaked out.

Dammit. I wish he'd have come home five minutes later and got an eyeful of what Peach looks like when she's being fucked over the arm of the sofa.

"Where's Clark?"

"Napping."

Preston briefly disappears and then returns with a stack of papers. Fucker totally left those on purpose so he could come back and see what we were up to. Fine by me. If he keeps trying to catch Peach and me doing something he won't approve, he'll eventually be successful.

Peach comes into the living room after he's gone a second time. "That was wrong, and it can't happen again."

"Agreed. Because I won't keep fucking another man's fiancée." That's why I have to get Preston out of her life.

She sits in the chair across from me and puts her head in her hands. "I'm a horrible person."

"Not true. Not even a little. And no matter what you have going on in your head, I'm with you, and I love you. Always."

Peach loves me. I know she does, but she's letting *him* stand in the way.

She lifts her face and looks at me. "You came to talk about Clark. We should do that."

"Okay. I want joint custody." For now. But that'll all change after we're together as a family. *Family. I love the way that sounds.*

"Every other weekend isn't going to work. I'm still nursing him, and he doesn't take a bottle at all. Ever. And I don't want him to. I plan to exclusively breastfeed for as long as possible." I can add determined to the long list of things I love about this woman.

"Every other weekend won't work for me either. I need to see him more often than that. I've already missed too much."

"Then what do you suggest?"

If she's going to use nursing as a reason to keep him then I'll use it as a reason for her to stay too. "If he were taking a bottle, you'd pack them up and send them. When he's with me, you'll pack you up and come along."

"Beau. I'm engaged to Preston. He'll have a shit fit. I see your logic, but there is no way he will agree with that." She mumbles under her breath, "I'm not sure I agree with it either."

"Would you prefer he have a shit fit or we go before a judge and have him or her decide our fate?" I'm sure she knows it won't look very good that she kept Clark from me since birth.

"So you're agreeing?" *Come on, Peach. Say yes.*

"I'm agreeing to try it. That's all I'm committing to. How many days are reasonable?" Every day.

"What's your schedule? Do you write full-time or what?"

"I try to write four days a week. Do you remember Emery Whitworth, the student who called me when we were in Jamaica? She and I grew quite close during our pregnancies. She comes over and keeps Clark for six hours those days. What I pay her helps with her tuition fees. But, not having any family support, she gave her baby up for adoption. Being in Clark's life has helped her heal. Emotionally."

After my experience with Caroline, I know how important it is for a young pregnant girl to have a supportive adult in her life.

"I want three days a week." I have no idea if she'll go for that or not. That means spending a lot of time with me.

"Three days is almost half the week." I know. And it's not near enough.

"Do I need to remind you that you're getting all seven with him?"

"No. I'm aware but that's going to disrupt my life a lot."

"Then give me two. You can use your days with me to write. I'll take care of him and you'll nurse him when he's hungry." It's really a great plan for both of us.

"Sheez, Preston is going to hate this."

"Preston can kiss my ass." I mean that from the bottom of my heart.

She laughs. "Okay. We'll give it a try and see how it goes. But I'm making no promises. And no more of what just happened."

I laugh. "I make no promises either, Peach." I don't need any of her false guarantees, because I already know how this is going to play out. I'm taking what's mine.

"I'm serious, Beau. Hands off."

Yeah . . . that's not going to happen.

CHAPTER 15

BEAU EMERSON

WE GATHER AROUND MY PARENTS' TABLE FOR SUNDAY DINNER. IT'S A DIFFICULT feat to get the seven of us together, but my mother insists we do it once a month. No questions. Each of us knows the last Sunday of each month is reserved for family, per order of Darby Emerson.

I've been sitting on the news about Clark for two weeks. It's nearly killed me, but I've held out because I want my parents and siblings in the same room when I tell them about him. With a family this size, it's easier that way.

"I have some news to share." I never make announcements so I easily gain everyone's attention. "I've recently found out that I have a child—a five-month-old son."

Everyone ceases eating and stares at me.

"Who'd you knock up?" Judd asks.

"Her name is Anna James Bennett. I met her in Montego Bay last year. We were inseparable for nine days."

Hutch laughs. "Sounds like you really connected."

"Aren't you clever?" Smartass.

"It's a gift."

I need them to understand Anna James wasn't just a piece of ass to me. I love her. "I can honestly say that the nine days we spent together were the best of my life. Ever."

"I bet they were," Wilder says.

Mom gives my brothers *the* motherly stare. It shuts them up every time. "I hear a but in there somewhere." *Typical mother intuition.*

"We had a huge misunderstanding, and she left without saying goodbye. She came to me after discovering the pregnancy but saw me with Phoebe. She thought I was happy and didn't want to ruin it." I leave off the part about her seeing me with both of my lovers and the fact she refused to bring our child into a poly relationship.

"You sound unhappy about that." Mom is baiting me. And I'm biting.

"I'm full of regrets. A series of unfortunate circumstances caused me to miss everything—going to the doctor with her, being there when he was born, the first five months of his life." I'm sick about it.

"But you're in his life now?"

"We've made an agreement about visitation. I get to see him two days a week."

"That's very generous." I know. She probably could have pushed the envelope and given me much less.

"I asked for three but I was pleased when she agreed to two."

"Is she the woman you introduced me to when we were FaceTiming?" Caroline asks.

I nod. "That's her."

"She's lovely."

Beautiful. Breathtaking. "She is that and so much more."

"What is his name?" my mom asks.

"Clark Beauregard. They call him Clark." Thank God. "You're going to be shocked when you see how much he looks like me. Our baby pictures could pass for twins." I consider showing her the pictures on my phone but seeing her grandson for the first time in person will be so much better.

"She named him after you although you were not together?" My mother is beaming, clearly happy to know Peach has carried on the Beauregard tradition.

"She loves that name. Don't know why."

"Because it belongs to you, but I'm guessing she didn't give him your last name since you weren't there when he was born?"

"He's a Bennett, for now, but I'm going to talk to her about changing it to Emerson." I need to give her time to let all of this sink in. I don't want to push too hard, too fast.

"What is her situation?" I know where Judd is going with this. He's asking if she's a gold digger.

"She's a former high school teacher turned author." I look at my sister. "Her pen name is A.J. Clark. Ever heard of her?"

"Holy shit!" Caroline yelps. "You have a baby with A.J. Clark?"

"She wasn't A.J. Clark when we met."

"What is your status with her now that Phoebe is out of the picture?" I hear the optimism in Mom's voice. She's so hopeful I'll find that special woman to marry and start a family. And I have.

"I love her."

A fork drops onto someone's plate, making a clanking noise, and a soft gasp leaves my mom. "Have you told her?"

"I did but she's with another man. Engaged." I despise admitting that.

"Beau, you can't sit back and do nothing. You love her, and she's the mother of your child. You have to fight for her and your son." Mom's not saying anything I don't already realize.

"I know; I'm going to. I'm already making plans."

"When do we get to meet Clark?" Mom is beaming.

"We're still ironing out the details on what days since she has a book release on Tuesday. She's asked me to wait until later in the week. I was hoping I could bring him then."

"You already know you can bring him anytime. I wish you could go get him right now."

"Me, too, Mom. I miss that little guy like crazy." And his mom, too.

~

JUDD AND HUTCH are on their knees installing the new hand-scraped wood flooring in our latest flip. Definitely worth the extra money. Potential buyers are going to love it. "That looks really high end."

"Well, here comes lover boy," Judd says.

"Fuck you." I knew I was going to catch shit from my brothers about my announcement last night.

Hutch moves from his hands and knees to a kneeling position and sits back on his feet. "Judd and I have been talking about your news, and we're curious. How does one living your kind of lifestyle go to a hedonism resort in Jamaica and fall in love? We thought that place was only about kinky sex."

"It is but it also happens to be where I found the right woman." And had lots of sex, some of it a little on the kinky side.

"But she's vanilla. And you're not. How's that gonna work out?" I'm a little surprised to hear Judd use the word *vanilla*. I didn't know he used that in his vocabulary for anything other than ice cream.

"I'm willing to give up my lifestyle for Anna James. If I have her, I don't need any of that shit."

"You said she's marrying another dude." I don't need Hutch to remind me.

"Not gonna happen." *Hide and watch if you don't believe me.*

"Judd, get the popcorn because I think we're gonna get to see a free show." This is my life, and they're laughing about it.

I don't have time for this bullshit. "Dickheads."

"Just kiddin' with you, bro. I can see how much you love this woman. I hope it works out for you."

I check the time. "I gotta run. Anna James and Clark are coming at three."

"Tell me again what time we're supposed to be at Mom and Dad's."

"We're going over at six, but y'all come around seven." I want Mom and Dad to have time with Peach and Clark without the whole gang. Plus, I don't want her to be immediately overwhelmed. My family can be a little much at times.

"Hey, Beau," Judd calls out. "Wanna come over to my place for some beers after the game tomorrow?"

"Sorry. Can't." I have a date with my son and his mother. "Maybe fishing next week?" I haven't taken the boat out in a while.

"Sure. Just let me know."

THE SLAM of a car door alerts me to Peach and Clark's arrival, so I sprint outside to offer help getting him out of the car, carrying his bag, whatever she needs me to do.

"It's all right. I've got this." *Miss Independent.*

"I know you've been doing this without my assistance, but I want to help." I need her to see my eagerness to be a father to Clark.

"Thank you." She holds out the carrier for me to take.

I sit on the sofa and place Clark's carrier on the cocktail table in front of me. "Hey, little guy. I'm very happy to see you again."

I look over at Peach. "And you, too." I can't believe how much I've missed them.

"The book release went well?"

"Oh, God. It's been a crazy week for me. I'm sorry I wasn't able to make it over sooner. I'm sure you've been anxious to see him." *Peach wants me in his life. She trusts me with our son. Now, I must convince her she can trust me with her heart as well.*

"It's okay. I know you couldn't help it."

"The book is getting great reviews, so I'm relieved."

"Of course, it is. It's a great story, Peach. It's ours." *Does Preston know our hot sex inspired what she wrote about?*

I haven't read the new book yet. I hear it's the second part of our story told from the male point of view. My view. "I plan to read the new book."

She covers her face. "Oh, God, Beau. Don't."

She's nuts if she thinks I'm not going to crack that puppy open as soon as I'm able. "It's my point of view. I want to know how you think I saw us."

"It's fictitious, Beau." *It's not. She wrote the story through my eyes. I want to know what she believed.*

"Don't be surprised if Caroline pulls out a copy for you to sign. She and her friends are huge fans. In fact, she's the reason I discovered *Hede*."

"Has she put it together, that Ben's character is based on you?"

"I hope not. That would mean she had figured out I used to be poly. As in, past tense."

Clark fusses so I take him out of his car seat. I've been dying to get my hands on him all week.

I recognize the offensive odor the moment it hits my nose. "Uh oh."

"What?"

I turn him around, and we make the discovery together. "Oh, dear, Lord. He's never done anything like that," Peach yelps.

Clark's covered in shit halfway up his back. "That, by God, is the worst case of Hershey squirts I've ever seen."

"Ah, poor thing. He's on antibiotics. The doctor warned me this might happen."

I'm alarmed at once. "Clark's sick?" She didn't call and tell me anything about him not being well or a visit to the pediatrician.

"Just an ear infection."

"He's my son. I want to know these things. I would have gone to the appointment with you had I been told." I don't mean to sound like an ass, but I am annoyed she didn't tell me.

"I'm sorry. I didn't consider that." She hasn't had to answer to anyone about Clark for five months. I guess I shouldn't be too upset with her.

"If you're truly remorseful, I think you should volunteer to clean him up."

"Sorry, Daddy. You're not getting off that easy." I love the way she just called me that.

"I'm already holding him so go run a bath while I take his clothes off. Second door on the left." He's covered so badly in shit I'm convinced I'll need a shower when we're done.

I pass his little naked butt off to Peach, and she places him in the water. "I have an emergency bag in the car. There's baby wash in it."

"Caroline brought over a basket of baby supplies. I'm sure there's some in there."

Lotion. Baby powder. Butt paste. "Found some."

"I bought that outfit especially for tonight. I wanted him dressed well when he meets your family. I'm not sure I have anything decent in his bag. It's probably just an emergency onesie." She sounds so deflated.

"This qualifies as an emergency." A code brown.

"I know but he should look his best. I don't want your family to think I don't take pride in the way I dress him."

She's worried about what my family thinks of her. *Caring about them is an extension of her caring for me. Right?*

"I have something he can wear." And my family will absolutely love it.

"You've been baby shopping?"

"Don't get too excited. I was in the campus bookstore with Caroline and couldn't resist getting him some Georgia Bulldogs stuff."

She laughs. "I should have known you'd put him in something like that as soon as you could."

"I was saving it for game day."

"Which is when?"

I had planned to discuss that with her tonight. "Tomorrow."

"At least you're not in a hurry."

"I'd really love it if you and Clark would come to the game with me and my family tomorrow."

"You want a five-and-a-half-month-old at a football game?"

It's about so much more than that. "Game day is family time for the Emersons. And Clark is an Emerson."

She doesn't argue he's a Bennett so I take that as a sign it could be okay to bring up his last name. "I wasn't around when he was born. If I had been, he would have taken my name."

"I know." Her initial reaction isn't to argue. Thank, God.

"I want him to be an Emerson. Legally."

"I knew you would. You're his father so he should have your name. But you probably ought to know Preston isn't okay with it." Again, Preston can kiss my ass.

That prick probably thought he was going to adopt my son as his own. Wrong. "He doesn't get to have a say about my son's name."

"I wish you could be a little less difficult when it comes to him. He's going to be my husband and Clark's stepfather. It'll be easier on all of us if you can get along."

My attitude is upsetting her, so I'll keep my opinion to myself about Preston's future status in our lives.

"Will you come to the game with us?" Tomorrow is my day with Clark. We've already agreed.

"Sure."

She takes Clark out of the bath once he's spick and span and wraps him in a towel. "I must confess I'm a little embarrassed about meeting your family."

What does that mean? "Why?"

"I only knew you a few days when I got pregnant."

"You didn't do it by yourself. I was right there with you, happily going along. They know that."

"It doesn't say a lot about my virtue. And then I kept Clark from you. They can't think I'm a very nice person."

"Don't worry, Peach. My family is going to love you and Clark as much as I do." I didn't really intend on saying anything about loving her. But it's the truth.

"You can't say that kind of stuff to me."

"Why can't I if I'm being honest?"

Peach sighs. "I'm marrying someone else. There shouldn't be another man saying he loves me."

"But I do and I'm not going to stop telling you until you hear me."

"I do hear you."

I don't think she does. But she will.

My parents are waiting at the front door to greet us when we arrive at their house. "This is my mother, Darby, and my father, Will."

Peach is nervous. I hear it in her voice when she speaks. "Very nice to meet you. I'm Anna James."

I take Clark from Peach and turn him so my parents can see him. "And this is your grandson, Clark."

My mother puts out her hands to take him. "My God, Beau. It's like looking at you as an infant all over again."

My mother hugs him, rocking side to side, as she kisses the top of his head. "He smells so good."

Peach and I look at one another and smile, saying nothing about the shitty mess we had on our hands an hour ago.

My mother goes to Peach and hugs her. "Thank you for giving us our first grandson."

Peach smiles but doesn't respond.

"Look at his outfit, Darby. He's definitely one of ours because he's ready to cheer on the dogs." I can tell my dad is proud.

We go into the living room and spend the next hour letting my parents get to know Peach and their grandson. I see her gradually ease but stiffen again when my mother asks about the type books she writes. "Umm . . . romance."

My mom reads all the time. I hope she doesn't decide to pick up *Hede*. I already don't like that Caroline has read it.

"Not your speed, Mom."

"Shut up. You don't know anything about my speed. Need I remind you I have five children?"

That's more than I needed to hear. "No ma'am."

Caroline and Ashlyn are the first to arrive. Of course, Ash has her bunny in hand.

I haven't seen my niece in a while so I take her from Caro to make the introduction between the two Emerson grandchildren. "You see my baby, Ashlyn? This is your cousin, Clark. You're going to be good friends one day."

Ashlyn squeals as she reaches out with grasping hands for Clark but I pull her back. She loves to hug very tightly. "I don't think he's quite ready for her kind of love."

Ashlyn needs a distraction. "Hey, baby girl. Show Anna James your toy."

Peach beams. "Is that the bunny I bought for her?"

"It is. If you'll remember, she wasn't much older than what Clark is now when you bought it for her. Favorite toy ever. She won't give it up for anything."

Caroline punches my arm. "You told me you bought this for Ashlyn."

I shrug. "I lied. Anna James did."

"You couldn't have chosen anything she would have loved more. That bunny is her best friend," Caroline says.

"So glad she has enjoyed it."

While we wait for my brothers, Caroline grills Peach about the new book and any future projects she's willing to talk about.

Judd, Hutch, and Wilder arrive one by one, and I'm amused by their reactions to Peach. None of them can take their eyes off her, but I get it. I'm the same way.

Cream lacy dress. Boots. Loose curls. Gorgeous.

"Bro, that is a hot piece of ass. I totally understand why you'd want to hold on to that," Judd says. "Give me a girl like that, and even I'll settle down."

Peach is a beautiful woman but that's not what draws me to her. "I want to be with Anna James because I love her."

"I think we can all agree it's easier to love someone who looks like that."

I look at her standing in the kitchen with Caroline, Ashlyn, and my parents. "It's easy to love her, period."

CHAPTER 16

BEAU EMERSON

I GET TO EXPERIENCE THREE OF MY FAVORITE THINGS AT THE SAME TIME: THE woman I love, our son, and Georgia Bulldogs game day. Doesn't get much better than this.

We're tailgating on campus before the game. It's almost October but still blazing hot. It's barely midday but Clark is already soaked with sweat. He's fussy so Peach and I take him into my parents' RV where it's cool.

"He's getting hungry. Can I go into the bedroom to nurse him?"

"Sure."

I walk to the back with her and open the door. She brushes against me when she squeezes by. *Fuck. Even her simplest touch has the power to send me into orbit.*

I've never seen her nurse our son. But I want to. "Is it weird that I want to watch you feed him?"

"Weird? No. Awkward? Yes."

I can guess what she's thinking. "Although I'd love to see your perfect tits again, it has nothing to do with that. I've missed every part of his life. Even the little stuff like this. It's not a good feeling."

I step out of the doorway to give her the privacy she wants. "It's okay. You can stay."

She's already said it would be awkward. "I don't want to make you uncomfortable."

"And I don't want to be the reason you miss the little stuff you want to be a part of." The corners of her mouth turn upward. She uses her hand to gesture for me to enter. "Come in."

I step inside, pull the door shut, and sit next to her on the bed.

Clark latches on and his hand goes for a strand of Peach's hair. At first, I think he's going to yank it but instead, he rubs it between his fingers as he nurses. The bond I see between them mesmerizes me. I'm a little jealous. "Does he always play with your hair like that?"

"Yeah. It's his thing. Has been since he was old enough to reach out for it."

"Those are the kinds of things I should know about but don't." And Preston does. That pisses me off.

"It'll come in time, Beau." No, it won't. Not if we're together two days a week for only a few hours.

Preston reminds me very much of Heath. He's in the picture claiming what I consider mine. I hate it and I can't do anything about it because it's what Peach has chosen.

Clark finishes eating. "We should probably head up so we don't get caught in the last-minute rush."

I like having Peach and Clark in this place with my family and friends. For a moment, I can almost pretend she's here because she wants to be with me, and not as part of our arrangement for visitation.

"This is nicer than the suite I visited with my friend."

"There are some even better ones but this is where we like to be. Our friends are here." Peach doesn't yet understand this isn't only about our immediate family. This is where we come together with our family friends as well.

"Want something to eat?"

"Oh, God, no. I'm stuffed from tailgating but I'd love some water. I have to be careful to stay hydrated when I'm out in the heat or my milk supply declines. And this little guy won't be a happy camper."

He is his father's son. "Men typically aren't happy when their food supply is taken from them."

I spot Daphne Clayton when I go to fetch Peach's water but it's too late to dodge her.

"Beau!" She's so fucking loud, always doing whatever it takes to gain people's attention.

"Hi, Daphne. How are you?"

I look to Judd for help. He laughs while expanding his cheek out with his tongue and imitating a blow job with his hand. *Motherfucker.*

I wish Mom would see that and slap the piss out of him. Because she totally would, right here in front of God and everybody.

Our family has been friends with Daphne's our entire lives. She's several years younger than me so I always looked at her as a kid—until we were older. She started pursuing me when she was sixteen, but I never looked her way until she came home from college one Christmas.

We fucked. And I found out quickly she was a leech. She still is even though it's been more than ten years after the fact. *Still regretting that one.*

"I want to know when you're going to give in and hire me to stage one of your flips." Never. I couldn't stand to spend that kind of time with her.

"I don't pay Kay for staging my houses. We trade out."

"How do you trade out with that ol' bag?" Kay is a nice lady so that comment pisses me off.

"She gets jobs from my clients because I recommend her services. In exchange, she stages for me." It's a sweet deal that works well for both of us.

"I can do a better job."

"I can't afford you." Lie.

"Bullshit, Beau. I know how much money you make." That's where the bullshit comes in. She has no damn idea what I make. I don't talk personal finances with anyone.

I look over at Peach and notice her watching us before she quickly looks away. "Maybe I'll give you a call sometime."

"You should do that. You already know I can show you a good time." I was referring to business so she'd leave me alone. I definitely didn't mean I'd call her for personal reasons.

Daphne comes up on her toes and kisses me. "I have some people to see but we'll talk later." No, we won't.

I hope Peach didn't see that kiss.

"I grabbed spring but would you prefer sparkling?" Fairly sure she prefers the fizz.

She takes the bottle from my hand and turns away. "It's fine. I'm sure you were distracted while you were trying to decide."

I have to be transparent with Peach if she's going to trust me. "That was Daphne Clayton. Would you like me to introduce you?"

"Why would I need to meet her?" She's staring me down, giving me that look I see from my mom when my dad's done wrong.

Damn. I think she may be jealous. *That lifts my spirits.*

"I think it's important for you to know everyone who will be around Clark."

"Why would Clark be around that woman?"

"Our families are friends so we see each other at functions." More often than I'd like.

"Thanks, but I can do without an introduction. Her voice grates like nails down a chalkboard."

I chuckle. "I'd agree with that assessment."

My mom comes over, grinning sheepishly. "Can I borrow my grandson? I want to show him off."

"Of course," Peach says as she hands him over to my mother.

"I'll keep him in the lounge where it's cool if you want to sit in the stadium seats."

"Want to?"

"Sure."

I always sit in my stadium seat for at least the first quarter. I don't like to be distracted by all the chitchat in the box's lounge. Peach, however, is more than welcome to have all of my attention.

Today's game is on ESPN so there's a lot of time for conversation during commercial breaks. "What happened to Meredith and Grayson?"

"Oh, lawdy. Things were rough for a while but they worked through their problems. Thank God. And now Clark has given Mere a bad case of baby fever. They started trying for a baby this month." A girly squeal follows. "I hope she gets pregnant soon so our babies can grow up together."

I'm not sure how compatible an infant would be with their lifestyle. "Are they still swinging?"

"Linc scared the shit out of Meredith. And Grayson. It opened their eyes to all the bad shit that could happen so they made the decision to never do it again. As far as I know, they've been monogamous since Jamaica. And couldn't be happier." God, she's so damn beautiful when she smiles.

I miss this. The ease of casual conversation like we had in Jamaica.

"I contacted the general manager of Indulge after I was home and told him what Linc had done. He was blackballed and will never be allowed to return. Neither will Carl Dennison. I reported him as well after you told me what he did." It's not near what he deserves since I consider his actions the reason Peach and I aren't together now.

"That's good but they both need red warning labels around their necks for the rest of the world's safety."

"Won't argue with that."

She looks at her hands in her lap, picking at the polish on her nails. "Have you been back to the resort?"

Phoebe and Zoey bugged the shit out of me to go, but I couldn't pull the trigger.

I grasp her chin and force her to look at me. If Peach is going to ask me that, she's going to look me in the eyes when I answer. "No. Haven't set foot down there since last July. I couldn't bear being there because I'd see your face everywhere. I let my membership go."

She takes a sharp inhale of breath.

I feel a hand on my shoulder. "Beau! You're on kiss cam. Kiss your girl," my mom's best friend, Marlana, says.

I hear the chorus of "Kiss Kiss" and quickly turn to see our picture on the big screen. I turn back, and without permission, I lay on her one of our best kisses ever. And she lets me.

She moans lightly and I feel her lips, against mine, spread into a smile.

Our entire section erupts into cheers and catcalls.

I release her and smile. "Sorry. Had to be done per ordinance of the kiss cam."

Her mouth remains slightly open and she's staring at my mouth so I lean in and do it again. After a moment, she shrinks away.

"Beau," she whispers before looking around to see who's watching. She sucks her bottom lip into her mouth and then wipes it with her hand. "You shouldn't have done that."

It's true. Nothing tastes sweeter than what you can't have.

"I disagree."

I stand to cheer for the Bulldogs, not giving her time to plead her case because it'll do no good; she won't convince me it was wrong. *I fucking hate I can't do that whenever and wherever I want.*

Four touchdowns for the Bulldogs, with two of them in the last quarter. It's another huge win for us, and I'm stoked. Maybe that's why I put my arms around Peach and surprise her with a full spin, causing her to squeal. "Beau!"

I return her to her feet. "Good grief. This family is obsessed."

"I wasn't kidding when I said we were hardcore fans. But this is how we like to spend time together. It works. Keeps us close."

"It's nice."

"So, you don't think you'll mind your son growing up as an Emerson?"

"I'm glad he's part of your family. And I'm happy to see how easily he was accepted."

"He's one of ours. Of course we accept him."

"I realized today how hurt you are about missing the first five months of his life. I was wrong for keeping him from you, and I'll forever be sorry about that. He needs his dad."

"I was angry at first but I realized you were doing what you thought was best for him. But please understand that, as his father, I'm going to do what's best for him, too." It's not even a choice really. I'm done with polyamory. Peach is it for me. Peach and Clark.

"You are already a wonderful father to Clark."

"Thank you. I'm pleased to know you think so." It would kill me if she thought otherwise.

"I let my pain influence my decision to not tell you about him. But I'm glad you found out; he would have missed out on knowing his daddy. And that would have been such a shame."

Daddy. I melt hearing her call me that.

The game ends, but I have several more hours during my visitation. Today has been easy. Anna James effortlessly fit into my family, and everyone adores Clark. How could they not?

Doing nothing but doing it together is something I've looked forward to all week. I just want to spend time with my son and talk to Peach. For me, that's the cherry on top of my sundae.

I pull into my drive and see a car I don't recognize. "Don't know who that is."

"It's Preston. I hope nothing is wrong."

Fucker doesn't need to think he's going to show up at my place and intrude on my time with Peach and Clark. I've waited all week for this.

"I'll take him in so you can see what's going on."

Clark and I go into the house, and I take him out of his car seat.

He's fussy and has been for half an hour. I think he's ready to eat again. "I know, dude. I feel the same way. I want Mommy in here with us, too."

Peach is outside with Preston much longer than I like. When she finally comes in, I can tell she's been crying. "What's wrong, Peach?"

I'm expecting her to say there's been an accident or someone has died. She doesn't. "Preston was at the game with some colleagues. He saw us on the kiss cam."

Oh. I'm not really sure what to say about that. I'm not sorry I did it, but at the same time, I don't want Preston giving her shit about it since I'm the one who kissed her. "Do I need to talk to him?"

"God, no. That will only make things worse."

She fidgets with her engagement ring, twisting it on her finger. The stone is puny. Nothing like the diamond she deserves to wear. *I'd put the kind of ring she deserves to wear on her finger. Everyone would know she was taken. Mine.*

"If he were a man, he would have come to me and settled this. Not jumped on you about something I did." *What does she see in that bastard?*

If this were the other way around and I was the fiancé, I would pull baby daddy aside and set him straight on some boundaries. But Preston is a puss.

"He's upset I didn't make you quit." He's not wrong. She didn't make me stop. Either time. In fact, I think she was on the cusp of initiating the second kiss.

"I need a minute to freshen up."

She disappears to the bathroom. I stretch out on the couch with Clark on my chest just the way I used to with Ashlyn. I turn on HGTV to my favorite fixer-upper show.

Peach stays in the bathroom for a while before returning. "I can't believe you have little fancy soaps in your powder room."

"Wasn't me. Kay did that."

"Who's Kay?" she asks.

"She's a stager I use when I get ready to put my flips on the market. She came in and spruced the place up after Phoebe and Zoey left."

"I guess they kept your house in order while they were here?"

"Fuck, no. They didn't lift a finger to clean. Kay came in to help me straighten up the path of their destruction."

"They were so messy you had to hire a professional to clean up after them?"

"Not exactly. I called them after we were together in New York and told them to get out. They trashed my house."

"That's horrible."

"Worth it to get *their crazy asses* outta here."

"You really did break it off with them for me."

I don't know why she's surprised. "I told you I would."

"I didn't know if I should believe you or not."

"I did it after you left my room, even before I knew about Clark, because I so desperately wanted us back. I still do, Peach."

"Please don't say things like that."

She turns away, but I'm not having it. "Look at me, Peach."

She hesitates but does what I tell her. There are tears in her beautiful eyes.

"Peach, I'm in love with you. I don't want you to marry Preston. I want you and Clark to stay with me. So, I will continue to tell you often how much I want and love you."

CHAPTER 17

BEAU EMERSON

TEN WEEKS IS A LONG TIME TO WATCH THE WOMAN YOU LOVE BE WITH ANOTHER man. The empty pillow beside me a reminder she isn't here but next to him. I've sworn every night to let her go, but I wake loving her more than I did the day before.

Surely she's been fucking him. Knowing that is far more hurtful than I could have possibly imagined. *I never cared this much when Erin fucked Heath.*

I'm tired of the pain. I have a vile desire to lash out so she can hurt the way I do. I know it's wrong. I'm not supposed to want that for my beloved. I should always want happiness for her. But I don't if she can't find it with me.

I'm a selfish bastard.

It's my day with Clark, and Peach has an approaching deadline with her editor, so she's working in my office. I know I shouldn't disturb her but Clark's down for a nap and we need to talk.

I tap on the door. She doesn't hear me since she's wearing earbuds, so I enter. She jolts when she sees me and then removes one of her headphones. "Sorry. Didn't hear you."

"Didn't mean to startle you."

"It's fine. Clark okay?"

"Yeah. He's asleep. I was hoping we could talk while he's down." I hate doing this when I know she needs to be writing, but I'm on my own deadline.

"Sure." She closes the top of her laptop. "What's up?"

"The wedding is soon." I die a little more each day as it approaches.

Wrinkled forehead. Narrowed eyes. I've seen that look before, and I'm guessing her wheels are spinning fast, trying to decide where I'm going with this. "Yes. It's creeping up on us."

"I can't do it anymore."

Those wrinkles deepen. "Can't do what?"

"Hold out hope for us. It's time to get realistic."

She sighs. "Oh." *That's all I get?*

"There are only so many times I can tell you I love you without hearing it back before you break me. I don't know the exact number but whatever it is, I'm almost there. I have one more "I love you" left in me, and I'm going to use it today."

"Beau . . ." she whispers, but says nothing else.

I go to her, pulling my office chair away from the desk. I drop to my knees in front of her. "I know you're scared, but I'm offering you my heart and asking you to take a chance on me. I swear on my life, you won't regret it. I will be the man you need me to be. Your friend. Your lover. Your husband." That last word sucks the air right out of her.

I want to be married to this woman. Very married.

"I'm asking you to trust me with your heart. I will not let you down." *This might break me, but I need her to know how serious I am.*

Tears spill from her eyes and I use my thumbs to catch them. "Please, don't cry. I never want to be the one to cause you tears."

I lean forward, pressing my lips to hers. She opens her mouth, allowing my tongue inside to meet hers in an erotic dance.

This kiss is different. It tells me things she can't or won't say because she's frightened of us.

I cradle her face with my hands. "Come to the bedroom with me."

She looks so pained. "You know I can't do that."

I press my forehead to hers. "Please."

"Beau . . ."

"Let me make love to you."

I look into her eyes and see her conflict. I know she wants us physically—she's such a sensual woman—but I fear she may not accept us emotionally. "Let me make you come until you shatter into a million pieces."

She closes her eyes and takes a deep breath. When she looks back at me, she nods.

I hold her hand, leading her from my office to the bedroom. I fear the whole way there she'll change her mind and back out.

I stop next to the bed and walk behind her. I snake my arms around her body and kiss the back and side of her neck. Goosebumps erupt over her skin beneath my lips. *This. This is what I want every day.*

I haven't touched her like this in almost three months. "It's been torture having you so near, yet untouchable."

"Touch me any, and every, way you want." Her voice is nearly breathless.

I want to lift her dress and bend her over the side of the bed so I can pound into her, punishing her for what she's put me through the last three months. But my yearning to make love to her overpowers my darkest desire.

I lift the hem of her dress and rub my hand up the back of her thigh. "I've missed these legs being wrapped around me."

She reaches overhead and grasps the back of my neck as she leans against me. *I love how she does that.*

She rubs her bottom against my crotch. If I wasn't hard before, I am now.

I haven't fucked since she was in my bed in New York. I think it's the longest I've ever gone without sex. "God, I've missed you."

I bunch the bottom of her dress in my hand and push it up until it's over her head. I start at the center of her neck and kiss down to the back of her bra. I push the straps from her shoulders as I unfasten it.

She turns in my arms and grasps my shirt, pulling it off and tossing it to the floor. She flattens her palms against my chest and rubs my pecs, causing my nipples to harden. Dropping down, she sucks one into her mouth.

I lift my face to the ceiling and close my eyes, savoring the feel of her mouth on my skin.

She yanks open the button on my pants and pushes them and my boxer briefs to the floor.

The only clothing left is her panties, but not for long, when I push them from her hips and they fall to the floor.

We move onto the bed. I feather kisses down her chin and throat until my mouth finds one of her nipples. Something between a moan and the sound of my name escapes her mouth when I suck.

I take my time with both breasts before dragging my face and mouth down the center of her body to reach her hipbones. I kiss each of them and everything in between before dragging my nose over her groin. I inhale deeply. "Mmm, you smell so good." Sweet with a hint of debauchery.

I'm kneeling between her legs and a thought occurs. I flatten my palm against her chest between her breasts and slowly glide it down, over her belly where our child once resided. I drag my fingers over the stretch marks on her lower stomach.

There isn't a single part of her body not worth kissing.

She pushes my hand away. "Don't. I hate them."

She probably thinks I find the marks unattractive but it's the opposite. These lines are proof that a part of me was once inside her. Nothing is sexier. "Your body carried our son and gave him life. I wish I could have watched you grow with him."

She laces her fingers through my hair. "I'm sorry."

I kiss her over the top of her pelvic bone before journeying south. "We're done with regrets."

I lick straight up her center. "Ahh!"

She squirms beneath my mouth before finding a steady rocking motion. "I love your mouth on me."

Mmm, I love the way she tastes.

My fingers glide up her thighs and find her hands. She laces them with mine as she lifts her head to watch me. Our eyes meet only for a moment before she throws her head against the pillow and arches her back from the bed. She lifts her hips closer to my mouth and squeezes my hands tightly as her entire body stiffens. "Ahh, Beau!"

Her body trembles and then goes completely lax, panting as though trying to catch her breath. "My God, you're magnificent at that."

I scale her body, kissing my way up until I hover above her.

"I want you inside me."

"No more than I want to be inside you."

I nestle between her legs and stare at her eyes. Everything in this moment feels different, as though we're the only two people in this world.

I press my erection against her, and our eyes share a silent conversation our mouths don't dare interrupt. She wants to be closer, the same as me. Skin on skin, nothing between us.

I swallow hard when I barely push myself into her slick opening, giving her time to object. It's my way of asking, without words, before entering her body completely. I'm giving her an out if this isn't what she wants.

She grants me permission by lifting her hips against me. I glide into her slickness and squeeze my eyes shut as I hiss, "Fuck, Peach. You feel incredible. So much better than I dreamed."

She tightens her muscles around me as I move in and out with methodical slowness. I savor the full sensation of being inside her unsheathed. It's a damn shame I have no memory of doing this the first time, but I will never forget this moment.

I watch her beautiful face as I move over her. I'm certain I've never felt closer to anyone in my life. Ever.

I make love to her, the way two people in love should. Slow. Deep. Significant. The affection I have for her is overwhelming. I love this woman with all my heart. She owns me, body and soul.

We're heart to heart, and I fade into her until I don't know where I end and she begins.

"I'm getting close." I feel I should warn her in case she wants to ask me to pull out. She answers by locking her legs around my waist. I couldn't free myself from her tight hold if I tried. It's fine by me. I want to mark her, to make her mine.

Surely this means she is mine.

I bury my face against her neck and push deeply within her body, holding steady when I spasm, filling her with a part of myself. She locks her arms around me and squeezes her legs tighter. It's in this moment I know he's her past. I'm her present. Her future.

"I love you, Anna James," I whisper against her ear as I pour every part of myself into her.

This is it. She knows, after this time, I have no unrequited "I love you" left in me.

I lift my face from her neck and look at her eyes.

Nothing.

She doesn't utter a word, but her silence is loud and clear. This is her telling me she doesn't love me. Doesn't want me.

And this time, I believe her.

She's choosing him. *Fuck. Fuck. Fuck.*

I pull out of her and push up to sit on the side of the bed, my back turned to her. "That was the last time you'll get to tell me no. I'll never again ask you to love me." No more begging. No more pleading.

I stand and pull on my pants.

"Beau . . ."

"No." I don't want excuses or explanations. And I can't bear hearing how she doesn't trust me, or how she loathes the life I've lived.

I despise the man I once was. His choices are robbing me of the thing I want most in life.

I say nothing when I leave the room. Not even when she calls out to me to come back so we can talk.

I can smell her all over me. She's on *and* under my skin. But, fuck. Everyone has his or her breaking point, and I've met mine.

I'm stupidly in love with a memory, an echo of days forever gone.

"I'm done."

I won't lose myself trying to hold on to someone who doesn't care about losing me.

Ours hasn't been a love story, as I thought. It's a fucking tragedy.

CHAPTER 18

ANNA JAMES BENNETT

I love Beau so much it hurts. I wanted to say those words to him so badly. But I couldn't.

Against my will I've fallen into a love I think I'll never be able to recover from.

I was very aware of what Beau wanted from me when I agreed to go into his bedroom. And it was far more than sex. I knew, yet I went anyway, knowing all along I wouldn't be able to say those three words he wanted so desperately to hear from me.

I'm so fucking selfish. I let him make love to me because I wanted one more, one last time with him.

Beau Emerson is a wild card. And the things I desire from him will destroy me in the end. He has the ultimate power to ruin me. That's a precarious scenario, one I won't leave to chance. That's why I'm choosing the assured route.

Preston Mitchell is safe.

Shit. Beau said he wanted to be my husband. My fucking husband. It's been five days since he professed that to me. I still can't begin to wrap my head around it.

I love you, Anna James. Those words bind me to him tighter than any chain.

Together, Beau and I are the equivalent of a flame meeting gasoline. We burn so hot it's impossible to be extinguished. But with a scorching fire, someone always gets burned. I can't let it be me.

I haven't seen Beau since we made love, but he's all I've thought about since. Who am I shittin'? He's all I've thought about since leaving Jamaica. There's never a time when he's out of my head.

Preston has to know something is going on with me. I haven't let him touch me since I was with Beau in New York. That's a long time, even for us.

I use work and deadlines as excuses, always saying I'm too busy or I'm brainstorming about a new story. He doesn't complain, but any man would have to question a fiancée uninterested in sex.

Clarification: I'm plenty interested in having sex, and lots of it, but not with him since Beau came back into my life.

Beau's visitation with Clark has cycled around so it's his day with him. I must admit I typically look forward to their time together since I get to tag along. But today is different. I have to face Beau for the first time since I hurt him. I don't look forward to that.

I let myself into Beau's house as I've been doing for the last couple of months. "We're here," I call out.

"In here."

I put Clark's bag on the couch as I pass by on my way to the kitchen. "Want a sandwich?"

Beau has a production line of bread, cheese, and deli meats. "No. I ate before I came."

He wipes his hands on a towel and reaches for Clark. "Hey, buddy. I missed you this week. Come 'ere and see your daddy."

Watching Beau grow as a father to our son is beautiful. And sexy as hell.

He kisses the side of Clark's face. "Seems like he grows an inch from one visit to the next."

There are four sandwiches on the counter. Beau eats like a horse, but even he can't put away that much food. "Hungry much?"

"It's a picnic, of sorts. There are some local musicians playing at Piedmont park today. I thought we might go over and hang out."

"That sounds like fun." I love live music.

"I thought it would be nice for you to get some peace and quiet so you could work uninterrupted."

Oh. I'm not invited. "Sure. I have a deadline, so that would be great." Lie.

I wasn't planning to work today. I guess it's a good thing I brought my laptop.

"Just you and Clark?"

"No. My friend Daphne is coming with us."

Daphne? The name is familiar, like maybe I met her at one of the family functions, but I can't place who she is. "The name rings a bell, but I can't put a face with it."

"Tall redhead. I think you said her voice reminded you of nails grating down a chalkboard." Ugh.

"Of course. No way I could forget her." Although, I'll keep trying.

She's the one who kissed Beau at the football game. He didn't seem receptive, but maybe there was more to it than I thought. I'm surprised by the flip my stomach does when I consider that prospect.

It hasn't even been a week since he said he loved me, pleaded for me to love him back, and now he's going out with her. Right in front of me.

This is why I choose safe.

I'm getting left behind while Beau takes our son on a picnic with another woman. I didn't see this one coming.

He's acting as though five days ago never happened.

He told me he was done. Now . . . I think I believe him.

I need a minute to absorb this. "Sorry. I drank a ton of water on the way over. I'll be right back."

I speed walk toward the bathroom. It's a race against the tears collecting in my eyes. *Don't let him see you cry, Anna James.*

I use a folded tissue to absorb the tears from the corners of my eyes as I recall the things he said to me.

I'm offering you my heart and asking you to take a chance on me.

I will be the man you need me to be. Your friend. Your lover. Your husband.

I'm asking you to trust me with your heart. I will not let you down.

I love you, Anna James.

I don't understand how he can say those things, mean them, and then go out on a date several days later. I can't sort that one out.

I return to the kitchen when I'm finished having my meltdown. "Everything okay?"

Shit. Do I look like I've been crying? I need to get away from him ASAP. "Of course. I'll be in your office if you need you."

I'm staring at my laptop screen when the doorbell rings. I cringe. I don't want to see or hear that big mouth but I'm forced to do both when Beau brings Daphne back for an introduction. "This is my son's mother, Anna James Bennett, soon-to-be Mitchell."

Soon-to-be Mitchell. Hearing Beau say it so nonchalantly hurts. It's as though he doesn't care at all.

"Congratulations on your upcoming nuptials." I don't even have it in me to thank her.

She turns her attention on my son. "Oh! My! God! He's the cutest little thing ever!"

Poor Clark is looking at her with a frown threatening to turn it into a cry at any moment. *I know the feeling.*

"Thank you. We think he's pretty adorable."

She leans into Beau and grins at me. "Just like his dad."

I'm instantly pissed off. That was intended to taunt me.

Beau is grinning. I hope it's because he's proud to have his son compared to him and not because his date is trying to push my buttons.

I don't want to see them another minute. "You should probably get going. Piedmont has terrible parking."

I get up to kiss my boy goodbye. "Mommy will see you in a little while."

I'm sitting in Beau's office trying to work but the words won't come. I've literally worked on the same paragraph, with a few minor changes, for fifteen minutes. At this stage of the game, I've learned that when it's not popping, it's time to walk away for a little while.

I close my laptop and think about how I would kill for a glass of Wittmann Westhofener Morstein Riesling as big as my head. That might help the words flow.

My first book was based on my experience with Beau at Indulge, told through Emma Jane's eyes. The second was Ben's point of view. Now, I've been asked to write their HEA. And I'm fucking uninspired. How do I write about something I've not experienced?

This book is supposed to be a modern-day fairy tale filled with breathless moments. And sex. Lots of it. And babies.

I'm just not feelin' it.

Feeling a little snoopy, I open Beau's desk drawer. Nothing interesting there so I move down to the next one. *Hmm. What is this?*

I flip the picture frame over. "Ah, Beau." It's a framed photograph of us with the dolphins. *I haven't seen this picture since I stowed my copy away in the box never to be opened again.*

I find a stack of six pictures beneath it, all of us. Four in Jamaica.

One at my book signing in New York, the day he found me. The last of him and Clark in the hotel lobby the morning they met. All worn with frayed corners.

Fuck.

I go to Beau's bedroom and sit on the edge of his bed. I grab his pillow and bring it to my nose. I inhale deeply. God, it smells so good, just like him. I fall back and squeeze it to my chest.

My life sucks.

I thought the heartbreak I felt when I fled Jamaica was the worst but my world split down the middle when I saw him with those two fuck-tarts.

I hurt so badly afterward. *Is that how Beau has been feeling these last few months seeing me with Preston?*

I had a year to get my shit together. And I did. I found a friend and companion I trust and feel secure with. But then Beau inserts himself into my life and all that goes to shit. He has been making me question everything for months.

Now, I see him with someone else and the problem is clear. I may have fucked up when I didn't tell him those three words he wanted to hear.

I have to talk to Preston.

~

PRESTON IS AT HIS PLACE, feet propped on the cocktail table with papers spread all around him. He looks up and peers at me over his reading glasses. "Hey, you. Whatcha doing here?"

"Beau took Clark to the park. Wasn't much need for me to stay at his place since they weren't there." I leave off the part about Daphne. I hate admitting, even to my own fiancé, that Beau is with another woman.

"Grading papers, eh?"

"Yeah. I have to return these Monday."

Preston never uses his teaching assistant. He doesn't have it in him to relinquish the control. God, he can be uptight.

"So, you'll have to go back to *his* house?" Preston refuses to say Beau's name.

"Yeah, but not for a while. There are some local bands playing at the park. I figure they'll be gone a few hours." Clark will let them know when it's time to come back.

Preston gathers the papers surrounding him and transfers them to the cocktail table. "We're alone. That's a rare occurrence these days."

I know what that means. He wants to have sex. "I need to talk to you."

He removes his glasses and tosses them on top of his papers. He blinks several times. "Sounds serious."

"It is, I'm afraid."

He pats the cushion next to him. "Come sit next to me."

I do as he asks. When I say nothing, he reaches for my hand, gently squeezing it. "You've been so distant, Anna."

"I know." Things have been so different between us since Beau came back into my life.

"Talk to me. Tell me what's going on and where your head is."

The tears come before the words. "I can't marry you."

"Because of *him*." His voice breaks on the last word.

"Yes," I whisper.

Preston leans away from me. He inhales deeply before releasing the breath slowly. "Have you slept with him?"

I want to lie so badly because I'm ashamed of what I've done. But I have to tell him the truth; he deserves that much. "Yes."

"How many times?"

"Twice."

He says nothing as he releases my hand.

"I'm so sorry, Preston. I didn't mean to hurt you." I mean that.

"Do you love him or was it just sex?"

I feel so guilty. "I love him."

He nods. "Of course, you do. You always have, and I knew that, but I thought we were in the clear because he wasn't around."

I thought the same. "You know I never intended for him to be in my life again."

Preston leaves the couch and stands with his hands on his hips staring out the window, his back to me. "Have you told him that you love him?"

"No." But I've wanted to so badly. I've held back, believing if I didn't, I wouldn't be such a horrible person. Such an unfaithful fiancée. I thought I deserved to suffer in silence for being in love with another man. But the truth is I couldn't help it. My head didn't choose to love Beau. My heart did. I couldn't stop if I tried. And I did try. But it was useless.

Preston is a friend. He's safe. I could marry him and probably never know a day of hurt for the rest of my life. But I'd also never know what it is to have legs impatient for him to be between. To be unraveled down to my last thread of decency. To have the breath knocked out of me because I've fallen in love so hard.

I can't help myself.

I want mad passionate love, even if it's harder and hurts more. Even if it comes at a price.

"Has he told you he loves you?"

"Yes." Many times.

"I believe he does." He stares out the window for a long time.

"You're breaking my heart, Anna." Breaking his heart is breaking mine.

"I'm so sorry." I don't know what else to say. There are no words to make this better.

"You're aware of the things he likes, yet you choose him anyway, knowing in the end, he will destroy you. Hell, Anna. He went right back to that lifestyle after you. I don't understand why you'd choose to inflict that kind of pain upon yourself."

I'm glad he went back into a poly relationship after me. I don't think I could have handled him being in a one-on-one relationship if it wasn't with me. I want him to save that part of himself for us.

"Beau and I were separated because of lies he had no knowledge of. He was ready to commit to me then, but things got in the way. I believe him when he says he'll give up that lifestyle. If I didn't, I wouldn't put my heart or Clark's in his hands."

I'm still talking to his back. But maybe that enables me to say the words he needs to hear.

"I want you to know I wouldn't have survived and thrived during the last year had it not been for your friendship. I hate how much this is hurting you, but I can't go into a marriage without giving it 100%. That is what you deserve."

Preston finally leaves the window and comes back to me, taking my hand. "I can't change your mind, can I?"

I shake my head. "No."

He gently lifts my chin with his fingers so I'm looking at him. "I love you, Anna, and I want you to be happy, even if it's with him."

Dear, sweet man.

I have loved Preston, but not as he deserves. He has a heart of gold. How he can want what's best for me at this moment is beyond comprehension.

I place my engagement ring in his cupped hand and close it. With tears in my eyes, I say, "Your heart belongs to someone you've yet to meet, and she will be the luckiest woman alive to have it."

THAT WAS BRUTAL. I hated hurting Preston. He's such a kind and loving man. I truly want the best for him, and that's not me.

I go back to Beau's house. My two guys and the loudmouth have beaten me there. If I didn't figure it out by seeing Beau's Hummer in the garage, I'd know because Daphne's horselaugh echoes through the house when I enter the front door. So fucking annoying. I don't know how he can stand listening to her.

"I'm back," I announce.

I go into the living room and find Beau and Daphne cozy on the sofa. One look at them and I'm consumed with jealousy. *Can he tell?*

I must admit I'm a little perturbed to see Clark happily sitting in her lap. I feel a little betrayed by my eight-month-old.

Clark sees me and immediately squirms in her lap, reaching for me. I happily take him from her. "Hello, my sweet boy. Did you enjoy your day at the park with Daddy?" I purposefully leave off Daphne.

Beau's smiling. He likes it when I call him *Daddy*.

"I think he did. He may be a fan of music."

"I'm glad you had nice weather. How was the music?"

Of course, she's the one who answers. "Oh! My! God! It was so good!"

She rambles on for five minutes about complete nonsense before Beau's able to get a word in. "There was a guy who put a reggae twist on a lot of popular songs but he also did an acoustic cover of 'Falling' by Iration."

"Ah, I'm sad I missed it. That's one of my favorite songs." Beau and I danced to it at the reggae club in Jamaica—while I was falling for him.

"Ugh! I hated that reggae shit." She babbles on again. I block out most of it but she regains my attention when she places her hand on Beau's thigh. "Are we still going to Café Intermezzo after they leave?"

At least she's subtle about putting her foot on my ass and giving Clark and me a shove to get us out the door faster. Too bad. I'm not going anywhere. "Beau has Clark until nine o'clock."

"You mean Beau has Clark and his mother." Daphne looks at her watch and sighs loudly. "And that's over three more hours."

Wow. One would think she's ready to be rid of my son and me. Can't imagine why.

I need a break from Miss Loud Mouth. "Baby boy, I bet you're ready to nurse."

"Dear, Lord! You still breastfeed him?" She sounds so disgusted. "Are your breasts super saggy?"

It's an inappropriate question so I decide to give her an impolite reply. "My tits are fantastic. Aren't they, Beau?"

Beau bursts into laughter. Daphne, not so much. "She's right. They're pretty spectacular."

Bam, Daphne! In yo' face.

The look Daphne gives Beau is priceless. I'm pretty sure it could qualify as a death stare.

Clark and I go into Beau's bedroom to get away from big mouth. Poor little thing has probably had all he can stand. Beau should be ashamed for forcing that on him. "I bet you're exhausted from hearing all that hot air, aren't you, sweet boy?"

I stack the pillows on Beau's bed the way I like them and get comfortable.

I know it was only a few hours but I'm never away from him for this long. I didn't like it. "Mommy didn't have fun while you were at the park today."

"Mommy didn't have fun?" Beau's standing in the doorway.

"Eavesdropper."

Beau comes in and stretches out on the bed next to Clark and me. Even after three months, he still likes being with us during his feedings. "Where did you go while we were out?"

He needs to know my engagement with Preston is off. But not this way. We should be alone for that discussion. I have big plans for what

I hope happens afterward. "I went home because there was something important to take care of."

"Right." He sounds pissed off, or hurt, and I can guess why. He thinks I went home to have alone time with Preston. And I did, just not for the reason he thinks.

"We need to talk."

He props his head in his hand. "I'm listening."

I wish we could have this conversation right this second. I'm anxious to tell him. "Not now. And definitely not with Daphne here. I need your undivided attention."

"Sounds serious." That's the second time I've heard that tonight.

"It's very important."

I see fear grow in his eyes. I don't want that. "Have you changed your mind about our custody agreement?"

I have. I want Beau to be a full-time father to our son. "This isn't a conversation to have now."

"Then when?"

"Can you come over tomorrow night?"

"I can if I don't have a heart attack between now and then, worrying you're going to take my son from me."

I need to put Beau's worries to rest. "I'm not taking Clark from you. If anything, I want you to see him more."

Beau's face and posture relax. "You don't know how happy that makes me. Two days a week isn't near enough time with him. I feel like I miss everything."

"Beau!" I cringe at the sound of her voice coming from the living room.

"She doesn't sound too keen on you being back here with me while my spectacular breasts are on display."

He looks at Clark nursing. "God, they are splendid."

He gets up to leave. "What I wouldn't give to touch them again." There it is. The glimpse of hope that he hasn't moved on from me to her.

"Beau?"

He stops and turns back to me. "Yeah?"

I'm dying to tell him not to sleep with her tonight after I'm gone. But what right do I have? "Nothing."

"You don't get to tease me like that. What is it?" He's grinning. I think he knows he's tormenting me by having her here. *And he's loving it.*

Damn bastard, whom I love.

I shake my head, saying nothing.

"I want to know what's on your mind."

I'm going for it. If he tells me to fuck off, then he does. "Don't sleep with Daphne tonight." Or ever.

His face beams. "Never intended on it."

CHAPTER 19

ANNA JAMES BENNETT

"I HAVE A HUGE FAVOR TO ASK YOU."

"You know I'll do anything for my best friend." She says that now. Let's see how she feels tomorrow morning.

I hate asking Meredith to do this. It could possibly be the worst night of her life. "I need you to keep Clark."

"That's not a huge favor." She claps her hands together like a happy child. "And I'd love to."

She hasn't heard the rest. "Overnight."

My son has never been away from me for more than a few hours so I have no idea how he'll react to being separated from me for a full night. "It might not go well, Mere. You might want to kill me and then run to get your tubes tied."

"What are you talking about? Clark loves Grayson and me. He's used to being around us so he'll be fine." True. He has spent a lot of time with Mere and G but I've always been around, too.

An overnight stay means Clark will have to take a bottle tonight and in the morning. It's still new, and he's not entirely crazy about them, so it could go bad, fast.

"I wouldn't ask if it weren't important." My happiness is dependent on how this night goes.

"What's going on that you need a whole night away?"

"I broke off my engagement with Preston." She doesn't seem the least bit surprised.

"Finally came to your senses." Meredith and Grayson liked Preston fine but they knew he wasn't *the one*. Beau is.

"Beau doesn't know yet. I asked him to come over tonight so we could talk." Just saying those words aloud gets me excited.

"Don't you mean so you can fuck his brains out?" Such a Meredith comment.

"Well, that, too, after I tell him." It's ridiculous how much I'm looking forward to doing that.

"Do you have something special to wear?" It's just like her to be thinking about that.

"I wasn't planning on wearing anything."

"As much as he might like it, going to the door naked will be a dead giveaway. You gotta make him sweat for a minute."

I'm pretty sure he's been sweating it out since last night, considering he has no idea why I've asked him over. Or maybe he does since I told him to keep it in his britches last night.

"What about one of the lingerie sets he bought you in Jamaica? Do you still have them? That would be a sexy walk down memory lane."

They're packed away in a box I never open. "I have all three. Two have never been worn."

"You need to change that. Tonight."

He chose them so they must be the style he likes. "I think I'll wear the champagne one with rhinestones." It's super sexy.

"With matching, sparkly fuck-me pumps. You have to."

I can't argue with her on that. "Done."

I'M SHOWERED, shaved, fluffed, and puffed. My hair and makeup is perfect. I'm wearing a charcoal wrap dress with the chosen lingerie beneath it. All I need now is Beau.

He's late.

Thirty minutes. An hour. An hour and a half. His phone goes straight to voicemail each of the dozen times I've called over the last hour.

Beau wouldn't be a no-show. He knows I was planning to discuss something important tonight. I don't believe he'd stand me up. *Was I too late? Is he really done?*

Something is wrong.

My phone rings. It's a number I don't recognize but the voice on the other end is familiar. Beau's sister. "Anna James. It's Caroline."

I immediately know something has happened. "What's wrong?"

"Beau's been in an accident. He's asking for you."

My heart takes off in flight, pounding in my chest, my ears, throbbing in my hands. "Is he okay?"

"It was a pretty bad accident. An eighteen-wheeler ran a red light and T-boned him on the passenger's side. They're still running tests, but he doesn't have any life-threatening injuries. That's all we really know right now."

"I'm on my way."

I drive far too fast to the hospital, especially considering Beau's there because of an accident, but I manage to arrive in one piece.

I rush into the emergency room and find the Emerson clan. Caroline sees me and leaves her seat, diverting me directly to Beau's observation room in emergency department services.

Despite the gentle smile on her face, I can see how concerned she is for her brother. He is so loved. "Mom's with him right now, but she'll give you the visitor pass and swap places. He wants you. He's been very vocal about that."

He hasn't been moved to a hospital room or admitted. I think that's a good sign. It means they've not found any serious injuries. *A miracle.*

Caroline calls Darby to meet us so we can swap places. "Oh, God, thank you for coming, Anna James. He's been having a fit for us to get you here."

"Of course. I want to be with him." Darby looks surprised to hear me say that.

"He's refused pain medicine because he said he wants to talk to you before he's out of it."

"Good grief."

"I know. And he's agitated because he's hurting so badly. Not pleasant to be around right now."

"Don't worry. I'll talk him into taking something."

He was T-boned by an eighteen-wheeler. That puts horrific images in your mind. I imagined the worst during the drive over so when I walk in, Beau looks much better than what I conjured in my head.

Minor cuts and what appears to be emerging bruises are scattered over his face and chest. The cut above his right eye looks deep. I'm no doctor but I bet it will need stitches. Since a sheet covers him from the waist down, I can't see what's happening there.

I go to his side and grasp his hand. "Are you okay?"

"Much better now. Where's Clark?"

"With Meredith and Grayson."

He looks disappointed. "I guess the hospital isn't a place for a baby."

"I had already left him at their house before Caroline called. I made the arrangements with Meredith this morning for him to stay over."

"You never leave Clark with anyone." I've never had a reason to before tonight.

"I know. I'm hoping he doesn't give her hell."

"Why did you send him away overnight?"

I rub my thumb over the top of his hand. "So we wouldn't be interrupted."

"You must have a lot to say."

He has no idea. "I have plenty to say."

"Then start talking."

I had such romantic plans for us. I wanted to tell him I loved him and then make love all night until we fell into exhaustion. "This isn't how I want to do this."

"Well, this is where I'm going to be for a while. And I want to know what you have to say."

"I'm not saying anything until you agree to take something for the pain."

"It'll make me sleepy. I might not hear everything you tell me." He's being such a hard ass.

"It'll take a good thirty minutes to work and it's not going to cause amnesia. You'll remember everything we talk about." I press the nurse call light without his permission. "He's ready for pain medicine now."

I'm all set to talk once Beau is medicated, but the hospital staff has other plans. "Radiology just called. They're coming to get you for X-rays."

"Now?" He sounds so irritated.

His nurse laughs. "Yes, sir. Now, as in the next few minutes."

Beau looks at me. Every line on his face expresses annoyance. I hope it's not with me because I made him take the pain medicine.

"I'm sure it won't take too long."

As promised, radiology arrives within a few minutes to take Beau. "Don't go, Peach."

I'm happy to hear him calling me Peach again. I was Anna James to him during our last two interactions.

"I'm not going anywhere. I'll be right here when you get back."

Beau is rolled from the room, and reality hits me. I'm overcome when I consider what could have happened.

He could have been killed tonight. I hate to consider the outcome had he been driving anything other than that huge black tank. He might have died not knowing how much I love him. The thought devastates me.

I go into the bathroom to fix my face. I look like a raccoon. A fucking mess. So much for looking my best when I tell him how I feel.

I'm on my third trip to the bathroom to clean under my eyes when Beau returns.

"We're back," the radiology staff member announces as he rolls Beau back into the room.

I put on a smile, not wanting to alert him to the meltdown I just had. "That didn't take too long."

Beau's eyes look tired. I have no doubt he's fighting the drowsy side effects of the medication. "Is your pain better?"

"It's okay but they think my ankle is probably broken. Gotta wait for a radiologist to read the X-ray."

I go to the side of the bed and pull the sheet away so I can see his leg. His right ankle is swollen and purple. "Sheez, that looks bad."

"I've known better days."

Seeing his injury sparks more tears. I try to hold back but it's impossible. I cover my face to hide my ugly cry from him.

"Come 'ere, Peach." I sit on the side of the bed, and he pulls me into his arms. "I can't stand to see you cry."

I bury my face into his shoulder, careful to not hurt him. "God, you could've been killed. Clark wouldn't have a father." I hesitate a moment before verbalizing the rest of my thoughts. "And I wouldn't have you."

"You didn't have me anyway."

I twist so I can see his face. "But I want you. I have since Jamaica, and I've never stopped."

"What about Preston?"

"I broke off the engagement."

"When?"

"Last night. That's what I was doing while you were at the park."

That brings a smile to his lips. "Is that why you invited me over tonight?"

"Yes. Because I wanted to talk about us."

"I'm hoping you want to have that conversation where we both admit what we had was good."

It wasn't good. It was wonderful. "I don't like what we're doing. I want to be with you every day. And not just as your son's mother."

"You already know what I want to hear from you."

He wants to hear me say I love him but I need to hear it from him as well. "You told me you didn't have another 'I love you' left for me."

"Wrong. I told you I didn't have another 'I love you' without hearing it in return."

"I'm asking you to tell me again."

He breathes in deeply and releases it slowly. "I love you, Anna James."

I reach up to touch his face, running my finger beside the cut above his right eye. "I love you, Beau Emerson. And I don't want to spend another minute apart."

"I've waited a long time to hear you say that." Beau's lips meet mine but our kiss is cut short when his doctor comes in.

"Well, Mr. Emerson. The good news is we didn't find anything serious or life threatening. Bad news is your ankle and two ribs are fractured."

I've always heard broken ribs are painful.

"We'll splint your ankle until you can see an orthopedic doc next week but the rib injury is going to make using crutches painful. No worries. We'll give you plenty of medication for the discomfort."

Beau is all business while the doctor is in the room, but that ends the second she's gone. "Sounds like I'll be down for a while. I think I'm going to need someone to sponge bathe me."

"You have a mother."

"I also have a girlfriend who says she loves me."

I'm pretty sure I surpassed that title when I gave birth to his offspring. "A girlfriend? I don't think so. I'm at least baby mama status."

"I hope you know you're much more to me than my son's mother."

"I know I want to be more."

"That's a conversation I want to have very soon but not here. And not after I've been given narcotics."

I don't want to be interrupted by medical staff or have Beau under the influence while we discuss our future, either.

Future. I like that word a lot. It gives me hope.

It's morning when Beau is finally released from observation. I twisted and turned in the bedside chair like a contortionist, trying to find comfort. I finally stopped fighting it and crawled into the hospital bed with Beau at three o'clock, after he'd been begging me for hours.

Getting him in and out of my SUV wasn't fun, but Beau insisting on a shower before he gets into bed is even less entertaining. "I have dried blood in my hair and sweaty balls. Be a peach and help me out?"

I swear this man can talk me into anything. "Well, I guess you don't deserve sweaty balls after what you've been through."

My sister broke her leg when we were in high school. I had to help her wrap it when she showered so I'm a little familiar with what to do about Beau's partial cast splint.

"Take your clothes off and get in with me."

Yeah, right. "How do you think you're going to do anything on one leg?"

"I'm not asking because I want to fuck. Well, I do, but there's no way that's happening. My ribs are killing me. I need help washing off."

"Hang on. Let me see if I can find a clip for my hair." Success. I find a ponytail holder so I twist it into a messy bun on top of my head.

Beau watches me remove my wrap dress. "Dammit, baby. Why'd you have to be wearing that underneath your clothes?" I haven't heard him call me that since we were in Jamaica. *I've missed that. I've missed him.*

"I'm wearing this because I had big plans for you last night before you became fender meat."

"Not my fault, Peach. I absolutely wanted to be with you last night."

"I know, Beauregard." Our Peach and Beauregard endearments are helping heal my heart.

"I can't believe I'm about to say this, but I love hearing you call me that. I've missed it."

"Good."

As badly as I hate it, there's nothing romantic about this shower with Beau. It's strictly about getting him clean before he crawls into his bed. And expressing. *I'm about to explode.*

I turn off the shower and reach for a towel. "No more sweaty balls. I think you're good to go."

"Thank you. I'll wash yours anytime. All you have to do is ask and I'll repay the favor."

"If I ever ask you to wash my balls then you better know we have a problem."

I go to his dresser and realize I have no idea how his clothes are organized. "What do you want to put on and where do I find it?"

"Underwear top right. Athletic shorts bottom left. No shirt."

"Got it."

I'm pulling his underwear and shorts up his legs. "I get the privilege of dressing two Emerson men."

Beau stops me, cradling my face to press a kiss to my lips. "Thank you, again, for changing Clark's name to Emerson."

"He's your son. I wanted him to have your name."

He kisses me a second time. "He's *our* son."

Maybe I'm imagining it but it almost feels like something unsaid is hanging in the air.

I tap Beau on the hip. "Stand up, Mr. Emerson. Yo' baby mama need to pull up yo' shorties."

It takes all of forty-five minutes from start to finish but Beau is clean and in bed. I'm worn out from handling this oversized toddler.

Beau takes another pain pill and we both crawl into bed. I'm thankful Meredith had a good night with Clark and has offered to keep him for the day since I'm a fucking exhausted wreck.

Neither of us say a word before giving into the darkness hiding behind our lids.

~

It's midday when I open my eyes again. Beau's reaching for the bottle of water I left out of his reach on the nightstand. "Stop, Beau."

I know it must be killing him to stretch his torso like that. "You should have asked me to get that for you."

"You looked so peaceful. I didn't want to wake you."

I go around to his side of the bed. "This one's warm. I'll get you a cold one."

"You don't have to do that."

"I don't mind." In Jamaica, Beau did anything for me. He is the most accommodating and generous man I know. Despite his bossiness, which I kind of love, looking after him is easy.

Beau chugs half the bottle of water. "Thanks, baby. I needed that."

"I like it when you call me baby." I've never told him that before.

"Then I shall do it more often."

"And I shall tell you I love you more often."

Both of Beau's dimples make an appearance. "Tell me now."

I roll over and move to kneel next to Beau, my hands on either side of his head, so our bodies are crisscrossed. I press a kiss to his lips. "I love you, William Beauregard Emerson. And I will never say no to you again."

"You'll never tell me no, again, eh?"

"That's right."

"So, if I do this," he slides his hand up the back of my thigh, "you won't tell me to stop?"

"I won't."

"And if I ask you to move over here on top of me, you'll do it?"

He has several broken bones. He can't be serious. "Beau. You were in an accident with a huge truck. You have multiple fractures."

"Don't care. I want you. I need to be inside you." He reaches for the back of my neck to pull me closer and then groans in pain.

"See?"

He puts his hand to the right side of his torso then quickly removes it. "You remember when you asked me to fuck you hard and dirty? I did it because I knew it's what you needed. Now, this is what I need. To be inside you."

He catches a lock of my hair between two of his fingers and rolls it around them. "Please, Peach."

Again, I won't tell him no, because I truly don't want to. I want him inside me too.

I rise and move one leg over his pelvis so I'm straddling him. I lean forward, my elbows pressed into the pillow on each side of his head, and kiss his mouth. He places his hands back on my thighs and moves them upward until they reach my bare cheeks. "You slept beside me all morning with no panties on?"

My mischievous grin spreads. "Seems as though I did."

I move to kneel between his legs. I hook my fingers into his waistband and tug downward so he doesn't have to do too much lifting. I'm sure that wouldn't feel great to his fractured ribs.

I drag his bottoms to his feet. When I finished pulling them over his splint, I lower my body to his, bringing us close enough to touch, but without the pressure of my weight against him. "I know you like to fuck hard and dirty but you're going to have to settle for sweet and gentle."

"All that matters is that I'm inside you."

I grab the hem of his T-shirt I'm wearing and pull it over my head, tossing it to the floor.

He places his hands on my stomach and glides them upward. He palms my full breasts, making my nipples become erect beneath his touch. "Peach. You are so damn beautiful. You blow my fucking mind to shreds."

Beau has the ability to make me fall in love with him over and over again.

I move my hands beneath my hair and lift it into a messy pile on top of my head as I rotate my hips, moving my wet entrance back and forth over his erection. "I'm going to die if I'm not inside you in two seconds."

I grasp the tip of his cock and position it at my center. My body sinks down until he's completely buried inside me. I lean back, placing my hands on his thighs for leverage, and begin riding him in a slow, deliberate rhythm. "Are you okay?"

"Fuck, yes. That feels amazing."

Beau's hand slides between us. His fingers rubbing my clit is so welcome. *Divine.* His touch is magical, and he knows just how to hit that sensitive spot perfectly. "Ohh . . . right there."

He's rubbing harder, and I'm riding faster. Turns out this isn't as sweet and gentle as I expected.

"Are you already close?" he asks.

"Yesss!"

"Me, too."

When I come I sink deep, and my muscles tighten around Beau. "Ohh . . . ohh."

He grasps my hips and groans loudly as he spasms inside me.

I'm fairly certain he shouldn't be doing this in his condition. No way this is doctor approved.

He grasps my arm when I move to get up. "Where do you think you're going?"

"Just to grab a wet wash cloth." Ah. The messy repercussions of foregoing the condom.

I return to bed and crawl over him. I prop on my lower arms, one on each side of his head, so we're face to face. He grasps the sides of my head and kisses me like crazy. When he finishes, he holds me so we're staring at one another. "Marry me."

He's jumping the gun because he almost died last night. "Beau . . ."

"Open the top drawer of my nightstand and take out the black leather box."

No way. He has not bought an engagement ring for me. Except I know he has when I see the ring box in his drawer . . . sitting right next to the condoms we didn't use.

I hold it out for him. This is his gig. I'm going to make him work for it.

He takes it from my hand and cracks it open. Inside is a beautiful cushioned-shaped diamond surrounded by a halo of smaller ones. "Beau, it's stunning."

"Anna James Peach Bennett, love of my life, and center of my world. There's only one thing I want to change about you. Your last name. Because you're it. This is it for me. Will you marry me?"

Since the day I met this man, he's been able to talk me into anything, but this is the one thing he doesn't have to persuade me to do. Be his wife.

I want to hold this man's hand in fifty years and say we made it.

I want our children to believe we're soul mates—because that's what kids do—and then find out when they're grown they were right.

I want our story, the real one, to have a happily ever after.

I crawl over to straddle his body, careful to not hurt him. I lower my face to his. "Yes. A million times yes. I will marry you."

The path leading Beau and me to happiness hasn't been conventional. Getting to this place was hard. But I'm glad. It makes it all worth the wait to give him my heart, because in him, I've finally found my true and beautiful.

EPILOGUE

BEAU EMERSON

I DASH TOWARD THE DOOR OF PEACH'S WRITING CAVE BUT CLARK IS FASTER. HE bursts through and runs to her, throwing his arms around her leg. "Mama," he whines.

I know, little buddy. I miss Mommy, too, when she's on lockdown, racing to beat a deadline.

Peach looks up from her computer. All smiles. She removes her earbuds and closes her laptop. She puts her arms out for our son. "Hey, baby boy. Come 'ere and see Mommy for a minute."

A two-year-old doesn't understand why his mother is in the same house but he can't be with her. Sometimes it's hard for me to comprehend as well.

"Sorry. I tried to catch him but the little stinker got away. He's fast."

She pulls him onto her lap, wraps her arms around him, and laughs. "Tell me something I don't know."

"Well, I can but it isn't good news."

She sighs and shakes her head. "One guess. Flip troubles."

Exactly. That's what the fuck it always is. "Judd called. We have a disaster at one of the new renos. Something with the foundation."

She wrinkles her nose. "That doesn't sound good."

"It's probably going to cost a fortune." And eat up a big chunk of profit.

"I'm going over to check it out. Want me to take Clark so you can work in peace?"

She kisses the top of his head. "As much as I hate it, I really need you to."

"No problem. Are you close to finishing?"

"At the end of the last chapter."

Thank God. I understand the wee hours are when the house, and Clark, are quiet but I'm ready for my wife to come to bed at bedtime instead of staying up half the night working.

"Maybe tonight we can work on that new project we discussed?"

"I have to start edits as soon as I finish this chapter. It's going to be tough getting that done before we leave on Friday." Clark interrupts her when he wiggles out of her lap. "What project are you talking about?"

"Our baby-making venture."

She smiles. "Ahh. Someone's anxious to get to work on that?"

"I really am, Peach." I've been wanting to try for another baby for a while, but she's been reluctant. I understand. Her body healed months ago but she needed more time to recover emotionally from the baby we lost earlier this year.

She was only a couple of months along when she miscarried. The doctor assured us it was random and not a predictor of future problems. *Thank God.*

My job as Anna James's husband is to protect her and our child. Our children. But what happened was completely out of my control. I'd never felt more helpless.

It was a dark time. But our loss brought us closer.

Now, things are much better.

Beauregard, I'm ready to try again. I think it's time we make a brother or sister for Clark. I was so happy to hear those words from Peach last week.

We leave on our Jamaican getaway this weekend to the Grand Rose, the boutique resort where we honeymooned. "Maybe we'll make another Montego Bay baby. I sort of like the first one." Even if he is a pistol.

"Yeah. He's a pretty cute lil' guy. I wouldn't mind having another like him."

Me either, but I hope the next one is a petite fair-haired girl with blue eyes the color of the luminous lagoon. Just like my incredible wife.

Clark streaks by chasing Kermit. He loves that cat, but I'm not so sure his affection is requited.

I reach out to catch him. "Come 'ere little buddy. Let's give Kermit a break."

I toss him into the air and catch him in a cradle hold. "Want to go see Unc Jid?"

"Unc Jid," Clark shrieks. He's crazy about my brothers. All of them. Caroline and Ashlyn, too.

"Want me to bring dinner home since you're cramming?" I know the routine. Peach is usually the cook in this family. Except when it's manuscript crunch time. Then, it's takeout every night, and I'm the delivery guy.

"That would be great, baby." She looks thoughtful. "You up for sushi and hibachi?"

I can always do Japanese. "Sure. Want the usual?"

"Yup."

I tickle Clark under the chin. "Chicken fried rice for you, little dude?"

Clark squeals and wiggles in my arms. I love that he's ticklish like his mom. That's one of the few things he got from her.

The rambunctious, fearless road runner trait he got from me.

"Okay. We'll be back in a couple hours."

Huge chunks of the subfloor are gone. Ripped up completely. What a fucking mess.

Judd wasn't kidding. This is going to cost big time. We can kiss our generous profit goodbye on this job.

But it's the nature of the beast on these kinds of projects. No risk. No profit.

Clark wiggles to get down. "No, Clarky. You can't get down here. Too dangerous. You could fall through those holes in the floor."

"Where is Unc Jid, Clark? Want to call for him?"

"Unc Jid," Clark calls out.

Judd knew I was coming. And his work truck is outside. He's probably hiding because he doesn't want to hear what I have to say about this shit.

I walk toward the back of the reno.

Dammit. The deeper you go, the worse it gets. I don't even want to know what this is going to cost.

Well, Judd and Wilder's asses can get ready to do the work to cut expenses. They're the ones who insisted we buy this dump. They're going to be the ones to get it in shape.

I enter the master bedroom and go to the en suite to evaluate its potential preservation.

"You like getting fucked like this, don't you?" Judd smacks the woman's naked, lilywhite ass.

Holy shit.

I cover my son's eyes and immediately begin stepping back.

Motherfucker. I did not need a visual of Judd bending some redhead over those ugly pink counter tops.

Dickhead knew I was coming. Hell, he's the one who called me and told me to come. So, why is he doing a lewd infusion with some ol' girl when I get here? And with my son? Asshole.

But I know the answer. He's ball's deep because he can be. Single life.

Clark and I hang out in the front yard while Unc Jid finishes his business.

Well, I'll be fucked!

"Hey, Beau! And hey to you, little cutie. You've grown since I saw you last."

Fucking shit disturber. "Hey, Daphne."

"You're just the person I came to see." It didn't look like that five minutes ago. *Does the woman have no shame?* "I have some clients looking for a house. Want to work together?" No fucking way.

I'll be happy to find a house for the client, but I'm not working with Daphne. Even if nothing happened between us the day I took her to the park, I'd be asking for hell at the house if I agree to work with her.

I take out my business card. "Have them give me a call."

She stuffs it into her purse. "Sure thing."

Daphne looks over at Judd. "You need to talk Beau into letting me decorate this house."

That's Daphne. Always pushing herself on people when she's not welcome.

Judd winks, one of his signature moves. "I'll talk to him."

Hell, no, we won't.

"Keep me in the know about what's happening with my clients." Sorry. Won't be doing that.

Daphne gets into her BMW and waves goodbye as she pulls away.

I put Clark down to walk in the yard.

"You skeezy motherfucker." I whisper the last part.

"What?"

"You know what."

Judd laughs. "You'd have tapped that ass, too, if she'd thrown her pussy on you like she did me just now. Oh, wait." He puts his hands into the air as though he's having an epiphany. "You did hit it."

And I've wished a million times I could erase it from my memory. And hers. "You don't even know how bad you're going to regret doing that. She's a leech."

"Nah, it'll be okay."

"Well, just remember I told you so."

Dumb fucker. That quick fuck is going to cost him.

"And we're not using her to decorate." Just so he knows.

"Well, fuck, no, we're not. I wouldn't do that to Mama Kay."

Judd needs to find a girl. And fast. It's the only way he's going to get Daphne off his back.

PEACH and I are staying in the presidential suite at The Grand Rose. Same room we honeymooned in eighteen months ago.

Those are good memories. But I'm betting we're about to make better ones this time, the kind we'll take home with us in her tummy. *We're going to make a baby.*

I take off my shirt and trousers while I wait for Peach. I'm only wearing my boxer briefs when she comes out of the bathroom and stops in the doorway, leaning against the frame. She shifts her weight to one leg and places a hand on her hip, pushing her tits up.

Black baby doll top split up the middle. Bare belly. Tiny black triangle between her legs. Fuck-me-now facial expression.

Ultimate prelude to baby-making.

"What does Daddy think?"

"Daddy likes."

I walk toward her, and she moves to meet me in the middle of the room. I'm overcome by the love I feel for this woman when I consider what we're doing. Again. This time, intentionally.

She puts her hands on my hips and walks us toward the bed until the backs of her legs hit the mattress. She sits and glides to the middle. She lifts her foot and curls her toes around the waistband of my boxer briefs, pulling them, and me, in her direction. She uses her index finger to coax me. *Fuck, my wife is hot.*

"Get up here, Beauregard, and put a baby inside me."

I crawl up her body, taking my time as I leave a path of kisses, beginning at her belly. When we're face to face, she grasps the back of my neck. "Kiss me."

She pulls me down so our mouths meet. Her mouth is making love to mine. Slowly. Deeply. Lovingly.

When she stops, I pull away to look at her face. "I love you, Anna James Peach Emerson."

She stares into my eyes as I hover above and runs her fingertips down my cheek. "And I love you, William Beauregard Emerson."

I kiss the side of her face and move my mouth down the length of her neck before unfastening the ribbon holding this beautiful package together. I can't resist placing a kiss between her breasts, over her heart.

If we conceive tonight, it'll only be a matter of months before she puts a newborn to these breasts to nurse. *And I'll get to be there for everything this time.*

When I'm finished removing her top, she lifts her bottom and I drag her panties down her legs. She returns the favor by hooking her toes in the waistband of my boxer briefs and pushing them down. I kick them away when they hit the top of my feet.

With legs parted, I nestle my body between them until my hard cock is against her warm, inviting pussy. She lifts her hips and my tip glides just inside her. She squeezes her legs and brings me closer. *I love when she does that. Coaxing me in.*

I press my hand into the mattress so I can wrap it around her lower back. I lift to pull her hips upward and sink as far as possible. Deep.

I'm moving inside her slowly and my hands skim the underside of her arms. I push them over her head and lace my fingers through hers. *Our hands are joined as one, just like our bodies.*

When I release her from my imprisonment, I move my palms down her body. Her legs are bent on each side of my hips so I spread them farther apart and back. *God, I love being inside her like this.*

Peach moans when I slide my hand between our bodies to the point where we become one. No beginning. No end.

I know her body as well as my own. She needs more than penetration to come so I find that spot—the one that drives her crazy every time I touch it—and stroke my fingers against it.

"Yes. Right there. Just like that."

Her breath quickens as she grasps my back and pulls me against her tighter. She grinds her hips upward so I know I'm right where I need to be.

Her legs tighten, and I know what's coming next. Her inner walls tense around me, rhythmically squeezing my cock. Once. Twice. And then again over and over until I lose count, because I'm lost in my own world coming apart. Exploding.

I thrust deeply one last time, spilling a part of myself inside her. My wife. My love. Mother of my children. My forever.

I'm braced on my elbows as I hover above her. I'm still inside, unmoving, while I remember the times when Peach has been her most beautiful: that first night when she sat at my table at the Indulge restaurant, our reunion in New York, seeing her with our son for the first time, watching her walk down the aisle to become my wife, and now lying here beneath me as we try to conceive another baby.

So fucking beautiful it hurts.

~

"Mmm . . . ohh . . ." I hear Peach moaning as she tosses in bed. Haven't heard that in a while.

"You okay?"

"Sss . . ." I hear her sucking air through her teeth. "Ooh . . ."

I sit up to turn on the lamp and see her lying on her side with her legs pulled into a half-fetal position. "Are you going into labor?"

She's covering her face with her hand. "Mmm-hmm. And it's bad."

Her due date isn't for another week. She went three days past due with Clark. I guess I expected a repeat.

Shit. I've been preparing myself for this for months, but I don't know what to do. "When did you start hurting?"

"Maybe two hours ago."

Two hours? How did I sleep through her moaning and tossing in pain for that long? "Why didn't you wake me?"

"I thought it might be a false labor. I didn't want to get you up if it wasn't the real thing." My selfless Peach.

She looks like she's in a lot of pain. "What do you want me to do?"

"Help me change into my yoga pants and a T-shirt so we can go to the hospital."

I grab my phone to call Mom while I fetch her clothes. "Hey, Nana. It's show time."

"Be right there."

I help Peach into her clothes. "Let me brush my teeth and pull my hair up before we go."

"Okay, but hurry." I'm not at all comfortable with hanging around here. She was already dilated three centimeters the last time she saw the doctor and I've heard second babies come much faster.

"Uh oh."

I don't like uh ohs. "What is it?"

I go to the bathroom door and find Peach sitting on the toilet. "My water just broke. Get me a towel."

I don't know a lot about having babies but I think that means things are progressing. "Did that happen with Clark?"

"Not until I was at the hospital." Peach looks at me and laughs. "You're white as a ghost. You okay?"

"I'm fine." *Lie. I'm scared shitless.*

"You've whined for more than two years about missing everything with Clark. Don't even think about wussing out on this one."

"You're going to make sure you give me the full experience, aren't you?"

She nods. "Oh, hell to the yeah."

We arrive at Women's Hospital and Peach is taken to an observation room where a nurse comes in to check her. Glove on, her hand disappears under the covers. "Looks like someone's staying to have a baby. I'd call you every bit of five, almost six centimeters. Are you planning to get an epidural?"

"No. I go natural."

The nurse looks amused, almost as though she thinks Peach doesn't know what she's getting herself into. "Have you done that before?"

"Yes. I did it without an epidural when I delivered my first baby."

"All right then."

She's tough as nails. "I know you can do it without the epidural, but I hate seeing you in pain."

She reaches out and cradles my face. "I'm okay. Really." Peach is the one giving birth, and she's comforting me. That's just like her.

"It's a good kind of pain." That doesn't even make sense to me but it's my job to support her decision.

"You're gonna rock this, babe."

An hour of panting and heavy breathing passes. And not the good kind. "I gotta push."

A herd of nurses and a doctor fill the room after Peach's nurse examines her.

Holy shit. This is happening fast. Not just her labor and this baby's delivery. The whole pregnancy from that night in Montego Bay.

Surprise! We're pregnant.

Guess what, Clark. You're getting a baby brother or baby sister.

Baby looks perfect on the ultrasound.

Beau! I felt the baby move.

Put your hand here and feel how hard this kiddo can kick.

I didn't miss a thing this time. I loved every minute of watching our child grow inside Peach.

"We're about to meet our new son or daughter. I'm so glad we didn't find out the gender."

"Well, we're about to know because this is happening."

Oh fuck. Reality hits me. I'm about to be Daddy to another little person.

Peach moves into position, her legs bent and apart, hands wrapped around the backs of her thighs. "Pressure's building. Oh God, I've got to push."

Peach pushes through the next contraction. "Look down here, Mr. Emerson, if you want to see the top of your baby's head."

Seriously? You can already see the head after one push? I thought this would take a long time. Peach said it did with Clark.

I get on my toes and peek over the drapes at her bottom. I've seen it like this countless times but never with something so surreal happening. "It looks like you're about to give birth to a peach. This baby has no hair."

"Ahh. My poor baby is bald?"

The doctor adjusts the lighting. "I see hair. It's just really light."

I lean down and kiss her forehead while we wait for the next contraction. "I love you so much."

"I love you, too." She strokes my face with her hand. "I'm glad you didn't miss out on anything with this one."

"Me, too."

"Another one's coming." Peach takes a deep breath and blows it out before taking another and holding it. She pulls her legs back and her face turns beet red as she pushes with all her might. She stops midpush and releases her legs as she bows from the bed. "Omigod, there's so much pressure. I'm burning. On fire."

"Don't stop, Anna James. Keep going and this could be the last time."

She takes a quick breath and gets back into position to push again.

"Look down here, Mr. Emerson, if you want to see your child come into the world."

I lean over Peach's leg and watch our baby's head come out of her body. The baby came out face down but the doctor rotates her so she can suction the mouth and nose.

I see her face for the first time. *Just like Anna James.* "This one looks like you, Peach."

I've never seen anything more amazing. "What a beautiful little face."

"Let's get the other end of this baby out and see if we have a boy or girl." The nurse pushes against Peach's leg and motions for me to do the same with the other. "Push, Anna James, push!"

I see the determination on her face and know her next push will be the last. And it is.

I hear a gush of fluid and then a piercing cry. *Our baby's first sound.*

"Want me to tell or show you what this baby is?"

"Show," we say in unison.

No tally whacker this time. "A girl baby. And she looks like you."

I kiss the top of my sweet Peach's head. "You did that

beautifully." *She is amazing.*

Our daughter is placed on Peach's bare chest, tucked inside her hospital gown. Skin to skin.

I stroke my finger down my daughter's cheek and remember doing this to Clark when he was smaller. "I already love her to pieces, just like I do Clark."

"I know."

Georgia Rhea Emerson. Our little Georgia peach.

Three years ago, a beautiful girl was seated across from me in a hedonistic resort restaurant. She wasn't doing anything but sitting there. Head lowered. Blushing. Turning my world on its head. A stranger who would soon come to mean everything to me. She didn't play hard to *get.* She was simply impossible to *forget.* I love her so much that at times she doubts my sanity. But she never doubts my passion.

I followed my heart and it led me back to her.

Once, my vanilla girl.

Now, my forever girl.

Our true and beautiful.

The End

ACKNOWLEDGMENTS

Thank you to my sexy husband for being a sexy takeout delivery boy when I'm on lockdown in the writing cave. #truestory. Your support means the world to me. I love you and our children more than I can say.

Danielle Sanchez of Inkslinger PR, thank you for working diligently to promote me and my work. Fours releases together, so far. It's been a great year, baby.

Georgia's Peaches, thank you for your love and support. I adore each and every one of you.

Marion Archer, I truly enjoy working together. You're incredibly talented. Such an advocate for the reader. I love that about you.

Karen Lawson, you are sharper than a tack. What wonderful *final eyes* you have. Such a pleasure working with you.

My readers, there wouldn't be a reason for me to do this if I didn't have you. Thank you for all your love and support.

Beloved bloggers, thank you for hard work promoting me and my books. I'm grateful for every ARC reading, review, and post you've made. I appreciate your precious time and effort.

My dear friends Samantha Young, Amy Bartol, Shelly Crane, and Rachel Higginson: Thank you for the late night talks and every word of advice you share. I can't wait until our next retreat.

ABOUT THE AUTHOR

GEORGIA CATES

Georgia resides in rural Mississippi with her wonderful husband, Jeff, and their two beautiful daughters. She spent fourteen years as a labor and delivery nurse before she decided to pursue her dream of becoming an author and hasn't looked back yet.

Sign-up for Georgia's newsletter. Get the latest news, first look at teasers, and giveaways just for subscribers.

For the latest updates from Georgia Cates, stay connected with her at:

@georgiacates

georgia.cates.9

www.georgiacates.com

authorgeorgiacates@gmail.com

THE *Beauty* SERIES

The *Sin* Trilogy

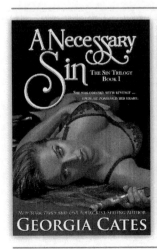

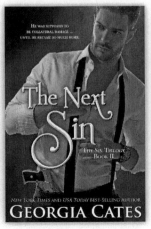

THE VAMPIRE AGÁPE SERIES

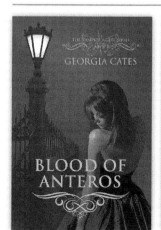
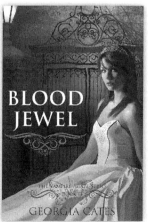
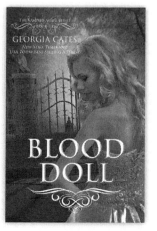

Made in the USA
Lexington, KY
01 February 2017